PRAISE FOR *UNRAVELED*

"This book has rocked my world!"

—**Chelsea (Starbucks & Books Obsession)**

"I absolutely could not put this book down. [It] is hot hot hot and sweet and at moments leaves you heartbroken...Definite 5 stars from me. If you haven't picked up this series —its a must!"

—**Becca from Becca the Bibliophile**

"Very emotional and very sexy story!"

—**Andrea from The Bookish Babes**

PRAISE FOR *UNSPOKEN*

"A sexy and sinful new adult read you don't want to miss!"

—**Katy Evans, *New York Times* bestselling author**

"Bo was a fighter, but, ahem, wow, he was also quite a lover! That boy was sex on a freaking stick!! Even aside from his hotness factor, though, Bo 〵 .... (AM). He was a wonderful fri all around good guy with her.

PRAISE FOR *UNDECLARED*

"[I] can't wait to read the next installment in the Woodlands series, the characters, storyline and gushing romance were all wonderfully written and Jen Frederick's writing is extremely engaging—she is definitely an author to remember and this is a book I'm more than happy to add to my favourites list!"

—Obsession with Books

"Noah Jackson was perfect in every way! He was compassionate, considerate and sexy as hell! His old school values mixed with his slight debauchery made him a perfect alpha male and you can't help but adore every part of his character."

—Craves the Angst

Titles by Jen Frederick

The Woodlands

UNDECLARED
UNSPOKEN
UNRAVELED

Hitman Series
(with Jessica Clare)

LAST HIT

UNRAVELED

Jen Frederick

PEAR TREE LLC

UNRAVELED

This book is a work of fiction. Names, characters, places, and incidents are the product of the author's imagination or are used fictitiously. Any resemblance to actual events, locales, or persons, living or dead, is coincidental.

PEAR TREE LLC
100 N. Pleasant Hill Road
Warner Robins, GA 31093

jen@jenfrederick.com

Cover Photo © Per David Wagner, WagnerLA
Cover & Interior Design by Meljean Brook

ISBN-13: 978-0991426713

First Edition: January 2014
CreateSpace Independent Publishing Platform

www.jenfrederick.com

To C. Sherrill, you'll probably never know the influence you had on my life but that junior year of high school when you made me read everything from Beowulf to Shakespeare to Ayn Rand changed me forever. Thank you.

To my family, as always, thank you for allowing me time to write. Your understanding and patience is endless and I love you both for it.

ACKNOWLEDGEMENTS

It's hard to know where to start because there are so many people who are so important to this book that it is hard to know where to start. First, though, special thanks must go to my beta readers. These are folks who read my work often more than once during the revision process. Without their help, Unraveled wouldn't be the book that it is today. Thank you to Brie, Elyssa Papa, Kati, and, last but certainly not least, CeCe. CeCe, your insights were amazing. Thank you for pushing me to dig deeper.

I'm blessed with an amazing circle of writerly friends including Daphne who listened to me talk about the plot and helped me discard some really bad ideas and for just being an amazing friend and Jessica Clare and Katy Evans who not only helped me over rough spots in the manuscript but whose hand holding during release week help to keep me sane.

To AW, I don't know how you do it but your editing pen is magical. I appreciate the numerous times you read through this manuscript because every suggestion made this a better book.

Meljean Brook, I don't know why you have all the skills in the world. It's unfair. You can create amazing covers and print designs but also write more magically than most of us mortals. Thanks for being a friend.

Lisa at The Rock Stars of Romance, you've been with me since the beginning. I can't believe the journey we've had together. Thank you for non stop support. And to Michelle at All Romance Reviews, our facebook chats are the highlight of many of my days.

Thank you to all of the bloggers who participated in the blog tour and/or reviewed Unraveled and to all the reviewers who've left reviews and readers who've read our book, your support is amazing.

Finally, to the MGL. I hope to be reading a book from every one of you soon.

UNRAVELED

ONE

Gray

"Y̲ou sure I can't give you a ride, Sgt. Phillips?" the sixty-year-old woman I'd sat next to on the airplane asked for the fifth time.

"No ma'am," I replied promptly. "Where can I put these for you?"

"Right here is just fine." She pointed to a luggage cart.

"I'd be happy to carry them to the car for you." The cart might be easy for her to maneuver but lifting the heavy luggage into her trunk by herself? Not happening.

"My son is picking me up and I promise I won't lift a thing."

I looked around skeptically but didn't see anyone but my own ride. I gave Bo Randolph a chin nod of acknowledgment but held on to the carry-on bag that looked like someone had puked flowers all over it.

"What's up, man?" Bo bumped my fist in greeting and then pulled me in for a hug.

"Just making sure Mrs. Kremer gets to her car in one piece."

"We're waiting for my son," she chirped. "And there he is now." Mrs. Kremer's son looked to be balding and forty. One glance from Bo and we silently agreed that despite her son showing up, we'd still be helping them out. Over both their protests, Bo and I picked up the luggage and placed it in the back of the four-door sedan. Mrs. Kremer gave us both a kiss, leaving behind the smell of lilacs and baby powder.

"Always the good Samaritan," Bo joked as we walked to his crackerjack box of a car.

"You helped."

He just shook his head. "Only because I'd have looked like a fool standing there while you hauled her luggage around."

"She looked frail," I protested. "Besides, you and I've both carried far more weight over much longer distances. Enough about the woman, let's talk about your damn car. Will my pack even fit in there?"

"Yes, princess, it will. How come you didn't ask Noah to pick you up if you hate my baby so much?" He hit a button and a sorry excuse for trunk space appeared at the rear of the vehicle.

"I didn't want to make you cry. You're an ugly crier," I said. I threw my seabag and pack into the trunk and wedged myself inside the even tinier interior.

"True that. Seriously, forty-five days? How'd you manage that?"

"How do you think? I'm a lucky fuck."

"So The Honorable Dennis Phillips came through?"

"Guess so." My old man was on the House Armed Services Committee and had pulled some strings to get special dispensation for me to take forty-five consecutive days of leave at the beginning of summer. The fact that it went through was helped by the fact I'd taken almost zero leave for the past six years and that I possessed a spotless record, but it was still a big deal. Other Marines would have killed to have even half that many days off in the summer. Literally knifed me in the gut. I shifted in the seat, which was too narrow for my six-foot-one, two-hundred-and-five-pound frame. "This car is too fucking small for you."

"I like 'em tight." Bo stroked the leather dash of his sports car.

"Given your dick is so tiny, it's no wonder you need 'em small.

AnnMarie's still a virgin then?"

"What?" He jerked his hand back and glared at me. "No talking about AnnMarie and sex. Besides, I saw you staring at my junk plenty while we were in A-stan."

"Because you whipped it out every five seconds."

"Can't help that my dick's so big my regulation pants couldn't keep it in."

I shook my head but knew I was grinning like a loon. "Missed you, man."

"You too," Bo said, smiling back. "Forty-five days is going to be gone in a blink of an eye."

"I know." My grin dimmed a little. This wasn't entirely a vacation. My exact orders from Congressman Phillips were to pull my fucking head out of my ass and sign my re-enlistment papers or start applying for college. He wanted me out and my grandfather wanted me to stay in. I felt a little like a sorry bone between two angry pit bulls.

I had eight years under my belt, a new meritorious promotion to staff sergeant that I wasn't sure I deserved, and some serious doubt about whether being a career Marine was the right choice for my future. During our family Christmas, I had made the mistake of mentioning that evaluating everyone's "knife hands" while running during physical training didn't hold a lot of meaning—and Dad had pounced.

"There's plenty of room for you outside the Corps," he'd said.

Then Pops had bristled. "Corps was good enough for me and good enough for you. No sense in planting doubt in the boy's head where there was none before."

Match to kindling, the two had gotten into one of their heated arguments. Having two career Marines scream at each other like they were trying to make the other break first had resulted in Mom leaving the table in tears and my two older brothers glaring at me. I'd wanted to sink under the tablecloth but since I'd started it, I sat there and took it like the man I was supposed to be.

Since then I'd told Pops that my commitment was as sound as ever and Dad that I'd think about college. When Bo and Noah, two former Marines in my platoon, invited me to spend my leave at their posh pad with a bevy of college coeds at the ready, I fled before the yelling could start again.

"You really in a tizzy about whether to re-enlist?" Bo asked, surprise evident in his voice.

"Marines don't get into tizzies," I scoffed. "We get angry. Also drunk. Shitfaced. Tired. No tizzies, though."

"Which one are you?"

"Tired. I'm supposed to shit or get off the pot."

"Is shitting staying in or getting out?"

"We all know that re-enlisting is for the motards who can't stop wearing all their USMC gear off the base, have more than one Marine tattoo, and can recite the Marine Hymn by heart."

"So you, essentially."

I slunk down in the seat and pressed a thumb to my temple. "Which is why I should get out before I become one of those Marines that we all made fun of when we were lance corporals."

"What's the real problem?"

I pressed harder. "The real problem? Let's see. I didn't sign my re-enlistment papers yet, causing Captain Billings to call my dad, who then decided to gleefully tell Pops he had lost. They yelled. Mom cried. Oh, and my ex is sniffing around again." And it sucked being responsible for people instead of just equipment, but I didn't admit that last one out loud.

"Do whatever you can to make your mom stop crying," Bo advised. "If mama isn't happy, ain't no one gonna be happy."

"Maybe." The sad truth of it was that someone was going to be unhappy. Because I cared about all of them, that sucked. Hoping to change the subject, I said, "You fuckers better have something good planned for me every day."

"We said you could come stay with us and hang out, not that we'd be your cruise directors."

"All I want to know is whether AnnMarie and Grace are bringing some single friends over. I'm a Marine on leave. I need some special attention."

"AnnMarie's neighbor's got a thing for guys, I'm pretty sure."

"Yeah." My interest was piqued. Both Noah and Bo had been

single in the Corps and for two years after they separated. The minute they'd moved up here to go to Central College, they'd each hooked so tightly to a girl that neither could move without the other feeling it. I hoped it wasn't something in the water. I didn't need or want that kind of complication. But hot girlfriends meant hot single female friends and that was all good in my book. "Hot? Good personality? What?"

"He's bi-curious, according to AM."

I groaned. "Sorry. Gray don't play that way. What about AnnMarie's roommate? Seem to remember that she had a tight ass and body."

"Taken."

"Do you know any single women?"

"I'm not a pimp either."

"You suck."

"That was your fantasy, wasn't it?"

"How did you end up with such a classy piece like AnnMarie?"

"Dunno but if you fuck it up for me, I'd have to kill you." He was dead serious. That was another thing that just didn't make sense in my world anymore. Bo had once been the biggest skirt chaser in our platoon. It didn't matter if the girl was big, small, or Martian, he'd do them. Now all he could talk about was one chick. And if that didn't set a lad's mind spinning, I didn't know what would. It confused me because all I knew of women was that they'd cheat on you the second your back was turned. I learned that lesson early on and *that* cheating girlfriend had been my last.

"You've discovered my evil plan. I'm here to lure your girl back to San Diego with me." I rolled my eyes. He knew, like all the guys in my platoon, that I didn't believe a relationship with a woman could ever survive repeated deployments or a twenty-four-month unaccompanied tour to Okinawa or some other overseas duty station.

"You still believe in the no-relationships-while-serving thing?" This time, it was Bo rolling *his* eyes.

"It's not a *thing*. It's a truism. *Semper Fidelis* only matters within the Corps. Feel free to fuck your brother's girlfriend, sister, mother, so long as you're true to the Corps." The bitter taste of infidelity always sat on the back of my tongue no matter how many times I tried to swallow it away.

"That's healthy."

"Thanks, Oprah. I'll let you know when I need more relationship advice."

"Just pointing out that the odds aren't much better outside the Corps, if that's one of the reasons you're thinking of not re-enlisting."

"Does Noah have to suffer your Dear Abby musings?" Noah Jackson and Bo were my kind of Marines. They fought hard and didn't complain, but they knew how to have a good time when we weren't busy picking sand out of our asses.

Noah was the more serious of the two and I'd thought he would have made a career of the military, but his ambitions were different. He wanted to build an empire and you couldn't do that on a military salary—no matter how much combat pay you received. We'd both signed up for every possible tour we could in all the most dangerous places. My burning ambition was to have as much adventure as possible. Unlike Noah, I didn't need to own the world to be happy. These days, though...I wasn't exactly sure what I needed.

When I was ten, Pops had given me a knife engraved with *Semper Fidelis* on the blade. He'd retired after thirty years in the Corps, and my father had made it to twenty. But neither of my two older brothers were interested, and so it had fallen to me to carry out the tradition. After years of hearing whispered stories of bravery and honor and brotherhood, I couldn't wait to wear the dress blues and the white gloves and carry that damn sword. Because I enlisted during war time, I got to do things that had *meaning*.

Since the troop drawdown, though, I'd felt...unmoored, to borrow a Navy term, as if I was standing on ever-shifting sand. People I'd known for a long time were changing. All around me, guys were settling down, picking out furniture, and going to flea markets on the weekends. They did couples things, like couples' showers and shit like that, and while I didn't want to go to those damn things, I felt like everyone else was moving on and that I was just stuck, spinning my wheels like I was some stupid groundhog that should be put out of my misery.

I don't know what it was, but every time I had gone to sign

those re-enlistment papers, I couldn't bring myself to do it. On one side, I had my pops and my commanding officer, Captain Billings, warning me about how boat space was shrinking and that even for an exemplary Marine like myself I could be squeezed out if I didn't hurry my ass up. On the other side sat my dad, who sang an entirely different tune—that I should get out now while I still had time to go to college, find a job, settle down.

Then there were the men in my platoon. Good men who would place their lives in my hands. I wasn't just making sure that my weapon was ready now but that theirs were too, and that was a responsibility you didn't take lightly.

"Nah, you know Noah doesn't speak unless it is absolutely necessary," Bo said, answering my earlier question. "His frozen yogurt palace is always stuffed full of estrogen. We could swing by and scope out the women there."

"I thought you'd said that the only females in Noah's shop were a mess of teenage girls and soccer moms."

"So? They're still females."

"My choices are to be a pedo bear or cougar bait?"

"Better go cougar. They're in their sexual prime. They could teach you something."

"Let's just head to your place." Upon arriving, I pulled my gear out of the trunk and followed Bo into the home he shared with Noah and three other guys—one complete with full floor to ceiling plate glass windows at the rear that overlooked a pool. The weather was great here. I'd missed the beach back in San Diego, but I needed to get away. The more distance I put between the base and me, the better I felt. Right then, I wanted to pound some beer, ogle some women, and relax.

A loud noise like a gunshot echoed, and I immediately ducked down to my knees, throwing my bag in front of me. I looked for Bo, but he was propped against the counter, crying with laughter.

"I'm so sorry." AnnMarie leaned over me—her long dark hair nearly touching my face. "We just popped the champagne."

I looked around and saw a group of people with shocked faces and a few girls in front holding a sign that said "Welcome, Grunt."

One of Bo's roommates (whose name I didn't remember) stood frozen with the bottle in question, champagne dribbling from the open neck like he was pissing all over the floor. Noah broke from the group and pulled me to my feet because Bo—the asshole—was still laughing.

"Sorry, we weren't thinking." Noah tried to look repentant, but I could see he was fighting a big-ass grin too. The crowd had recovered, and he started introducing me around.

"You fuckers." I laughed, because it was funny. You could take the Marine grunt off the base, but you couldn't eliminate his reaction to close-quarters fire. "If I didn't know better, I'd think you planned that."

"Bo would've had to frisk you to make sure you didn't draw on us." Noah shook his head. "We both know he'd have liked that far too much."

One little blonde who'd been part of the sign committee murmured a few words I didn't catch. I thought her name was Alice or Amy or something like that. I'd met her before when I'd come up for a weekend to see Bo and Noah's set up.

"What's that, sweetheart?" I had to double over to talk to her. Some guys loved a good height disparity. I preferred a taller women. Easier to have sex standing up.

"You guys are all so mean to each other. Noah made us write grunt on your sign." She stuck her lower lip out, which might have been an invitation to do something, although I wasn't sure for what.

"Grunt is a good thing for a Marine. You have to pass infantry school, otherwise you're in the rear with the gear," I explained. After eight years of being enlisted, I spent most of my time with other Marines or Marine wives and Marine girlfriends. I didn't love explaining things to civilians but part of why I'd come here to see Bo and Noah in the Midwest was to get away from the military folks, clear my head, and come up with a life plan. God, I sounded like Dr. Phil.

"What's infantry school?"

I reined in my impatience and started to explain when Grace came over and rescued me.

"Amy," Grace said. "Leave the pretty Marine alone. His glass is empty and you know how guys get when their glass is empty."

"They get thirsty?" Amy asked.

I kind of wanted to hear Grace's reply, but her eyes were silently telling me to get while the getting was good. I fled to the group out at the pool, which included Bo's girlfriend.

"AnnMarie, you got any cute, single girlfriends available for me?" Truthfully, I planned to keep my pants zipped the entire time I was here, but I figured people expected me to be a horndog—and I didn't like to let anyone down.

"There's a whole bunch of single women here." She waved a hand at the ever growing crowd. "We held this party just for you."

"I appreciate that, but I'm only here for a short time. Pick one for me. I want to use my time wisely."

"Oh no, not the 'why one-night stands don't make good sex' lecture." Bo groaned.

"What's this?" she asked.

"Ignore him. Bo doesn't like anything that requires thinking," I said.

"He's actually very smart." She looked adorably peeved that I was saying anything bad about her boy. While I enjoyed giving both my boys shit, I was happy that Bo was with someone who defended him so fiercely. I kind of wanted that. Someday. *Like in ten years*, I told myself.

"I can see you're still in the early stages of a strong infatuation," I teased, wondering how long it would be before Bo would carry AnnMarie off to have some dirty hot sex that we'd all hear because this house, as nice as it was, did not have enough sound proofing. I'd learned *that* the last time I'd come to visit. The guys in this house enjoyed the ladies, often and loudly.

"I want to hear this theory," AnnMarie said.

Bo flopped back and heaved a huge theatrical sigh. "Now we're in for it."

She put her hand over his mouth. "Start talking."

He must have licked her hand because she pulled it away with a yelp and wiped her palm on her shirt, giving Bo a dirty look. Yup, it was official. I was jealous of one of my oldest friends because of the easy relationship he had with his girl. Maybe coming here had been a mistake.

I forced my gaze away from the happy couple and onto the growing crowd. There were a lot of gorgeous women here, and many of them were eyeing me like I was top grade prime rib at an all-you-can-eat buffet. I'd be a fool not to take advantage of an offer.

I turned to AnnMarie to explain my theory. "It's not that hook ups aren't good but it's like the difference between a nice song and an awesome concert. One is a three-minute interlude. The other is an event. The better you know your partner, the better the sex is." My eyes surveyed the eclectic mix of students, construction workers, musicians, and gym rats that made up the new friends of my old friends. If I did hook up, I wouldn't want anyone who would form an attachment. My time here was temporary, after all.

"Maybe for you it's three minutes." Bo smirked.

"Whatever. You can't tell me it's not better with AnnMarie than anyone else."

"I was a virgin when I met AnnMarie," Bo said loftily. AnnMarie just rolled her eyes. "Besides, just because AnnMarie knows a girl, doesn't mean she knows her medical history."

"Why do you need that?" She quirked an eyebrow at me.

"I'm just careful," I replied. I didn't want to go into the long, sordid story about my past brush with a serious STI due to a cheating girlfriend. I'd come away clean, thankfully, but it had been a close call.

"Plus she has to be in the medical profession," Bo added.

"Jesus, she does not." I was going to have to take him to the ground because he'd forgot the kind of beating I could deliver.

"Your last three 'companions' were in the health field." Bo held up his fingers. I grabbed a couple and twisted them back as he tried to hit me with his other fist. AnnMarie grabbed at him and he subsided. Still, her scowl was directed at me.

"I'm not going to hook you up with any of my friends if you're dating someone!" she said disgustedly.

"I'm not seeing anyone," I assured her. "I'm just not into the bar hook up."

"Why's that?" This was a question from Adam, the one who'd popped the champagne cork. He had more tattoos than some of the guys I served with. I guess it went with his rock band lifestyle.

"Safety," I said.

"Too many chances of putting the stick in crazy?" another roommate asked. It was Finn this time, the guy who actually owned this house.

"No way. Crazy is awesome. Crazy in the head; crazy in the bed," Adam said.

I shook my head. "No. Disease. Pregnancy scares."

"Suit up, man." Adam tipped his head back and drained his beer. I waited until he was done to impart some much-needed sense. It was the same tip I gave to the new recruits.

"You can still get herpes on your ball sack."

Adam looked down at his lap and so did nearly every guy within listening distance. One by one, they all got up and left. Presumably to go look at their nuts. Bo gave me a nudge and high-fived me. Civilians, Marines—they were all the same in some ways.

Grace came wandering out and sat down next to us. "Where is everyone?"

"Checking out their balls," AnnMarie said. Her dry delivery made Bo and me crack up again while Noah looked on with a smirk.

AFTER ADAM HAD CONVINCED HIMSELF his gonads were in good health, he showed me where I'd be staying for the few weeks I'd be here.

"You sure I'm not putting you out or anything?" I threw my seabag and backpack down near the door in case Adam had changed his mind about letting me use his room. The place was pretty clean for being the bedroom of a twenty-five-year-old musician who lived with four other guys. Not military clean. There was shit everywhere, like two guitars in the corner and a mess of woven bracelets, heavy silver rings, guitar picks, and what looked like four or five different pairs of headphones on a dresser. But there weren't any empty pizza boxes on the floor or half-filled beers on the nightstand. Instead, it looked like the room of a guy who lived in his music.

"Nah, I'm going to bunk in the garage. It's where most of my instruments are anyway." Adam went over to the dresser and shoved everything off the top and into the drawer beneath it—presumably clearing space for my shit. "This is the bathroom." Adam opened the door to what I'd thought was a closet. Inside was a decent-sized bathroom with a shower, a toilet and a sink and another door. "Closet's through there. I tried to clear a little space for you." The closet looked like a denim factory. There were dozens of jeans piled on custom shelves and another full set of shelves with an unholy amount of boots and shoes.

"Not to be offensive, man, but you've more clothes and shoes than any guy I've ever met."

Adam gave a negligent shrug. "I like clothes. So sue me."

"I'll just leave my stuff in my bag." I didn't feel comfortable setting my gear up beside Adam's. I was only here for a short while and I'd had plenty of practice living out of my pack.

"Your call," Adam said. "Use what you want. The cleaning crew comes on Wednesdays at three. We all try to get out of here and leave them alone." He paused, looked around the room again, and then gave me another shrug.

The cleaning crew explained the decent state of the room. The shrug, however, was weird but I let it pass without comment because it wasn't any of my business. If Adam had been in my platoon, I would have probably had to ask nosy questions to make sure he wasn't fucking up his personal life so bad that it would affect his performance in the Corps. But he wasn't, so I shut my mouth, showered off the travel grime, and shrugged on a fresh T-shirt, cargo shorts, and sandals. Downstairs, the party seemed to be in full swing, with people littering the patio outside and some poorly playing a first-person action game on the big screen in the living area.

"You allow these atrocities to occur without retribution?" I asked Bo, who was leaning against the wall grimacing as the video game players missed kill shot after kill shot.

"I don't know them but we can dunk them out in the pool later."

"This is just a normal everyday occurrence here?" I waved at the mass of people moving in and out of the house toward the back patio and into the pool. Bo's gaze traveled around the room, stopping at AnnMarie talking animatedly to some girl I hadn't met. I had to nudge Bo out of whatever fantasy he was concocting. He jerked a little and then punched me in the arm. "The fuck?" I said, punching him back.

"I was having a moment." He scowled. Like he hadn't had a moment earlier when he'd dragged AnnMarie away from the pool for some private time.

"Let her be for a minute and maybe she'll miss you," I retorted. This riled Bo up and soon we were grappling on the hard wooden floor. He struck me twice in the ear. Bo had big fists but his larger body also made it easier to maneuver around him.

I'd gotten a choke hold around his neck and was pulling his head away from his shoulders when a huge stream of cold water hit my face. "Motherfucking what?" I yelled, dropping Bo. AnnMarie stood there with an empty pot, looking both exasperated and amused.

"You guys are acting like you're five." She tapped her foot by my head.

"Nah, I was still fighting like this when I was fifteen." I smiled, getting up and pulling her in for a hug. I pressed my wet body against hers for all of one second before Bo pulled me off. He and Noah picked me up and proceeded to throw me into the pool.

I kicked off my shoes and stripped off my T-shirt and shorts, throwing the whole lot up on the pool deck.

"Keep your panties on," Bo shouted as my clothing hit the concrete.

"No worries, man, I won't embarrass you by showing my package to all the girls here."

"No one wants to see your pasty white ass."

"I think you're more afraid that AnnMarie will see my giant dick and leave you." Predictably, Bo jumped into the pool. We started trying to drown each other, but I'd had too much training for that.

Bo's entry into the pool prompted the rest of the crowd to jump in and soon I was too interested in all the honeys around me to want to wrestle with Bo anymore. Noah tossed me a pair of swim trunks, and I changed under the water. We played pool games until I was too hungry to be distracted by all the bikini-clad coeds in the water with me.

"You really know how to press Bo's buttons," AnnMarie commented as I threw together a sandwich and wolfed it down in three bites.

"When you spend a few years stuck next to a guy 24/7, you get to know him pretty well," I explained. She handed me a soda and I drained that too.

"Did you hate it? Is that why you want to get out?" she asked, sipping at her drink.

I made up another sandwich before answering her. Part of me resented the question, but that's why I was here, and I guess everyone knew it. Answering their questions might help sort out the confusion in my own mind. "Everyone says you don't miss the service, you miss the men you served with. So no, I don't want to get out because I saw your man far too much in the desert.

"When you're deployed, you are always busy doing something, and you feel like you're doing something worthwhile. Whether it's going to look for insurgents or handing out aid. At home, some guys get to do embassy duty or presidential assignments, but a lot of us stay on base. When you're on base, you train, but it doesn't feel as…"

I paused, unsure of the word I was looking for. "Important?" I still wasn't sure what was making me feel out of sorts. "My pops— grandfather—says that the reasons for getting out will always outweigh the reasons for staying in." I laid my sandwich down, my appetite kind of gone.

"Sounds tough." AnnMarie made a clucking sound of sympathy, and I gave her a wry smile in return.

"Kind of a downer of a discussion for such a nice day."

She patted me on the arm. "Nope, not a downer at all."

She was lying, but we both left it at that. If I'd known the answers to AnnMarie's questions, then I wouldn't be here; I'd be in sunny Southern California with my boys at the beach. I picked up my sandwich again because I couldn't let it go to waste. I ate the whole damn thing methodically, without enjoying it. I was afraid that no matter what decision I made—getting out or staying in—it'd be the wrong one.

"How come you refer to Bo and Noah as Marines even though they've been out of the military for a couple of years now?" AnnMarie asked.

"Once a Marine, always a Marine," I explained. "It's the oldest, best fraternity in existence. I could be anywhere and if I yelled Marine in trouble, I'd have every Marine in the room lending me a hand. It's a brotherhood like no other."

"Sounds like you love it." Her eyebrows were raised in challenge.

"Yeah, I guess I do." I sighed. I did love my brothers. They would be the thing I missed the most about the Corps, but I also would miss the sense of purpose and the idea that I was involved in something bigger than myself.

Thankfully, I wasn't allowed more time for my dilemma to mess with my head because Bo sidled up to me with the fat grin that he wore when he was about to get us all in trouble.

"Want to go to a bar?"

"What about all this?" I nodded toward the crowd.

"Mal's going to stay here." Mal was another roommate.

I shrugged. Party here, bar there. Made no difference. "I'm going to trust that you have good things planned for me."

"Don't doubt it," he said, giving me a hard slap on my back.

TWO

Samantha

I FELT LIKE I WORE A SCARLET LETTER. NOT "A" FOR ADULTERER but "W" for widow. I thought the defining moment of my life was going to be when I married or maybe when I had kids. Instead, it came two months after the wedding, when the "casualty team" showed up at my door, expressing the sorrowful regrets of the Secretary of the Army. I doubted the Secretary of the Army knew who my nineteen-year-old husband was, and I seriously doubted the sorrowful regrets.

My reaction wasn't very graceful. A real Army wife would've stood stoically by while the two Army men in their service class "A" uniforms somberly delivered the news at the door of my condo. My response was first screaming at them followed by an ungraceful collapse on the floor and finally spewing snot all over their wool jackets.

Bitsy, my sister, tried to cheer me up months later by reading Internet articles of all the other ways I could've embarrassed myself. "At least you didn't stab anyone or try to burn yourself," she pointed out. I didn't question the veracity of those reports because it actually did make me feel better that there were a handful of people that took the news worse than I did.

At the funeral, the chaplain had held my hand, repeatedly murmuring, "You're so young." That was the refrain of my life now. Samantha Anderson, widowed so young. I heard it everywhere. At the grocery store, the library, and even at the stupid bar where I worked.

It seemed like people in my life placed themselves into two general camps. There was the camp, which included my family, that was ready for me to move on from the death of my best friend, only lover, and husband of two months. The other camp wanted to enshrine me as Will Anderson's widow forevermore. I wasn't at all sure what camp I fell into, but I knew I was lonely. I was tired of being a widow, and I was tired of bartending for a living, and I was tired of having to serve as Will's avatar for the family he left behind. I guess I was in the tired and lonely camp.

But I set that sentiment aside today to endure my monthly luncheon with Will's parents—David and Carolyn. Sometimes my brother-in-law Tucker showed up, but more often than not, it was just me. Last night, Tucker had called and explained earnestly that he just wasn't up for it this month—again. His inability to have any kind of emotional investment in his family was irritating on most days, but it was enraging on days like today. As if *I* looked forward to the monthly lunch.

"I'm so glad you came today, Sam." Will's mom patted my hand. That made one of us. It was a strained meal, what with Carolyn drinking her lunch, David criticizing her for it, and both of them wondering what I was doing to uphold Will's memory. The slight ache at my temples that had hummed in the back of my head when I woke up was spreading across the entire surface of my skull and face. I lifted a shaky hand to my temple in an effort to relieve the pain.

"Have you registered for your classes this fall, dear?" Carolyn handed me the butter dish.

"I did. I'm taking eighteen hours."

Carolyn tsked. "That sounds overly ambitious. Will wouldn't have wanted you to work that hard."

I slid a dollop of butter in the shape of a flower onto my bread plate and swallowed a sigh.

"Smart to try to catch up for lost time," interjected David. "Since your dad gets you free tuition, you might as well take as many credits as possible." If Carolyn had said the sky was blue, I swear David would have told her it was green. Mom said that David was a great law partner, but a sucky life partner. Lucky for Mom she got David as a law partner. It was Carolyn who had to live with him every day. He continued. "If you do eighteen credit hours every semester and at least twelve in the summer, you'll be on to law school in two years. You got a full year under your belt before you quit the first time."

I gave David a tight smile. He couldn't resist getting his jabs whenever he saw an opening. "Let's just take one semester at a time."

"You should start planning now what prerequisites you'll need to get your major and when's the best time for you to take those classes." David buttered his own roll and then pointed his butter knife at me. "Otherwise you'll be stuck waiting around an extra semester trying to finish out your degree. No need to waste more time. After all, wasn't going to college the reason you stayed here instead of moving to Alaska?"

Yes, David, stick the knife in deeper. Twist it around. I don't think you've caused enough pain yet.

"Will would be so proud," Carolyn added.

I fought back a grimace. He would *not* be proud. He hated school. Why else had he escaped to the Army right out of high school? What other reason was there to spend more and more time in the ROTC during high school, playing at drill on weekends? It was because he couldn't stand school. And he didn't want to be a lawyer like his dad. Like my mom.

"It'll be nice to finally have one of you kids join the firm." Carolyn smiled at me.

"If I don't," I demurred, "then Bitsy for sure will."

"Bitsy is whipsmart, but she's only fifteen. It'll be eight, nine years before she can join. You can be there in five, maybe even four if you apply yourself." David waved his knife at me again. The likelihood of anyone finishing college and law school in four years was so low that I wasn't even going to respond.

Not that it mattered to David. He could argue both sides of a topic for hours on end. I guess it made him a great lawyer, but he was a shitty dad. Reason two why Will had hightailed it out of here before the last high school bell had rung.

David must have recognized the ridiculousness of his statement because he set down his knife and leaned closer to me. "We're just anxious to get some young attorneys in so your mom and I can take some time off."

Carolyn leaned in on the other side, and I felt like they were squeezing me like a lemon. "Yes, dear. David keeps promising me that Austria river cruise and we can't do that if Anderson and Miller have no associates."

Will would've told you to hire some already and stop living out your fantasies through your kids. Mom has told me that I didn't have to sit through these lunches or all the other landmark days of Will's life with Carolyn, but if not me, then who? Tucker, who had abandoned family events long ago, showed up only at Christmas and then only for a few hours. He refused to play Carolyn's games, as he put it. But grief wasn't a game. My counselor had told me that everyone grieved in their own time and in their own way. Who was to say that Carolyn was somehow wrong just because it created more pain for others around her? Will had loved his mother and I just couldn't abandon her.

"I'll get there," I said. That was suitably vague. I'd agreed to go back to college, but I hadn't fully bought into becoming the legacy that David and my mom were looking for. Well, mostly David. Mom had Bitsy. And David? He had Tucker, who was supposed to have entered the firm a couple of years ago, but he'd bailed to become a tattoo artist.

"I'll be fine, though," I assured Carolyn. "After this summer, I won't be working at the bar anymore. Only classes."

The mention of the bar brought a disappointed moue to Carolyn's face, her lips puckering and flattening. Carolyn thought tending bar was too low class but I wasn't sure that folding shirts at the Gap was a more honorable occupation.

"What will you be studying then?" David asked. "I think literature would be a good basis for a law degree."

Once more David didn't need a response. He loved the sound of his own voice and it was just best to allow him to drone on about the different majors I could take to prepare me to be the best lawyer ever.

"Will would've loved this place," Carolyn said in between cocktails. I nodded but inwardly disagreed again. It was like Carolyn's vision of Will was remade into who she thought Will should have been instead of who he was. The food wasn't even that good but Carolyn felt like Will deserved this nice restaurant. As if he was keeping a scorecard in his afterlife of how we marked his passing. Year two. Spent at a two-star Michelin restaurant. Five cocktails. Twenty Kleenexes. A deduction for lack of crying from the wife. C+.

And lunch lurched on. I looked at the clock and then the waiter. *Please bring the main course,* I pleaded silently but he looked away.

EXHAUSTED AFTER LUNCH WITH THE Andersons, I wasn't prepared to face the same question that Mark, the manager, had taken to asking me every time I walked through the door. "You okay to work the bar?" He never looked at me as he asked. The floor, the bar top, the stage where the live band performed, all held more interest, but ordinarily I'd have my work face pasted on—the one with the fake smile and happy-to-be-here attitude.

Ever since I'd had the *episode,* Mark had been acting awkward around me. Apparently if you start sobbing just one time while salting a margarita glass, you're marked as a difficult employee, even if you showed up on time, didn't try to set up dates with the bar rats, and got along with the other staff.

Mark should have cut me some slack. The days around the anniversary of Will's death were always the worst. A newspaper reporter had contacted me wanting to know if he could interview me for a two-year retrospective on the war that wasn't a war anymore. Pass. I was still suffering the results of the nonstop coverage that had blanketed the city the first time Will died. Every year, they tried to kill him again. Or to at least make us suffer through his death again by reporting on me, his family, and the snuffing out of the promise of his young life.

It didn't help that a photograph of his mother and me at Will's funeral had gone viral. We'd clasped hands over the flag given to me by the Army Honor Guard during the service. Two generations of sad women captured in one picture.

Grief porn, Bitsy had called it. Just looking at the picture made hearts ache. I'd become the girl who was widowed before her twentieth birthday. So no, I didn't want to rehash to the media about how my nineteen-year-old husband was killed by an IED or comment on the growing epidemic of young widows. I'd hung up on him before he'd finished asking his question. But ever since the phone call in February and my subsequent breakdown at the bar, Mark had been uneasy around me, giving me looks like I was too emotionally unstable to work around regular humans.

But my bar persona was pretty good, I thought. I pretended to be happy, made appropriate jokes, and flirted with my co-bartender Eve because I couldn't bring myself to flirt with the men at the bar. I even slicked on mascara and painted my lips dark red so that I didn't look like a sad girl who'd lost her husband before she'd turned twenty. I wasn't the best-looking member of the staff, but I wasn't going to embarrass any of the Gatsby's ownership either.

"Do you think you'll be okay?" Mark pressed, shifting from foot to foot. Didn't he ever tire of that question? In the days and weeks following my breakdown, I understood why he asked. When I started crying, it had actually set off a chain reaction, and then the bar had cleared because it was too depressing. I got that it had been a bad night of receipts for Mark, but bringing it up every time I came into work seemed a tad excessive.

"I'm not on the rag if that's what you're asking." I decided to pretend like I had no idea what he was talking about.

"Fine." Mark threw up his hands and walked off in a huff. In a contest between which topic was least comfortable—talking about a girl's period or a girl's husband's death—I guess period talk won out. I finished wiping down the bar top and putting the glasses away. Mark would return. He just wanted to shake off the horrible vision that I'd popped into his head. I smiled a little evilly to myself. Maybe he'd associate periods with death from now on and never bring up either subject again.

Mark wandered back when I'd put up the last glass. "I'm putting you at the outdoor bar. You and Eve."

"Ten four." I gave him a salute. Eve was a good bartender; she was able to flirt just enough to make the guys feel handsome and strong without going so far over the line that her boyfriend, a bouncer here, felt threatened. Working at the bar meant I could concentrate on a constant buzz of activity instead of how fricking alone I felt all the time.

"Let me know if you have any trouble." Mark held the hinged part of the bar top up as I slid under.

"And then what?" I asked. When Mark just shrugged, I patted him on his biceps. He meant well, I suppose.

The band was good and it was a gorgeous evening, so the patio bar was hopping by eight that night. Our uniforms of short black shorts and tight white t-shirts that constantly got wet ensured that the bar crowd stood three to five deep at all times. Eve and I had taken to wearing tanks underneath our Gatsby's tops to avoid giving a free show to the guys, but they still showed up. I guess hope springs eternal.

"Did you see the eye candy Adam brought in tonight?" Eve waggled her eyebrows at me as she poured two draws at once. Adam was the son of the owner of Gatsby's. The table just to the left of the stage was always reserved for him and his crew. The patio bar was positioned on the right of the stage.

"Nope." And I hadn't. Despite my loneliness, actual guys didn't interest me much. They sometimes looked at me with lust in their eyes, usually after last call they'd come up to the bar hoping that maybe Eve or I would take up the offer that had be declined throughout the night.

I turned to look over at Adam's table, but per usual, I couldn't see anyone. I was too short. At five ten, Eve stood a good five inches taller than me and could generally see into the crowd. I'd have to wait until the crowd moved or the band took a break.

"Mmm." She'd spotted him again. "Tall, buff, buzz cut so short you can see his scalp?"

Eh. Eve and I had very different ideas of what was hot in a guy. Her boyfriend, Randy, was all neck, shoulders, and muscles, which was a good fit for her because she was taller. A guy like Randy felt overpowering to me. I liked them short and wiry, and none of the guys in Adam's group were that type. His guys were all buff and muscled, as if they were some traveling men's fitness troupe. And, worse, at least a couple of them were former military. I could just tell by the way they held their bodies and looked around constantly, as if they feared some mortar attack from the sky.

When I got back into the dating game, which I would someday when I stopped missing Will so much, I wouldn't be with another military guy. My perfect man was someone who loved statistics more than guns and whose idea of a grand time was shopping for a new ruler or pen. Maybe he'd even be a fellow knitter and we'd sit side by side on the sofa watching *Downton Abbey* and knitting each other socks. Those guys weren't coming to the bar, though. Some smart girls had already snapped them up and were hiding those treasures in their homes.

I'd shared this with Eve once and, after I'd finished my description, she'd shaken her head. "There are two rules for dating you should never forget. One, he should be strong enough so you can have sex standing up and two, never, ever date a guy who could wear your jeans. It's terrible for the confidence when you see your skinny jeans looking better on his ass than yours. Learn from my sad dating history," she admonished me. Randy sure fit both those rules and so did most of Adam's crew. I was making up my own standards though and tall, buff, brawny guys didn't meet them.

"You know him?" I asked Eve when I swung back her way after serving a couple of drinks.

"No, but I'd like to." She bit her fist in mock appreciation of his fineness. "Since I'm taken, I guess I'll have to leave him to you."

"I thought I was going to be the threesome in your and Randy's bed tonight," I teased, trying to divert the discussion away from Eve's supposed man candy.

"That's a threesome I'd like to see." One of the bar customers leaned against the bar, waving a twenty. The guys who came to Gatsby's in their hundred-dollar bargain suits were trying far too hard, but their clothing attracted a certain type of girl, and I hardly ever saw a guy with a suit go home alone. I wondered what the girls thought when they were taken back to the guy's apartment that he shared with three others. Probably the same thing a guy thought when a girl took off her miracle bra. Disappointment all around.

"It's a hundred dollars," Eve said to Mr. Suit, while tapping his twenty. "You'll need four more of these."

"A hundred for what?"

"If you give them a hundred, they'll kiss." One of our regulars who'd been sitting at the bar since five that afternoon explained the rules. When Eve and I worked, guys were always asking for sexual things. I never really understood why they hit on us. Did they think that their ten spot was going to buy our phone numbers? Or that their lame catchphrases like ""What time you getting off tonight?" were going to make us bend over and drop our shorts? My favorite was "When are you two going to kiss? I'll pay twenty dollars for that!" just like this joker.

Eve and I once said that we'd kiss for a hundred, and since then, we'd get offered the money several times a night. I guess it fueled some fantasy. A hundred bucks to kiss a friend? Too easy to resist.

Suit Man rounded up his friends and slapped a hundred dollars on the table. "Now kiss."

"Kiss. Kiss. Kiss." The chant rose up from the bar. Eve finished delivering four mugs of beer and I slipped the lime wedges on a couple of tequila shots before we met in the middle. She dug her fingers into my hair and whispered against my mouth. "Someday you oughta try kissing a guy." Then she gave me a wet kiss as I held on to her shoulders.

When we broke apart to the shouts of encouragement, I responded. "Only if I can make fifty bucks per kiss." Scooping up the money, I stuck it in my back pocket to split later.

She swatted me on the ass and turned back to the customers. Watching us kiss made them thirsty. When Maisey, the waitress serving Adam's table, swung by with an order, Eve grabbed her tray and started pumping her for information. I was a little ashamed to say I sidled down the bar so I could eavesdrop.

"Who's the big guy Adam brought in?" Eve popped the caps of three bottles and set them on the tray and took to making the rest of

Maisey's orders.

"Aren't they delicious? I'd like a go with all of them."

"At one time?" Eve mocked.

"Like you haven't thought about it," Maisey retorted.

"You ain't woman enough for all that man meat over yonder," Eve said. "Don't know a woman who is. But anyway, the new guy. What's his deal?"

"Some Marine on leave for a couple of weeks."

A Marine? *Yup, totally not interested.* I drifted back down to my side of the bar. Out of the corner of my eye, I saw Eve toss a sidelong glance my way while gabbing with Maisey. Eve filled the rest of the order and Maisey took off. Once Maisey was out of earshot, Eve came down to see me—a naughty look on her face. She was up to something. "Take a break. Maisey says that the band is finishing up the last song of this set." When the band took a rest, the patio usually emptied out as people went indoors to dance and hunt a different crowd. "Go on." She started shoving me out of the bar.

"No." I resisted but she was stronger than I was and before I knew it, I was on the wrong side of the bar counter. "Fine, I'll be back in thirty minutes."

"Take your time," she sang and turned back to help some patrons.

With the band still playing a cover of "Mr. Brightside" behind me, I easily made my way to the interior of the bar and headed for the rear exit. Maybe I'd sit in my Rover and read or work a little on the layette set I was making my mother's very pregnant administrative assistant. I'd been kind of slacking off since the good weather hit, spending more time on my tiny balcony enjoying the breeze and drinking ice tea than inside knitting, surrounded by all the artifacts of my dead husband's life.

"Samantha Anderson, I haven't seen you in ages!"

Teresa Bush, she of the unfortunate last name, came barreling toward me. Teresa, Will and I had graduated together. In high school, we were probably known as friends but I hadn't laid eyes on her since Will's funeral.

"You look great." Her skintight sparkly red dress was a little upscale for Gatsby's, but it matched the suits we occasionally saw wander in after work and then stay until closing. She must be enjoying a night away from her kid. At the funeral, I'd asked if she was expecting her second, and the glare she'd pinned on me had me feeling my chest for an open wound. I thought the black look she'd cast me was because I didn't remember her kid's name but Mom had told me later that I should never ask a woman if she was pregnant.

"You are looking…" She paused, groping for the right word. My mascara was likely making smudges around my eyes and I could feel my hair slipping out of its ponytail so Teresa was looking for an honest word to describe "mess" without being offensive.

"Like a bartender?" I offered.

She gave me a slightly superior smile, "Ha! No, good, really good. Gosh, I don't think I've seen you since the funeral. It's so good that you're getting out and being social again."

"I work here," I said blandly.

"Oh right." She tittered and then placed her hand on my shoulder to stabilize herself. "I just don't get out very often and I think I need to sit down. Come talk to me. It's been so long. Did you know I got a tattoo done by Tucker? Do you want to see it?" She started pulling down the bodice of her red dress. Alarmed, I looked around for Mark, thinking that he could call her a cab. It was early though, barely nine thirty. Poor girl must not get out much what with the kid at home. "Um, should I call you a cab?"

"Why?" She smiled drunkenly at me. "Are we going to go to another party? I can't believe you're here. You are so brave. So so brave." She hiccupped. "If my husband had died after just two months of marriage I think I would've died myself. You looked so fragile at the wedding. Or funeral. Which was it?"

My feelings of sympathy toward her were fast evaporating and I needed to escape. Like David, Teresa didn't need a response. She rambled on, telling me about her kid and how it was nearly impossible to get a night to herself and how the Mai Tais we served were delicious. I tried to look rapt while searching for a way to escape. One of my stupid reasons not to move to Alaska with Will when he went there to learn how to jump out of airplanes was that I didn't want to be away from my friends and family. But as Teresa described a life experience a thousand miles from what I knew, the pain of regret squeezed my heart tight.

I looked around for assistance, but no one appeared available. Heck, no one even seemed to be paying attention to us as she rattled on about how much food her five year old ate and how clever he was for using a fork. No one noticed my predicament besides a tall guy leaning against the interior bar with a smile dancing around the edges of his mouth. Below the short sleeves of his T-shirt, the muscles in his arms were well-defined, and they flexed lightly as he supported his weight on his elbows. He was probably too far away to hear what she was saying, but he found something amusing about my situation.

We stared at each while she talked on and on. She'd moved past my own personal courage and her child's dexterity to speak about her own bravery in having children given her small birthing channel. I felt Teresa wiggle her hips to draw attention to them but I couldn't look away from the guy at the bar.

As she talked on, I watched as he pushed slowly away from the wall while maintaining eye contact. There was something familiar about him, and for a second I wondered if we'd met before. He walked so confidently, his bearing erect. His arms were held just so at his sides, as if he was ready for anything. With purpose, he strode toward me. I would have remembered this guy if we'd met before. Even in my fog of grief, I would have been able to appreciate a guy who stood an inch or two over six feet tall and whose shoulders were so broad that I wondered if he had trouble fitting through an ordinary door.

Those shoulders tapered into a lovely V that would have made any other girl's mouth water. Good thing I was immune to those feelings. I could look, appreciate the work of art in front of me, and go home unaffected. If I hadn't been completely unsusceptible, I'd be in big trouble but, as I reminded myself, I liked slim, short guys, not men whose jeans could swallow me whole or who could hold me up while we had sex—which short guys could do anyway.

"Hey, sweetheart." The stranger bent down and brushed his lips against the side of my face in what seemed to be a kiss. It'd been so long that maybe it was just a puff of air against my cheek, but I thought I felt his soft lips touch my skin. Whatever it was, it raised a flock of winged things inside my stomach. "I've been waiting for you. Gotta introduce you to my boys."

My gaze flitted from Teresa's wide-eyed gaze to the stranger's, which I now saw was hazel. I ignored the flutter in my belly and the feeling, well, lower. It wasn't my heart rate that had accelerated. The pounding in my ears had to be from some other source. Hot males didn't affect me like they apparently affected Teresa, whose eyes had glazed over and who might actually be trying to sniff the guy. The man signaled to Steve, the indoor bartender, who came over and led Teresa to a chair. I watched the whole thing like I was in a trance.

The stranger cupped my elbow and directed me toward the patio, but I didn't want to go back to the patio. Strangely, I directed him down the hallway, past the bathrooms, and then turned right before an emergency exit door that was just an ordinary door, which all the staff knew, and probably some of the patrons as well. I couldn't extricate myself from his grasp if I'd wanted to. The touch of his calloused fingers against my elbow was as powerful as an alien tractor beam.

"I, ah, thank you," I stammered out.

"You just looked like you needed a rescue," he murmured, his mouth inches from my head. We were facing each other, his hand still holding my elbow. I swore I could feel his breath ruffling my hair and my whole body shivered from the sensation.

"Is that your gig? Rescuing folks?"

He stuck his tongue into the side of his mouth. "Yeah, you could say that." His eyes wandered over me, taking in my unkempt hair, mascara-smudged eyes, and slightly damp T-shirt, made wet by the constant handling of mugs, bottles, and shots.

Teresa may have been tipsy or drunk but she'd still looked immaculate. Her blonde hair, lighter than mine and perfectly dyed, had been blown out into the perfect summer beach wave hairstyle. My own hair was drawn into a simple ponytail and I was acutely aware of all the strands that had snuck out during my hours of work and how my fingers were pruny from handling all the liquids behind the bar. I wore sneakers, low ankle socks, black cotton shorts and a simple white T-shirt. Even the worst-dressed bar patron was more put together than me.

I smoothed a few strands behind my ears, an action that loosened his firm grip on my elbow, before I caught myself. What *was* I doing? Why should I care what this guy thought of how I looked? I tucked my fingers in my shorts pocket. My elbow already felt cold, missing his touch. I frowned at myself. This was so unlike me.

"Do we know each other? You look really familiar to me." I looked at him suspiciously.

He smiled broadly at me. "I don't think so but let's remedy that. Gray Phillips, from San Diego."

"Sam Anderson." I took his right hand in my right hand and shook it. "From here."

"You're working the patio bar, right?"

I nodded, still holding his hand, enjoying the feel of it. He had a nice grip, firm, calloused, but not too rough. And it was very large. Very, very large. Like I think it could span my whole waist. Before I knew it, I was pressing his large hand against my stomach. His eyes widened and his nostrils flared at my unthinking invitation, and before my good sense could catch up with my instincts, his head was lowering toward mine.

A faint scent of spice and ocean invaded my nose, the subtle smell drowning out the heavier smells of the bar. I should be smelling sweat from the dance floor and yeast from the spilled beer or maybe even ammonia from the cleaning supplies behind me but in this little corner my senses were filled with him.

"I've been watching you all night." His mouth was right above the tip of my ear and I felt something crack inside me—a fissure was forming in the mask I'd donned earlier today or perhaps his breath, his touch, his words were simply hastening the demise of the barriers I'd held between myself and everyone else for two years. Inside my body, it felt like there was an awakening, and every fiber of my being reached toward him, upward and outward as if I were a flower on the first day of a spring rain. I lifted my head to gaze up, wide-eyed and anxious with anticipation.

Some part of my brain was telling me that the storage closet was just two steps to my right and that the exit door was just beyond that. I knew my Rover was outside, and all three were safer than standing here almost in his embrace, but I couldn't hear the warning over the pounding of my heartbeat. He bent toward me, his face serious. Even in the low light of the corner, I could see the gold flecks feathering out from the center of his eyes.

"I'm going to kiss you now." His voice was deep and rough, and it matched the rest of his thoroughly masculine body.

"I know," I whispered back. And I wanted that kiss from Gray, even though he ordinarily wouldn't be my type at all. I wanted it more than I wanted to breathe. When his mouth molded against mine, it felt like bliss—as if my whole cold body had been submerged into a warm bath. If I thought I had been engulfed before it was nothing like I felt at that moment. My entire world—my thoughts, my feelings, my senses—were full of him. I tasted the mint and hops on his tongue. I inhaled the scents of cinnamon and bergamot and ocean of his faint cologne into my airways. I felt the calloused palm on my waist and then lower against the exposed skin of my thigh. His dense muscles were drawn tight under his skin and the fabric of his t-shirt and he felt as strong as a citadel. The moan that had been building since he first backed me into the wall escaped. It had been so long since I'd had the touch of a man's hand on any part of me, and I nearly wept at the pleasure of it.

Every square inch of my body felt sensitized, as if I'd been an unlit Christmas tree and I'd just been plugged in. I wanted to feel his hands all over, not just on that patch of thigh. I needed his touch in those secret places, those places I thought had calcified. I'd thought I'd been waiting for the smooth hands of an accountant but the longer, rougher fingers pushing the hem of my shorts up couldn't belong to a man who worked in an office.

His tongue and mouth broke from mine to leave a hot, wet path from my mouth, across my jaw line, and down to my neck. My leg lifted of its own accord and he took it as a sign to hitch me up higher until both my legs either dangled off the floor or wrapped around him. I chose to wrap my legs around him and was rewarded with a thick hard column pressing into my sex. We both groaned at the contact and I could feel his sound against my neck. The reverberations sent minor shocks throughout my nervous system. Holding me up against the wall, he began thrusting against me rhythmically, every impact of his hips making me hotter and wetter than I thought I could get.

I gripped him tighter with my legs and dug my hands into his hair, using every bit of his body as leverage. He held me up with ease, as if I were a feather. One hand was under my right butt cheek and the other was exploring my left side, pulling out my T-shirt, only to find the tank underneath. Needing his mouth back, I tugged on his hair and he took the hint immediately. He fastened his lips over mine and we devoured each other, still rubbing our lower bodies against each other as the bass from the dance floor pounded the floor boards.

Whimpering, I begged in moans and small cries for more. A familiar but almost forgotten tension was winding its way from between my legs outward. All thoughts of storage rooms and hallways and strangers were lost in the swirl of bright lights bursting behind my eyelids.

"I got you, baby," he growled against my mouth. "Just let go." And so I did. I closed my eyes and let those long-dormant feelings wash over me, spreading from the inside of my legs to the nerve endings in my toes and fingertips and the very top of my head. And he kept grinding and grinding and grinding against me, whispering in my ear how I was the hottest thing he'd ever held, how he couldn't wait to taste me, how he'd die if he couldn't be inside me tonight.

THREE

Gray

I'D GONE INSIDE TO TAKE A LEAK AND TO LOOK AT THE TOP SHELF row of liquor to see what kind of celebration drinks I could buy the boys when I'd seen the little blonde bartender from the patio. Her hair was caught up in a high ponytail that swung like a rope down her back. I'd already caught myself staring at her several times throughout the night as the crowd at the bar, which was mostly dick, parted and closed like a peek-a-boo game. The glimpses they'd revealed weren't half as interesting as the whole package. Standing about ten feet from me and caught in the grasp of another woman, the bartender had shot me a deer-in-the-headlights look. I couldn't resist helping a sixty-year-old grandmother at the airport, and I had even less fight against the unspoken plea for assistance from a twenty-something beauty.

I abandoned my liquor hunting and headed over. I'd had no plans to lead her down the dark hallway and dry hump her to an orgasm because, as I told the Woodlands crew earlier, these types of bar hookups were generally unsatisfactory. I'd thought to escort her back to the bar outside but when she paused and stared at me like she *knew* me, I felt a jolt. Suddenly I didn't want to take her outside where there were other people—other men—who would look at her and want her. I'm not sure who turned down the dark hallway first, but it was the right place for me to taste her full lips and grip her long ponytail.

Her lips had felt as soft and suckable as I thought they would be. She tasted tart, as if she'd had a vodka lemon shot. The hot cavern of her mouth made me think of other hot, wet areas on her body and I wanted to explore all of them.

There wasn't much thought in my head other than how kissing her wouldn't be enough. At the very least, I needed to get my hand under those shorts or under her shirt. I *had* to touch more bare skin but her shorts only went up so far and under her shirt there was more damn fabric. I really wanted to rip those shirts up over her head and draw one delicious tit into my mouth.

Before I could get any closer to her, I'd felt a trembling in her legs and her breath had started to come in harsh, jagged pants. She was so turned on by just the kissing, just the press of our bodies together, that she was ready to come right then. And I wasn't going to stop that. I pressed my hard-on with more force against her cotton-clad pussy and felt her explode.

Feeling her come apart in my arms just from kissing her made me feel like a giant, and it left me with a hard-on the size of California. Had I ever been a fool to say that a bar hookup wasn't good? Maybe I just hadn't had the right bar hookup. All my little rules about dating, hookups, and women were somewhere in a puddle under my feet. There was only one thought in my mind now. I needed to find us some privacy—immediately. Desperate to lay her down on any surface, I pulled away from the wall, holding her against me. Her body was lax in its post orgasmic state. There was a door just to her right.

"Sam," I whispered as gently as I could, not wanting to disturb her moment but desperate for some relief myself. "That room. Is it private?" Sam turned her head, still resting on my shoulder.

"Yes, storage room."

I started for the door before she got past the word yes. "I need you bad, Sam. Once we're inside, I'm going to strip off these shorts and stick my head between your legs and lap up all the juice your body just made for me." She shuddered and clenched her legs tighter around me. She liked the dirty talk. I'd have to remember that. We got to the door, and I leaned down to open it, not wanting her to let go. "After I'm done eating you out, I'm going to—" I never got the rest of the promise out.

"Hey, Mrs. A." A voice called from the end of the hall. "Mark's asking for you."

Sam jerked upright and pushed away from me. I let her drop to the ground as the words sunk in. *Mrs. A* as in *Mrs. Anderson?* I grabbed her left hand and raised it. Sure enough there was a fucking diamond on that hand and it was not a small piece of shit like some of the recruits bought at the local mall. "What the hell is this?" I asked, raising her hand between us. I never, ever cheated. I'd been on the other end of that shitty stick and wouldn't wish it on my worst enemy. Having discovered that I was making out with a married dude's lady made me sick.

"It's none of your business." Her face paled when she saw the ring. Probably afraid that her dirty secret was going to come back to bite her in the ass. She tried to wrench her hand away but I had things to say to her.

"None of my business, my ass." I got up right into her face. "You better hope your man doesn't come in here tonight because I will not hesitate to fucking tell him that his woman has absolutely no morals. I do not appreciate being dragged into whatever sordid little thing you've got going on with your bar patrons. Next time you feel like cheating on your man, consider taking your ring off first. It's a dead fucking giveaway." I flung her hand away as if it was diseased. She might be. My skank of an ex had tried to climb back into my bed with syph between her legs. "Or better yet, just break it off and stop trying to climb every available dick you think might taste good."

I stomped off before Sam could utter whatever excuses she was ready to vomit out. I was furious at her, but even more pissed off at myself. My dick was still as hard as steel, and it was aching from the lack of attention. It wanted me to run back to her, ignore the ring, and just let myself push inside what was probably a juicy pussy. She'd be a good fuck. Cheaters usually are.

If I'd taken a minute, just one minute, I could've easily checked out her ring finger but I was too busy staring at things like her lips and her chest and her ass. I was too busy fantasizing about grabbing that ponytail and wrapping around my hand while she rode me hard. The whole event just reinforced that bar hookups were a shitty idea. Heck, I don't think I'd mind sticking my dick in crazy so long as she was up-front and honest, neither of which applied to Sam Anderson.

Samantha

SHOCK HAD ME LEANING AGAINST the wall, weak as a kitten. Shock from having an orgasm brought about by activities I hadn't done since I was a teenager. Shock at being yelled at for cheating. I'd come into the bar as twenty-two-year-old Sam Anderson, widow, bartender, knitter. Now I didn't know who I was because I'd just nearly screwed a stranger in the storeroom of my place of employment. The first time I'd had sex with Will, I'd been so nervous because I thought his parents would come busting through the doors of the pool house. And now I was wrapping myself around a guy I'd never met before.

"Mrs A.?" It was Steve again. He was the only one who called me that here. Like Teresa, Steve had gone to school with Will and me and had started calling me Mrs. A in high school. At the time Will and I had thought it was funny. "You okay?"

"Yeah. Just fine," I lied and pushed away from the wall. Smoothing my shorts down and tucking in my shirt, I kept my gaze on the floor, not sure what I'd see in Steve's eyes.

"That guy causing you problems? He can be gone in a heartbeat."

"No, we just had a disagreement over…limes."

"Limes?" Steve asked skeptically.

"Um, right, well, he said I put too many limes in his Corona. He'd only wanted one and I guess I shoved two in there." I peeked through my eyelashes to see Steve frowning.

"Mark asked me to send you up to the VIP lounge."

"Thanks." The second floor held a small VIP lounge that Mark usually worked, ensuring all of Adam's dad's friends were properly served. It meant constant sucking up to old rockers who thought they were still the hottest thing on the billboard charts instead of musicians whose names not one person downstairs other than Adam could name. But I'd rather stroke the ego of these guys for the rest of the night than go downstairs and serve drinks with Gray about ten feet away the whole time. God, maybe I *was* emotionally fragile.

"Sweetheart, so glad you're up here taking care of me tonight," one of the regulars called out.

I gave him a wry smile because, for once, I was glad to take care of the older set. I was careful to treat them like they were still young and hot lest I hurt their feelings. "Me too, Ollie. Need me to top off that whiskey?"

"You know it."

What I'd just done in the hallway of Gatsby's was so incredibly out of character, so incredibly dumb—so incredibly *good*, dammit. I wanted to sit down by Ollie and cry my eyes out. Mark would certainly think twice, maybe even three times, about allowing me to work here if that happened.

It was like someone else had taken control of my body. I'd never, ever been into public displays of affection and here I was dry humping a stranger. Worse, he was a friend of Adam's who, for all intents and purposes, was like my boss. Sex wasn't even that important to me. I didn't own a vibrator. I rarely ever masturbated. Those urges rarely poked their head into my thought process. Sure, I missed Will and Will's body, but he'd been gone a lot, and I'd gotten used to being alone even before he'd died. Will had gone to Basic and then off to Alaska for training, and since I hadn't gone with him, I'd been by myself.

What I needed was a vibrator. It'd just been so long without any sexual release that a guy who wasn't even my type could get me off. Heck, Eve could've gotten me off in the hallway if she'd been rubbing me right. *It was just a normal reaction to long dormant feelings,* I told myself. Taking a deep breath, I straightened my shoulders and continued my internal pep talk. It was normal. I'd never have to see this Gray Phillips from San Diego again if I didn't want. He was visiting and would be going home after the weekend.

I liked safe and comfortable, not crazy encounters with strangers. New guys and new experiences were all overrated, amazing orgasm aside. I'm sure I could give that to myself. I'd try it tonight in fact. Right when I got home, I'd head for the shower and use the old variable water spray. Upstairs in the tiny VIP lounge, I wrapped myself in the memory of Will and my old friend grief, because even though its heavy weight made it hard to get out of bed in the morning and tried to smother me with memories at night, I had learned how to handle it. Working long hours at the bar on the weekends helped, and I hoped spending every waking minute studying once school started in the fall would have the same numbing effect. Either that or I was going to have to medicate myself with Vicodin and Xanax cocktails like Will's mom. We'd be a pair. But as awful as the grief was, at least I knew how to deal with it. The awkward feelings of attraction toward someone else were strange and unfamiliar and kind of terrifying and I just didn't need that in my life.

FOUR

Gray

I WAS STILL STEAMED WHEN I MADE IT BACK TO THE TABLE. THE band hadn't reappeared, and all the girls had left. Either dancing to some ABBA shit or going to the bathroom, I guessed.

"What's up, hoss?" Noah asked, clearly seeing I was pissed off.

"Nothing a little liquor won't cure." I picked up a new bottle of beer and drained half of it before setting it down.

"Someone call you a boot?" Bo wondered. Boot was what we called new Marines or stupid Marines, which were often the same thing.

"I wish." I tried to smile and joke back so I didn't ruin the evening with a shitty attitude. "I'm not even wearing any gear from the Corps."

"Another reason to get out, buddy. You can stop wearing clothes issued by Uncle Sam."

"That's not even in the top ten reasons why not to re-enlist."

"Glad to know you're making a list." Bo clinked his bottle against mine.

"The list to get out is always longer than the one to stay in."

"Sounds like you already made up your mind."

I sucked down my bottle. "Who knows? Maybe."

"Do you even need this vacation?"

"Even if I had made up my mind, I wouldn't say. Who's going to turn down forty-five days of consecutive leave?"

Bo laughed as I'd intended. With his attention diverted, I gave myself a mental shake. So I kissed a married woman. It's not like I knew that going in. Otherwise, it would've never happened. I wasn't going to allow one cheating woman to ruin my time here.

"Get out then. Come here to Central with us. It'll be like old times."

"Not everyone has a trust fund to fall back on."

Bo smirked. "Don't try that with me, son of a congressman. You aren't hurting."

"What's this?" AnnMarie and the rest of the girls had returned. By the looks of their freshly applied makeup, bathroom had been the right call. I tried to warn Bo to keep his mouth shut, but he'd already started spilling it all out.

"Gray's dad is the Honorable Phillips from the—what district is it?"

"Fifth," Noah offered. I closed my eyes in resignation. So much for trying to be anonymous. Whatever advantage I'd been trying to achieve through being in entirely different surroundings where no one knew me was lost, but I'd never told Bo and Noah I wanted anonymity so that was on me. I should have went white water rafting in Colorado for a month with a bunch of strangers. I should've packed less gear. I should've avoided that last conversation with my dad. I should've turned away from Sam Anderson's doe eyes. Lots of should haves.

Bo knocked me in the shoulder. "Hey, buddy, it can only go up from here."

"Thanks, man." I gave an obligatory laugh and tried to loosen up.

A few minutes later a rough group of guys showed up. Four of them, varying heights and hair colors, were sporting the same tattooed tough-guy look. They wore sneakers, T-shirts, and chains running from the sagging waistband of their ripped jeans to the wallets stuck in the front pockets. Tattoos covered nearly every inch of bare skin. One of them greeted Adam by knocking his forearm against Adam's forearm twice. Lots of civilians gave the military crap for their uniforms but everyone had a uniform. You only had to look around the table to see it. College kids wore the uniform of lazy carelessness. These newcomers' clothing, hair, and attitudes all indicated they were in the same tribe. Uniforms were everywhere; discipline, however, was not.

I balanced on my chair lightly and didn't pick up a drink, not wanting to be caught off guard if a fight started. Worse thing about being off base? Not having a weapon at the ready. My trigger finger itched and I scanned the grounds to see what I could use *just in case*.

"There's no danger here. Ease off Marine," Noah whispered in my ear. I gave him a rueful smile and settled back. Another chair was brought up and the guy who greeted Adam dropped into it while his friends wandered back into the bar. Our waitress brought out a glass filled to the top with a dark lager. Introductions were made around the table although it was clear that they were for my benefit. Most of the table appeared to have met this Tucker Anderson before.

When I heard his name I tensed up for another reason. Shit, I bet this was Sam's husband. She had a lot of nerve kissing me in the back hallway when her husband could've shown up at anytime.

"How's your dick?" Tucker asked Adam. "You laying off the pussy like I told you to?"

Was Tucker some kind of doctor that'd he be asking about Adam's dick all casual like? The rest of the table wanted to know the answer to the question.

"Thanks for your lack of discretion, buddy." Adam folded his arms and glared at Tucker.

Tucker spread his hands innocently in front of him. "I'm raising your dating capital." To the girls at the table, he announced, "Adam got his dick pierced."

He wasn't wrong. Almost before he got out the word "pierced" the entire bar tilted toward Adam. Even Bo and Noah's girls leaned toward Adam with interest in their eyes. The questions came fast.

"Did it hurt?"

"What kind?"

"How does it feel?"

And from our waitress, "Are you gonna show us?"

Bo looked at AnnMarie's avid curiosity and groaned. "Oh, sunshine, no. You wouldn't do that to little Bo, now would you?"

AnnMarie nestled back in Bo's arms and giggled. "Nah, only because you're not so little." That was exactly the right line to deliver and Bo laid a kiss on her that raised the temperature of the group about five degrees. My two boys settling down made me feel strange inside, a little empty. It was an unwelcome feeling and I drank the rest of my bottle trying to drown it.

Tucker abandoned Adam to target Finn next. "Thanks for sending your girlfriend's sister by. She's working out great."

"She's my ex, but thanks. Winter's very talented." Finn's voice held an odd oppressive note, like he didn't want to talk about it but Tucker was oblivious.

"You might tell her that." Tucker smirked. "Your ex-girlfriend was all over the ink shop yesterday telling Winter about how you two were about heartbeats away from registering at Target."

This reveal only made Finn's glower turn darker. Maybe Tucker wasn't oblivious. Maybe he was just an asshole. Not that this excused Sam for cheating on him. She should've chosen better in the first place.

"Lay off, Anderson," Adam said coolly and turned a warning gaze at Finn. No crazy shit in his bar, he telegraphed. Finn got the message and stared at the band, cutting Tucker out. Having lost his toy, Tucker scanned the bar and then turned to Adam. "Where's Sam? She said she was working tonight."

Adam gave a nod toward the second floor of the bar. "VIP."

"Why? She hates it up there."

Maybe because she's found an ounce of shame and took herself away from the scene of the crime. I shifted uncomfortably in my chair, the guilt scratching at my back. I had to come clean to this guy, but not in front of everyone.

"She doesn't hate it. Besides, I think it was too crowded down here for her," Adam said.

"Whatever. I need to see her. I think she's pissed at me," Tucker said.

"How come?"

"Why d'you automatically assume I'd done something?" Tucker complained, but he caved under Adam's cool stare. "Fine. I skipped out on the memorial lunch."

Adam and Finn cursed in unison.

"You're a douchebag. Your brother dies during deployment and you can't even bring yourself to go to lunch?" Adam punched Tucker in the arm. From Tucker's wince, the fist carried a bit more power than a friendly smack. Tucker must've felt guilty because he took the punch without retaliation. So maybe Tucker was a serious douche, but that *still* didn't excuse Sam from kissing me.

"Yeah, yeah, but seriously, I need to see her. When's she got a break?" Tucker asked.

Adam stared at him for a moment, kind of measuring him up. "You still got a thing for her? If so, you better start treating her right."

"Or else what? You're going make a move?" Tucker asked a little belligerently. This was like a goddamn telenovela. I looked at Bo and he wiggled his eyebrows. But seriously they were asking if Tucker still had a thing for his own wife? Were they separated? I wanted to stand up, yell time out and have everyone explain themselves because I was damned confused. The one thing I did figure out was I owed someone an apology and right now I had a feeling that apology needed to be given to Sam.

"No, dumbass. And I don't think you should either," Adam replied.

"Why, because of Will?" Tucker returned. More belligerence. Everyone at the table was watching this train wreck. We couldn't look away. "At least I'm not fucking sisters."

This was apparently directed toward Finn because he leaned forward immediately and shot back, "No, *you're* only trying to fuck your dead brother's widow."

Tucker's chair made a screeching sound when he stood up, fists at the ready. Finn had risen to meet the challenge and everyone on my side of the table tensed up. We were backing Finn. No question. But Adam stood and separated the two.

"Come on, Tucker, let's go upstairs." Tucker allowed himself to be dragged away while Finn stood glaring at the two of them. He kicked one of the chairs and then left the bar. A minute later, we heard the roar of a hemi engine as Finn drove away.

"Did I catch that right? Tucker Anderson is Sam's brother-in-law? And he wants in her panties?" Everyone nodded, wide-eyed. Yup, I'd gotten that right, which meant I'd gotten everything oh-so-wrong before. Well, shit. All the details clicked into place. Sam was a widow of a military guy who'd died over in the Middle East. Her brother-in-law was the crapbag who'd just taken off. And I was the fucker who'd accused her of cheating on her dead husband. I started toward the bar.

"Don't go there," Bo said warningly. "No need to save damsels you don't even know."

"Go where?" I pretended like I didn't know what he was talking about.

"She's got all she can handle if her brother-in-law is looking for a poke," Noah added.

"Ugh, can we not talk about that poor girl like this?" Grace interjected.

"Sorry," we all mumbled. It *was* low class. She'd made the ultimate sacrifice, losing her man in battle. That had to be respected and I wasn't leaving until I'd made amends.

Samantha

AFTER GATSBY'S CLEARED OUT, I came down and helped Eve cash out the patio bar. "The hottie that arrived with Adam left alone, or at least without a girl. Maisey was mad because he wouldn't even accept her number. Just said that she was too pretty for him."

I ignored her and sorted and arranged the bills so all the numbers were facing the same direction. Orderly things made sense. Knitting a precise pattern of stitches into a blanket or socks made sense. Trying to figure out a new man? That did not make sense.

"He came up to the bar a couple of times. Like he was looking for someone," Eve said.

My hand hovered over the bills for a moment as a little thrill inside of me surged up. He looked for me? *No, stop it*, I thought, and clenched my hand for a moment, the pain of my nails digging into my palm bringing me back down to earth.

Eve put out a hand to stop my counting. "Steve said you had a run-in with a customer and that's why you hid upstairs all night. The patron he described sounded a lot like Adam's new friend."

I closed my eyes for a moment and then opened them to see Eve still staring at me. "Yeah, it was him. I kissed him." I didn't tell her that I virtually dragged him down the dark hallway and then climbed him like a pole and rubbed against him like a cat in heat until I was left with wet panties and a whole lot of regrets.

Eve squealed and clapped her hands. "Oh, Sam, that's awesome. What happened next?" She placed her fingers under her chin for support and batted her eyelashes. "Tell me more. Tell me more. Did he put up a fight?"

I smiled at her use of the words from *Grease*. "No, Sandra Dee, he did not, but when he saw my wedding ring he was plenty pissed off."

"Oh no." She groaned and lifted my left hand. She grimaced slightly. "Do you think you're ready to take that off? You definitely don't want to be attracting guys who think it's okay to hit on married women."

"I hadn't even thought of it that way." I didn't know if I was ready to take off the ring. Removing the band seemed to signal that I was ready for other things—like another relationship, another boyfriend, another husband. Experimentally, I tugged at my diamond, but there was little give to it, the knuckle preventing the ring from sliding any further off my finger. *No, not ready for taking my ring off then*. But the memory of Gray's mouth on mine and the dirty words he'd growled in my ear made me think I was ready for something. The press of his body against mine was like taking the first sip of hot coffee in the morning. It woke me up and I was hungry for more. I knocked my head against the register. "I'm no good at this. It's just one of a million reasons why I shouldn't have been kissing Gray."

"No. No. It's all good. Is that his name, Gray? I like it. It's unusual."

"It's a color. Who names their kids colors?"

"Weird people. California people." Eve's boyfriend had arrived in the lounge and parked himself on a bar stool while I finished cashing out the drawer and she completed the bottle count.

"Opposites, then," Eve cooed. She let go of my hand so she could pat her heart.

"Don't go having us married in your imagination. I can't even get my ring off, which means according to you that I'll only attract the slimiest of slime." The beautifully cut facets sparkled even in the crappy lighting of the bar as I waved my hand in front of her face. "This is Carolyn's, you know."

"Will gave you his mother's ring?"

"Yes. But then David had to buy Carolyn a five-carat diamond to replace this one." I pulled the diamond around to the inside of my hand. "It all worked out."

"Are you going to see him again?"

Picking up the bills, I started counting again. "No. He was pretty angry. Besides, I could probably be used in an instructional video about how not to interact with males."

"Go up to him and explain."

"Explain what?" Randy interjected.

"Sam made out with a guy tonight down by the storage closet and then he saw her ring and got mad. I told her she should go and explain that she's not married anymore."

For a moment I was irritated that Eve was sharing but what the heck, a male opinion might be worthwhile. "What do you think?" I asked him.

"I'm not sure I'd feel comfortable kissing a girl who's got her wedding band on." He popped more nuts in his mouth, swallowed them, and added, "But if you want to see him again then an explanation is worth a shot. Be real obvious about it. Guys are dense. Go up to him and say 'Hey, boy, I want to do you tonight.'"

"Is that how you picked Randy up, Eve?" I teased.

"No way. He was even denser. I had to basically club him over the head and then drag him back to the car. Even then I had to climb onto him before he realized I was interested."

"Hey, no," he protested. "I just wanted to be sure you were sure."

"I couldn't have been a surer thing if you'd had paid for me." She shook her head in mock dismay. "But I took him against the car anyway."

"Against the car?" I was torn between being aghast and envious.

"If you haven't tried that position then I'm really sorry because up against the wall or door while he's between your knees, one leg slung over his shoulder is," she paused and shuddered, "un-friggin-believable."

I stared at her and recalled the truncated promise Gray had given me. Just the memory made me shiver. "I believe you. I think I'm turned on just by hearing you describe it."

"I know I am," said Randy.

"Can't wait for tonight, baby." She leaned over and cleaned his tonsils out. I watched them far too long to be polite. I realized then that I *had* been missing sex and more, real intimacy with another person. I missed what Eve had with her boyfriend, the right to have casual intimate contact. To hold hands with someone in public, to know that on all the important holidays someone was thinking of me. I'd missed it so much that I'd attacked a stranger in the hallway. Should I go after Gray and explain? Should I explore these feelings he'd roused? I thought I was immune to men and that my girl parts had shriveled because not one guy in the two years since Will died even warranted a second look let alone stirred sexual desire.

Eve must've seen my envious glance or felt my overlong stare because she broke it off and shooed her boyfriend away.

"It's been two years, why not give another guy a chance or at least just hook up? Get back in the game."

I looked down at my left hand and the diamond winked backed at me. "I don't know how."

"Go over to Adam's house tomorrow. Maisey said he's staying there for like six weeks. Or ask him over to your condo for coffee."

"Coffee?"

"Or a movie."

"What kind of coffee? And a movie? For someone I don't know." This sounded like terrible advice.

Randy snorted. "It's never coffee."

"What?"

"It's never coffee. Or even a movie," he elaborated. "You invite him over for anything and he'll know you're asking to have sex."

"I thought you guys were dense and that I had to ask for things straight up." Getting back into the dating pool was going to take a lot of effort. Probably more effort than I was interested in exerting. Yet... wouldn't it be nice to leave the bar and crawl in bed next to someone? The ache I felt in my heart may not be soothed, but the ache in the body could be.

"Everyone knows that an invitation over to her place for anything after, say, eight at night, maybe even seven, is a booty invitation. And vice versa." He shook his finger at me. "You should know this if you're gonna start sleeping around."

Thankfully Eve hit him so I didn't have to. "What?" He held up his hands. "I thought we were just tossing out advice to the poor chick."

"Don't even," she warned, "or you won't get any of what I was talking about earlier."

Randy sat back and motioned that he was zipping his lip.

I sighed. "It's okay. I need all the advice I can get. I haven't done this in, well, ever. I grew up with Will. I knew him better than I knew myself at times. This Gray guy, I only know he smells good." And other stuff that I didn't want to admit like how strong he was when he held me against the wall and how his rough calloused fingers on the bare skin of my thigh made me damp just at the memory.

"He's a Marine on leave for a few weeks staying with former members of his—whatever they're called—troop?"

"Platoon," I said flatly. I'd forgotten the most important thing about Gray—that was he was in the military and that I wasn't ever getting involved with another military guy. Not even for a casual, one-night hook up. Eve opened her mouth to say something, but I didn't let her. "Whatever argument you've got, just shelve it."

"You need hair of the dog," she told me, ignoring my admonition. "One military guy breaks your heart, get good loving from another to put it back together."

"Will didn't break my heart. He died."

"Same thing, honey. You've been heartbroken for two years now.

This could be the perfect antidote."

"You're crazy." I walked down to the other end of the bar and Eve followed me.

"I might be crazy but it doesn't mean I'm wrong. Trust me, I know heartbreak. You know I do."

Breaking my heart would've been Will leaving me for someone else. He didn't leave me. He went to serve his country. He still loved me. If he would have had it his way, we'd be happily married with a kid on the way. *Then why did he enlist? Why did he choose a dangerous military occupational specialty?*

Because he loved his country too, I told my little voice mulishly.

A cold cloth pressed against my temple. A quiet moment in the corner of the bar was what I needed to silence the voices, but I couldn't tell anymore which were speaking lies. The ones that told me he loved me or the ones that told me he didn't.

"He didn't break my heart," I repeated.

Eve kissed the top of my head. "Didn't say he didn't love you, honey, just that he broke your heart. This guy is perfect. He's a rebound guy—only around for a few weeks. You do him, get back on the horse, and you're ready for a real relationship then."

"Did you know, besides that insane moment earlier with Gray, that you're the only person I've kissed on the mouth since Will died?" I tapped my index finger against my lower lip. "So that's like twenty-six months, because I saw him the weekend before he deployed."

"Christ, girl, no wonder you were making out with soldier boy." Eve brushed by me to stick the cash drawer, minus the cash, back into the register. "You're like a bear waking up from hibernation. Try out someone else. Those big alphas can be a handful." She winked at Randy who grinned like a man well satisfied.

"Because I'm slow and doddering, like a bear?"

"No, because you're hungry. I'm afraid you'll try to feast on him in front of everyone."

Too late, I thought. "I can't even pull my ring off so I think I'm still hibernating."

Eve shook her head. "Nope."

"And you know this how?"

"Because before you wouldn't even talk about guys. I don't think you even saw that they were actual sexual beings. And now? Now you're actually asking questions. We gotta make sure you're pointed in the right direction for your hunt."

"I sound very predatory...and dangerous." They both laughed. I appreciated Eve's words, though, because they made my earlier reactions less embarrassing viewed through her perspective. "If I was interested, though, Gray is not my type. He's too tall and...bold. Plus, he's not even from around here."

"That's what makes him absolutely perfect," Eve declared. "Who cares what he does for a living? It's not like you are going to marry him. He's a rebound guy. You're getting your feet wet. Even better, you both know it's temporary."

Temporary. I rolled that word around on my tongue and after a moment I realized it didn't scare me. It felt alright. In fact, it made me kind of excited.

FIVE

Gray

WHEN EVERYONE BROKE FOR THE NIGHT AND LAST CALL WAS made, I sent Bo and Noah on their way, explaining I had an apology to make and I'd catch a taxi home. I'd tried to find Sam during the evening but she never returned to the patio bar, and I didn't want to make waves by asking Adam for access to wherever she was.

"Taxi service is shit here," Noah cautioned.

"What's the worst that could happen?" I said. "I'd have to run back to your place? I've done longer distances with a hundred pound pack on my back."

Bo and Noah shared a look and then shrugged and took off when they realized I wasn't going to change my mind. I loitered outside the bar, leaning against a brick wall, fading into the shadows. From my vantage point, I could see the exit but I was mostly hidden from view.

The door opened and Sam came out with her friend, and I pushed away from the wall and called out so I didn't startle her. She still yelped in surprise and jumped back, bumping into her girlfriend. So much for not startling her. I stepped into the light and held up my hands in surrender so she could see I was harmless—although I was aware that was a relative term. I could've taken both women and had them bound and in a car in less time than it takes a cop to piss.

"Jaysus," said the taller woman, holding her hand to her heart. "You scared the piss out of us."

"Don't you have anyone walking you to your cars?" My plans for Sam were momentarily distracted by the thought of these two young women out here in the night unprotected.

"Mark's here." Sam jerked her finger over her shoulder and out came a guy I noticed had been walking around checking things out. He was dressed in black slacks and a black button down shirt and looked like he weighed about a hundred and forty pounds dripping wet. He might require a little more effort, but the three were vulnerable. "And Randy."

Randy was clearly a bouncer, and he walked with heavy feet. He looked like he was all muscle, no technique.

I decided to make for Mark first, before I separated Sam from her people. Mark was the guy in charge, at least based on his clothes— black shirt button down shirt, black slacks, and dress shoes. Sam and the other woman wore shorts and Randy had on jeans and a T-shirt. "Hey, Mark, Gray Phillips. Friend of Adam's. We sat at the table to the left of the stage."

Mark nodded and held out his hand. He had a good handshake. I was tempted to squeeze it too hard but managed to suppress my stupid caveman instincts. I was trying to make nice here. I gave him my best politician's smile, which I learned from watching my dad for the last eight years—he'd worn it out until it was his default expression.

"I need to have a few minutes with Ms. Anderson here, if I can. I promise to return her in just a few." I gave his hand another squeeze and another smarmy "I'm a people person" smile. It worked for my dad, and I hoped it would work for me here.

Mark nodded. "Sure." He even gave Sam a little push toward me. She glared at Mark but no one made a move to stop me from moving her down the sidewalk into the darker edges of the boulevard.

She was resistant and I felt like I was dragging her. "Look, I'm sorry I said that stuff inside. I was worked up and caught off guard." I gave her a sheepish grin. "I'm pretty big on not cheating."

"I got that." She sighed. "I think it was just a mistake all around. I get why you were angry. I'm sure if I was kissing someone I thought was married, I'd have freaked out too."

I wanted to object to the freaking out thing. "Can we rewind and go back to the place we were before I insulted you thoroughly?"

Sam bit the side of her lip and glanced back at her tall friend. The tall friend smiled and waved, a get-going gesture. I waved back because Sam needed more encouragement from the look of indecision on her face.

"Did you really wait all night to tell me that you're sorry?"

No, I realized with sudden clarity, *I waited all night to see if I could convince you to pick up where we left off.* Then I laughed at myself for being a dick. So much for not liking bar hook ups. "Yeah, I guess I did."

"Where's your crew? Did they abandon you?"

"I told them to go on ahead."

"You have a car? The Woodlands is a ways out."

"Nope, but I'm fine."

She tapped the front of her neck and frowned at me. No one else was around now, just her, me, and the three waiting for her.

"How're you getting home?" she asked finally.

I rolled my shoulders to appear as relaxed and non-confrontational as possible. "I'm just going to call a taxi."

"Taxi service is terrible here." Her frown was getting deeper which was the wrong reaction.

"I really am sorry, you know." I ran my fingers over the side of her mouth, trying to coax a smile out of her.

"Me too." She tucked her face into my hand, almost like one of those kittens a few of us had found near a forward operating base in a ditch, abandoned by their mother. Those tiny things had been hesitant at first, but with a little milk and a tender touch had tottered on their little legs after us, always seeking one last pet. We'd given those kittens away to local kids.

"You going to drive me home, or am I going to have to hoof it?" We'd been beating around that bush, and I figured I should just come out and ask.

"I actually live near here." She gestured to the west of us but I didn't care where she lived, only that I was hearing her right. "Would you like some coffee?"

Coffee. *Shit yeah, I did.* "Ordinarily I don't go home for *coffee* after a night at the bar but yeah, with you, I'd like that."

"I've never had anyone home for *coffee* except, well, Will."

Will, her dead husband and fallen soldier. I pushed that image out of my mind. She was here with me and I still remembered the feeling of her shuddering in my arms. This time I wanted the trembling to happen when I was inside of her. I wanted to feel the shake of her body when I licked her pussy and the clench of her tight channel when I thrust into her. No one else would be there but her and me. "Lead the way," I said. "I'm thirsty."

She flushed slightly, waved to her friends and boldly took my hand, leading me down the dark alley with piss poor lighting behind the bar. I took a mental note to mention to Adam tomorrow that his old man needed better, safer lighting for the staff. Sam hit her key fob and the lights to an expensive European SUV blinked on and off.

"Nice wheels," I said. "You take this off-roading?" This vehicle was more my style than Bo's tiny sports car would ever be.

"Never," she said. "It was my mom's. I got it when I graduated from high school. It's actually pretty old."

"Still nice."

We chitchatted about cars and she knew surprisingly quite a bit about her own vehicle.

"I can even change my own tires," she said proudly after I'd teased her about knowing how much horsepower her Rover had.

"That's impossible," I mocked. "No girl knows how to do that."

"Whatever," she flicked her palm toward me. "My dad taught me because…" She trailed off.

"Because?"

"I've been alone for a long time."

The specter of why she'd been alone formed between us but if she was going to ignore it, then I was too, because I wanted this girl. We'd started something in that hallway and I was too stubborn to give up on whatever she had in mind for me. Plus, I had stuff to show her too. I'd made her those promises and I always, always delivered on my promises.

The trip to Sam's place took only a few minutes. She wasn't kidding when she said she lived close. It was one of those old brick factory buildings revitalized into lofts. The lighting here was shit too. I shook my head. Placing my hand at the small of her back, I watched the shadows so she didn't have to. She might be able to change her tire and recite the horsepower on her Rover, but she didn't watch out for herself like she should.

"Have you lived here long?" I asked as I followed her up the stairs to the second floor of the building.

"Three years," she replied. "It's small but mine."

I may have preferred taller girls, but there was no denying the shapeliness of Sam's ass as it moved underneath the cotton of her shorts. I remembered what it felt like in my palm—firm but pliable. I clenched my fingers unconsciously at the memory. I couldn't wait to take a bite out of it. The upside down heart shape was practically taunting me.

Surreptitiously, I reached inside my own shorts and made a small adjustment so my burgeoning wood wouldn't scare her or cause me unnecessary pain.

"Here we are," she murmured, throwing open the door to her apartment. I took a quick look around. There was a lamp lit on the far side of the room and a kitchen to my immediate left. I noted the table and the sofa as the only real furniture in the room. Her bedroom was either somewhere else or she slept on the sofa. "Do you, um, want coffee? I mean a real cup?"

I suppressed a smile at her artlessness. This girl was the farthest thing from a cheating, dishonest base wife. The same protective instincts I'd experienced before when she seemed under verbal assault by the blonde came roaring back. Reaching out, I tucked a few of the loose strands of honey blonde hair behind her ear. "No, what's right in front of me is more than enough." I rubbed the pad of my thumb across her lush lower lip.

She closed her eyes and raised her face to mine, and I took the invitation that she offered. Lifting her against me so I wouldn't have to stoop down, I molded her body against mine. My first kisses were light, to make sure she had time to change her mind, but when she licked her little tongue along my lips, my fire was lit. I'd had aged whisky with my dad that didn't taste as rich or as heady as she did. When her mouth closed over my tongue and sucked, my eyes rolled back into my head. There were other hot, wet areas of her body, and I ached to put my fingers there, and then my tongue, and then finally my rock hard dick.

"Ahhh," I moaned against her lips. She released my tongue but fixed her mouth against mine again. The flicks of her tongue against mine had me wondering what that fluttering motion would feel like against my cock. All the blood pooled in my waist as I envisioned her on her knees between my thighs, repeating those same butterfly touches and the same hard suck.

This time when I pulled up her shirt, I grabbed both the T-shirt and her tank underneath. She moaned when my hand made contact with her breast. It wasn't very big, but the nipple felt like the size of an eraser and saliva pooled in my mouth as I imagined sucking it into my mouth. I shoved up the material and pulled down on her bra in quick jerky movements until I had her plump little breast in my hand. Kneading it, I heard her moan and felt her clutch at my head. I got the hint. Pulling away from her mouth, I lifted her higher with one hand until I could place my mouth around her breast. Through her shorts, I swear I felt the wetness of her arousal. I sucked and she moaned harder, her legs nearly squeezing the breath out of me.

The sofa, I thought, *I need to get to the sofa.* I stumbled forward, my mouth still latched onto her breast, rolling her stiff nub around my tongue and enjoying the trembling that my ministrations were causing. Holding her, I used the mental map I'd created when I first walked in. The sofa was at ten o'clock. I headed to my left and then cursed when I tripped on something.

"Hold on, baby," I said, letting her breast fall out of my mouth. "Shit, what was that?" I looked down and saw a pair of worn out combat boots and the shadow of her dead husband rose up and killed my arousal. My hand slid out from underneath her ass, and I slowly released her down to the ground. She looked up at me in confusion, clutching me, and I felt the bite of her wedding ring. This wasn't going to work.

"I'm sorry." I looked around the room and catalogued more than just the furniture now. There was an assault pack in the corner and on the wall hung a weird flag with just stripes and a blank space where the blue field of stars should appear. The combat boots I'd tripped over looked obscene. The whole place felt like there was someone other than Sam living here.

"What's wrong?" She looked and sounded upset, the kind of upset you got when you were turned on and then didn't get to come. It was a bad kind of upset, the worst kind.

I ran my hand over my short hair and searched for the right words to explain it all to her. But I couldn't. I couldn't find the words for something even I didn't understand. I wasn't always a jealous guy, but I was feeling pretty jealous now—which was sick in its own way because who's jealous of a dead guy? If I told this girl that I felt like her husband was still here then she'd think I was loony.

At my hesitation, Sam slumped back away from me, wiping the back of her hand across her mouth. She released a thready breath and I cursed myself silently for doing this to her. A part of me wanted to just place her on the sofa and say to hell with it but I wasn't even sure I'd be able to get it up right now.

"I'm sorry," I repeated lamely. "I'll just call a taxi."

"No." She turned to me. "No. I'll drive you home." Her head tilted up in a recognizable expression of pride. Okay then. I'd shit on this whole experience for her and if she wanted to drive me back to Adam's place then I'd suck it up and let her do it.

Samantha

"WHAT BRANCH WAS YOUR HUSBAND in? Adam didn't say." Gray asked, trying to start up a conversation, I guess. I was feeling embarrassed and bit petulant but a twenty-minute ride from downtown to The Woodlands in uncomfortable silence wasn't a great idea either.

There was no reason *not* to talk about Will. After all, I was going home alone tonight like I had so many nights before. "Army."

"Soldier, huh? Where did he serve?"

"Afghanistan. Right at the end. You?"

"Same. What was his platoon? Maybe I knew him."

I told him but he just shrugged.

"Yeah, I didn't serve with a lot of airborne. I was a boots-on-the-ground kind of guy. Not that I don't enjoy jumping out of a plane."

"I've never seen the appeal," I admitted. Will loved it but Will was always the adventurous half of our pairing. He said I kept him grounded and I'd always been kind of proud of my plodding, somewhat boring ways. What a silly thing to be proud of. "Will wanted to be a pararescueman—a PJ. He said that there was nothing greater than falling out of the sky."

"PJs are awesome. Did he ever take you jumping?"

The unease I felt talking about Will had faded. It was kind of interesting talking to someone about the military who knew about it, knew the sorts of things Will was seeking when he was enlisted.

"No. We'd talked about it but then, you know..." I shook my head. Dragging up Will's death was just not a place I wanted to go. "How long are you here for?"

He didn't answer right away, maybe contemplating how messed up I was with my condo full of Will's old things, the ring still on my finger, and me pawing at his clothes. I wanted to tell him that I wasn't screwed up at all but that he'd surprised me. Or my feelings surprised me.

"Forty-five days," he finally said, giving me no insight into what he was thinking.

"Forty-five days?" I gaped at him. "So many weeks off! The only time I got to see Will for any extended period of time was between Basic and jump school. Even before he went to paratrooper training in Alaska I didn't get to see him that long."

Gray shifted uncomfortably in his seat. "I haven't signed my re-enlistment papers. My contract is up in six months."

The military had you sign contracts. I knew the first contract was usually for four years of active duty and then Will had said that they tried to lure you into signing new contracts with promises of a better job or more money or both. Gray looked to be in his mid-twenties, although he could be younger. Deployment in a war zone aged you, Will had told me. Young recruits would go over and return months later looking like they were ten years older "How long have you been in?"

"Eight years."

"And you're thinking of separating?"

I felt, rather than saw, him nod. He was reluctant to share his dilemma and why not? I was a stranger so I just drove on until we reached Adam's house. I stopped the Land Rover at the top of the hill but Gray made no move to get out.

"I can't decide. I think they gave me a meritorious promotion to staff sergeant because they want me to stay in. I don't deserve it." He was frustrated, not quite pulling all of his thoughts together coherently. "There's a lot more responsibility now. I've got to pay attention to the regs better. My dad, he says there are better things out there for me…" He trailed off, his indecision making him more attractive to me than all his alpha male posturing could have.

"When Will died, I dropped out of college, and I've never gone back. The last two years…I spent the time bartending, just marking each day as it went by." I watched him as he stared out the window, the air conditioning in the Rover making the only noise for a while.

"I took a community college course last fall when I got back from Afghanistan," he said finally, still looking out the window. He'd cupped the back of his head with one hand, rubbing the back of his neck to ease whatever tension had built up. "Other guys who'd gotten out said that community college was better because the students were older, but there's still such a big difference between me and the others. When I was running raids, they were watching epic battles between wizards and monsters. I felt disconnected. When I finished that course I didn't go back. I'm not sure college is for me. Both my dad and my grandfather were career Marines. I joined right out of high school. Every time I encounter civilians, it's like we speak a different language.

I get tired of explaining to everyone that not every military guy is a soldier," Gray grumbled.

I smiled. Marines were touchy about being referred to as soldiers. "Will obviously never had that problem."

"There are four branches of the military. Only one has soldiers."

At Gray's continued disgruntlement, I laughed out loud. "I know. Soldiers, sailors, airmen and Marines."

"Thank you."

We sat there for a moment in companionable silence and for once I didn't feel the need to rush to say something. Even though he wasn't touching me, I still felt a connection between the two of us. It could have been our shared experience but I couldn't remember the last time I enjoyed just talking with someone. A transient thought niggled at the corner of my mind and I asked the question before I could give it much thought. "Have you lost anyone?"

"A couple guys early on. But not a spouse," he said quietly. "I get that that's different."

His respectful tone made me feel somber. I looked out the window into the quiet night. There was little noise back here. The streets were illuminated by sporadic streetlights, and the only sound was the quiet rumble of the engine.

"A loss is a loss." I hated the measuring of grief.

"Can I ask you a question?"

"No."

"Seriously?"

"If you have to ask the prefatory question then you already know the follow up is a bad idea."

He'd repositioned himself so his back was resting against the window showing no signs of wanting to leave. Strangely my early frustration had given way and I wasn't anxious for the loss of his company either. Gray chewed on his thoughts for a moment and then asked his question anyway. "What's the hardest thing about being a widow?"

Ugh, seriously. I didn't want to talk about my sad situation with Gray anymore. I was beginning to feel like that poor young widow again instead of Sam, the girl Gray wanted to have coffee with—if only for a small window of time. Heaving an exasperated sigh, I leveled the most annoying military question ever at him. "Did you kill anyone?"

"Not even on the same level," he argued. I bet if I looked at him he'd have a pissy expression on his face.

Sighing, I gave in. "What do you want to know?"

"A pog in my platoon died during my second year. You know what a pog is?"

"In the rear with the gear. Persons other than grunts," I trotted out. I'd picked up some military lingo while Will was in. I'd wanted to be supportive and helpful even though I hadn't entirely agreed with his decision.

"Right, non-infantry. But damn good guys. Anyway, he had a young wife and a kid. I think she's twenty-three or twenty-four. Older than you, but not much. He died, and she was still around base. Everyone was super careful with her, and finally one day, she broke down at the PX and screamed that she's fine. Only obviously she isn't fine. Later I guess she goes home and swallows a bottle of pills and has to be taken to the ER."

I winced. "Horrible story."

"I knew him. I felt like he was one my guys even though he wasn't a grunt." A genuine sorrow weighted his words.

"So you felt like she was partly your responsibility?"

"In some ways. I mean, there's a big support network for military widows around the base and I went to visit her, but I felt helpless. I wished I could've done more. Plus, because he died, she was going to have to move off the base anyway."

His expression of regret tugged at me. "Maybe if you wrote her a letter about how vital a member of your platoon he'd been, she'd appreciate that," I suggested.

"Yeah, maybe." His hand reached up to rub the back of his neck again and he sighed. "Sorry for bringing it up."

"I've always thought that the girlfriends and fiancées had it worse." I wasn't sure why I was extending this topic.

"Why's that?" In the dim light I couldn't see his eyes but I felt them. He was not only listening to me but *hearing* me, and I understood him in return. My heart stretched toward him.

"Because they don't get the same consideration even though they were in love. I mean the difference between getting the funeral flag and the brass bullet casings was two months for me. Two months earlier and his mom would've gotten those things."

"So you feel guilty because you have them?"

"A little. Like I'm an imposter—like I don't deserve to grieve like others have. But I got the visit, the commemorative things, the people checking up on me." God, I couldn't believe I was sharing this stuff with him—this guy who I'd stared at, kissed, argued with. But he didn't turn away at all. He just kept looking and listening, like what I had to say really interested him.

"I never thought of it that way." He sat up but didn't stop looking at me. We were tethered now, our eyes hooked on each other. "So I shouldn't feel guilty for not following up with one? Or I should've checked up on more of them?"

"I don't think you should feel guilty either way, but if it bothers you, then you can do some things. Is it really your business? I hated it when Will had to explain why I wasn't going to move out to his base with him. I felt it was so intrusive."

"Anytime you have guys under you, their personal life is your business. It's a readiness issue. Is their head in the right frame of mind to go over?"

"That's really weird, isn't it?" I asked.

"Completely." He chuckled and then reached out to rub the worn leather steering wheel. I felt it too, like he was touching me, rubbing my arm in comfort. But it wasn't really enough. I wanted him to touch me again. "I appreciate you sharing with me, even though this must be a tough subject."

"When did you stop feeling grief over the loss of your friends?"

He gave me a sad smile. "Never. You never get over it. I lost them in the first year of deployment. Two guys, and I'll never forget them."

"Me either but that's good, right?"

"Damn straight." He moved his hand from the steering wheel to my face, tucking back the stray hairs that wouldn't stay put. I held my breath because I wasn't certain if I wanted to shake his hand off or turn and taste his entire hand. I didn't have to decipher my feelings for more than a second because he allowed his hand to drop back into his own lap. My twinge of emotion was a mixture of regret and relief.

"What do you do when you aren't mixing drinks?" His question caught me off guard and I wished I could say something adventurous like "I teach skydiving." At my hesitation, Gray wiggled an eyebrow. "Can't be that bad."

I released an embarrassed little laugh. "It's just so stereotypical. I might as well buy my red hat and dye my hair blue and call it a day."

"Now you're speaking another language."

"I knit," I admitted. "The most exciting thing I've ever done was to yarn bomb the lampposts at Central College's sculpture gardens."

"What's that? Throwing balls of yarn at something?"

"No, like putting sweaters on things secretly in the dark."

Silence.

"Not very adventurous, right?"

"Hell, who am I to judge?" he offered magnanimously. "It's creative."

I couldn't tell if he was interested or thought it was silly. "Not very exciting though, not like skydiving."

He shrugged. "You could've been caught."

"We had the administration's permission."

"Yeah, not very dangerous." He grinned at me and I caught a glimpse of white even teeth and crinkles around his eyes. It was a smile that made me feel warm and tingly inside. It made me want to smile back and so I did. "Knitting seems cool. Will you make me something?"

This made me laugh again. "That's everyone's response when I tell them I knit."

"Damn, I'm not very original. But does that mean no?"

"You don't think that it's a little dull?"

"Not really." He shook his head. "Has someone said that to you?"

"Not about knitting specifically. I'm just kind of a non-adventurous type of person. Will always said I kept him grounded." I always took it as a compliment as Will intended it to be.

Gray didn't comment on that, but instead he asked me, "What kind of things do you think are adventurous?"

"Jumping out of airplanes?" I peeked at him. Whatever had shadowed his thoughts earlier were gone. Instead, a mischievous smile was directed toward me, as if he had some grand idea. It made me smile in return.

"Jumping out of airplanes is good but there are a lot of other things we could do."

We? I liked the sound of that. "Like what?"

He gave me a mysterious look. "Leave that up to me."

"What happened earlier?"

The hand went back to the neck. Gray wasn't very difficult to read but this time I didn't think it was tension that made him grip his neck as much as it was embarrassment. "That was me being stupid and I'd like to make that up to you."

Was that like an invitation for coffee? I couldn't figure it out, but I wasn't sure I wanted to put the effort into mulling it over. I put the car into gear and coasted down Adam's driveway toward the house.

"I'm not agreeing to anything but if I did, what would I need to bring?"

"Wear sturdy boots. Shorts. T-shirt. Bring your knitting." He jumped out almost before I'd pulled to a complete stop leaving me with unanswered questions and an uncertain tomorrow.

I backed out and headed to my parents' house. In the driveway, I pulled out my phone to text Eve. She was either sleeping, having sex with Randy, or winding down by watching some television. Hopefully the last one, because I wanted some more advice. I hadn't been able to close the deal with Gray physically, but the car ride to Adam's house wasn't just meaningless small talk.

I asked him to coffee but he turned me down.

Way to go! And I'm SORRY! He's a douche. You are WAY too good for him. Where are you?

Oh, Eve, such a good friend.

Parents' house. Took him up to my condo. We were friendly then he decided to go home. Guess he didn't like the taste of my coffee.

I've had your coffee. You have great coffee. Randy says U should stay AWAY. Too Ducking dumb. God, I meant F UCKING. STUPID PHONE. R says guy who doesn't know a coffee invitation means sex can't find your C L I T anyway. STUPID PHONE typed CLOT.

He asked me to go on adventure with him tomorrow.

OH HE DID! He may be able to find the CLOT after all. UGH. U KNOW WHAT I MEAN!

He told me to wear sturdy boots, shorts, T-shirt, and to bring my knitting. Is that code for sex too?

There was no response right away. Had she passed out? Slipping out of the car, I headed into the house and to my bedroom. I was able to change, wash my face, and brush my teeth before I got a response.

We're STUMPED. R says he may be kinky bastard. May like outdoors sex. U be careful?

Should I stay home?

This time, she responded immediately. *NO! was the immediate response. GO and tell me ALL DETAILS tomorrow night. Bring condoms. Never trust other person.*

As I looked around my childhood bedroom, it occurred to me that I should've brought Gray here. There were no traces of Will in this room. My father had banned him from coming up here. Instead, Will and I had spent a lot of time in my parents' basement, making out and sometimes even having furtive, not terribly satisfactory, sex. The fear of my parents catching us made it too hard for me to relax. I think the thrill worked the other way on Will. He always finished hard and fast. But that was Will, hard charging and thrill seeking. He said my more sedate pace was what kept him balanced and I kind of took pride in that. Being his anchor.

My dad thought that as long as we weren't doing it in my princess bed with its sheer white bed hangings I was still untouched. Ironically, my princess bedroom had become a haven, a place I could escape the suffocating memories of Will and me. I'd spent a lot of nights here right after Will died.

Pulling the pink gingham quilted coverlet back, I climbed inside and tucked an old teddy bear next to me. The image of Gray as he effortlessly held me up flitted through my brain but I didn't want to be having a fantasy about him tonight. As I allowed exhaustion to pull me under, I wondered if my attraction to him was based on the fact that he was military and he reminded me vaguely of Will even though the two looked nothing alike. *Oh, Will. God, why did you leave me alone?* And I was alone—and so, so tired of it. The pang in my chest felt vaguely like guilt, and when I closed my eyes, my aching loneliness soaked my pillow.

SIX

Samantha

"NICE PAJAMAS. ARE YOU FIVE?" BITSY WANDERED INTO THE breakfast room as I was getting breakfast, or brunch to be technical given that it was half past ten in the morning. I glanced down at my Smurfette nightshirt and shorts and at the bowl of Cheerios I'd just poured.

"Yes, I am. What are you?"

"It's hard to believe you're the older sibling."

My response was to grunt into my cereal. I wasn't equipped to verbally spar with her on my best days, let alone one that followed an emotionally exhausting evening. I just wanted to eat my cereal and read the new messages on the knitting message board that I'd pulled up on my phone.

"We can't all look like fashion plates." I squinted at her, taking in the high-waisted shorts, off-the-shoulder midriff top, and high-heeled cork sandals. "Is this normal weekend attire for kids these days?" I gestured at her outfit.

"This is everyday attire for normal people." She set one hand on a bony hip and struck an I'm-too-good-for-this pose.

"Normal people are exhausting then." Shaking my head, I turned my attention back to my phone where I could read the debate about whether wool or acrylic yarn should be used for knitting baby booties and hats. I liked both and acrylic was very soft but lots of people thought babies should only be in natural fibers. That was about as an important of a discussion as I could handle this morning. "I told David you were going to be the one to take over the firm in eight years."

"Ooh, you had lunch with the Andersons?" She rushed over to take a seat at the table. "Was Tucker there?"

"You do know that Tucker is old enough to be your dad, right?" Bitsy's weird crush on Will's older brother was funny in theory but kind of scary if it was real. "Aren't there guys your own age you can date?"

"No one dates anymore, Sam." Bitsy sighed dramatically. Man, only a few years out of high school and I didn't even understand the mating rituals anymore. Coffee for sex and no dating. Actually, Will and I never really dated either. We'd moved from childhood friends to something more when we both realized that there were stronger feelings than just friendship.

"So what do you do? Hang out? Hook up? Cavort?"

"Cavort?"

"You know, fool around."

Even though she made no sound, I could tell she was rolling her eyes.

"Cavort is an old lady word," she mocked.

"I feel old," I said, stretching my arms out. "I feel eighty."

"It's because you hang out with old ladies all the time."

"They aren't all old ladies," I protested. She was referring to my grief support group, the Yarn Over Widows Knitting Club. "I think some of them are in their fifties."

"Mom's not even that old!"

"Husbands don't usually die when they're in their twenties," I pointed out, quickly regretting it when Bitsy's face fell. Hurriedly, I added, "Anyway, can you be sure to tell Mom that you're going to take over the firm when Mom and David are ready to retire."

She wrinkled her nose. "Ugh, no. I don't want to be a lawyer. I'm going to do something else."

"Like what?"

"Not sure, but it's going to be fun and awesome."

"I hope so, Little Bit." I wanted her to be happy. Hell, I wanted to be happy, I realized, but I think my little sister had a better idea of how to achieve her goals than I did.

"So was Tucker there?" She was like a dog going after a bone, persistent and relentless. Actually that was all Mom right there. I was more like Dad—letting things come to me instead of pursuing things.

"No." I shoveled the rest of my cereal into my mouth and then added more dry cereal to soak up the remaining milk. "At our last anniversary luncheon, Tucker yelled at his dad, and they almost got into a fist fight. Carolyn cried, and I wanted to crawl under the table." Two years ago, Tucker had started law school. When Will died, Tucker had dropped out and started inking people. Life was too short to live the life other people wanted for you, he'd told me. So I guess Tucker's dream was to be a tattoo artist, because that's what he was doing now. "But it'd be nice if he came to hold his mom's hand."

"Mom says that Carolyn needs to learn to hold her own hand." Bitsy took the cereal from me and poured herself a bowl.

Holding Carolyn up emotionally was an exhausting task and I wished Tucker would help me since his father wouldn't. "He's still a selfish jerk and way too old for you."

"Mom says I'm an old soul." No, Bitsy, I thought, *you're so bright, shiny and new my heart aches at your beauty.* I wished I still had that look. Instead, I felt dull and used and, after last night, rejected. When I had woken up, the memory of Gray telling me he had to get out of my condo was the first thing that popped into my mind—not the long meaningful discussion we'd had afterwards. The invitation to do something adventurous felt like a pity date rather than a genuine desire to spend more time with me. I felt foolish and embarrassed.

"What does Mom say?" questioned our mother as she walked

into the breakfast room dressed in slacks and a blouse. She must be meeting clients at the office today.

"That you work too hard," I said affectionately. Mom leaned down and kissed both of our heads.

"Someone's got to keep you girls in cereal," she teased and went over to make herself a cup of coffee. "Your father says hello by the way and would like for you to Skype him tomorrow." Dad was over in England teaching a summer fellowship on comparative American Lit at Cambridge.

A horn honked outside and Bitsy jumped up, kissing Mom goodbye and running out the door. A cloud of perfume and hairspray threatened to choke me as she sprinted past.

"Bad night?" Mom sat in Bitsy's now-empty chair and pushed the abandoned cereal bowl aside.

I considered lying to Mom, but I hadn't been able to get away with it when I was a teen and I doubted I'd get away with it now.

"Just felt a little lonely, I guess," I admitted.

She mmhmmed mysteriously but didn't say anything else, just sipped her coffee and looked at me like I wasn't spilling all my secrets. I knew this trick. She'd once told me that the best way to get someone to start talking was to be quiet because people hated uncomfortable silences. Trying to resist the pull of her unspoken command, I looked everywhere but her. After not even a minute had gone by, I started blurting it all out.

"I met a guy last night and he…" There were limits to what I wanted to share so I tried to think of some euphemisms to describe what he'd done, what we'd done together.

"You were making out with some stranger in the hallway of Gatsby's?" Mom offered with a choking laugh.

I pounded my head on the table. "Teresa Bush right? I thought she was too bombed to remember anything. She tried to pull down her dress and show me her tattoo, for crying out loud."

Mom nodded with a smile. "Yes, Teresa wasn't too drunk to remember seeing you being led away by a man god—I think that was the phrase that Teresa used—and then she watched as you…" Mom paused and tapped her chin, clearly searching for the most embarrassing way to put it. "Oh yes, acted out the first scenes in a porno."

"Mom," I moaned. "Really? I'm trying to eat. Don't you have people to sue?"

"The great thing about the courts moving to electronic filing is that I can sue people twenty-four hours a day, seven days a week. That means I can take time out to eat breakfast with my eldest daughter," she said cheerfully and then took another sip of her coffee.

"Oh my god, Mom."

"So I wondered why you weren't at your shrine with your man god but rather in my kitchen. Was it just a one-night stand? Or hook up, as you kids are calling it these days."

"I'm sorry, but I have to go outside and commit Seppuku."

"You girls embarrass so easily." Mom smirked at me and took a big sip of her coffee.

"Do you really think it is a shrine? My condo," I clarified. Within the walls pieces of Will were present. His old assault pack rested against my sofa and his combat boots were up against the wall. In my closet hung his combat and service uniforms. His mother and I had taken all of Will's things to the dry cleaners and they hung there, shrouded in plastic, beside the clothes that I used to wear—the flirty dresses and skirts, my skinny jeans, a whole floor full of sandals, sneakers and the occasional heels left over from school dances.

On the wall, covering an expanse of white-painted brick, was a large green felt where my nearly finished knitted American flag afghan hung. I'd finished all the white and red stripes but the blue blocked area where the stars should be had me stumped. I could either try to figure out how to do the intarsia stitch where I'd knit two different colors of yarn at the same time or I'd have to crochet the stars. Neither option enthused me. Tucked amongst all of Will's Army paraphernalia, was yarn. Lots of it. In a basket near the kitchen, under the sofa, and more upstairs. It was as if I'd tried to fill my life with yarn instead of people. My condo was filled with unfinished knitting projects, balls of yarn, and the relics of my dead husband. So yeah, Mom was right. No wonder Gray had freaked out.

Setting down her cup of coffee Mom studied me for a moment,

as if gathering her thoughts for an important argument. "I think that there is a lot of Will in your condo and that might make it uncomfortable for a new man." She pointed to my left hand. "Along with your ring."

I twisted the ring uncomfortably, hiding the shiny diamond in my palm again so only the plain band showed "I just…don't know what to do with Will's stuff."

"And you can't give it to Carolyn?"

"I tried, early on, but she started crying and said Will would've wanted me to have it. I just wanted her to stop crying so I didn't push it."

Mom pressed her lips together, suppressing her real feelings about Carolyn. "Just because you were once married to Will doesn't mean you're endlessly responsible for Carolyn's mental wellbeing."

Her use of the past tense when referring to my marriage with Will made me tear up. The two bowls of cereal I'd eaten started to clog my throat.

"I don't know why I'm tearful all of a sudden," I admitted. "You'd have thought that I'd cried enough during that first year to last me for a lifetime."

"You're starting to feel again. You were asleep for a long time. When you wake up sometimes it is painful."

Was that it? Was I just waking up and this Gray guy just happened to push the restart button on my libido? The fact was that I'd been thinking about the lack of physical intimacy more and more as of late. I'd like to think it would pass—an illicit thought of seeing him naked in my bedroom sent a minor shiver down my spine, a shiver that didn't escape the watchful eyes of my mom.

"Who names their kid Gray?" I asked.

Mom smirked. "Is that the hottie's name? Gray?"

"Hottie, Mom?"

"I'm down with your lingo. I have clients your age."

"Juvenile delinquents?"

"No, you're an adult. Full felonies for you." She nudged me with her shoulder. "Grayson is actually Old English meaning son of a bailiff."

"You're saying my name should be a color."

"I thought of naming you Blue but your dad wouldn't allow it."

"So I have a boy's name instead?"

"It's gender neutral. Just think of the advantages." She leaned toward me. "Will I get to meet the man god?" Mom got a lascivious look in her eye.

"Mom!" I said with outrage. "What would Dad say?"

"I'm married, not dead." Mom finished her coffee and picked up Bitsy's empty bowl and the coffee cup and headed toward the sink. "There's no harm in looking."

I harrumphed and then realized I sounded exactly like the old woman Bitsy had accused me of being. The discussion of Gray had brought to mind his broad shoulders, tapered waist and big hands. I swore I could still feel his tongue running down my neck and the pressure of his erection between my legs. I bit my lip and squeezed my legs to get myself under control. Thank God Mom's back was to me.

"Speaking of kids of lawyers, what are you doing, Sam? Not that I mind you bartending but is that really your life's ambition? I know you signed up for classes at Central because your dad got the tuition waiver but what is it that you're going back to school for?"

"I don't know." I stirred the milk left in my bowl a few times and watched the Cheerios swirl around the tiny current I was creating. Talking about the future was one way to kill any sexy thoughts. "It seemed like the thing to do. I can't even remember what it was that I wanted to study in the first place." I scrubbed my face with both hands. "I'm just tired of being sad all the time. I had all these excuses why I couldn't move to Alaska with Will and now I wish I didn't live here where everyone who knew me recognizes me as one part of a unit that's broken and missing a major piece. I'm Will's widow here."

"So move away. Start over," Mom urged. "You've got to stop living your life based on what other people think you should do. I get that you have regrets and that you wish you moved to Alaska so that you could have spent those months with Will together instead of apart. But that doesn't mean you have to spend the rest of your life trying to be the best widow possible because you weren't the best girlfriend or because you weren't the best wife or because you resented the hell out of the fact that Will decided to join the Army. You were both teenagers at the time. Just because you didn't move when he went combat infantry and jumped out of planes all over the world doesn't mean that you lack a spirit of adventure. Get out there and start living."

I stared at her, my mouth hanging open a bit. "How long have you been waiting to bust out that lecture?"

"Probably a good year." She sighed and pulled me against her.

"So long? Your restraint is remarkable."

"You weren't ready."

"And now I am?"

"Yeah."

"How do you know?"

"Because about two seconds ago you were shivering remembering the touch of a man's hand. I think that means you're ready to move on."

The old "eyes in the back of the head" trick. I wondered if that rear vision was something that you developed when you started gestating. "I'm not very good at taking risks," I said.

Mom shouted with laughter. "Honey, the biggest risk is loving someone. You of all people know that."

After that bomb, Mom kissed me and then left for her office.

My childhood home felt empty with Bitsy off with friends and Mom at the office. I left my dad a Skype video message and then headed down to my condo. For the rest of the morning, I sat on my tiny metal balcony with my knitting. Mom's admin assistant was having a baby and I was working on the newborn set for her. Will and I had been assiduous about the use of protection but there were several times after he died that I'd wished we weren't so careful and that I was sitting here knitting booties for our child.

But thoughts beginning with *I wish* and *what if* were a bad trip down the rabbit hole. That was the one negative about knitting. The mind tended to wander, and if I wasn't careful, I would start getting maudlin. Instead, I purposely focused on the streets, the river beyond, and the pure pleasure of having the warm sun on my face. The rays of sunlight reminded me of the smattering of gold flecks that had twinkled at me out of Gray's eyes.

I allowed myself the guilty pleasure of visualizing all of Gray—his wide shoulders, his firm touch, his soft lips. Rubbing my elbow, I imagined that I could still feel the imprint of his fingers on my skin. It'd been so long since I'd enjoyed the touch of a male other than a swift hug from a family member. Gray had smelled good too—some blend of earthy masculine fragrance overlaid by faint notes of spice and the ocean. I rubbed the tip of my tongue across my lips, remembering how his mouth felt hard and soft at the same time. How his tongue felt huge inside my mouth and how much I ached between my legs.

Was I really a risk taker? *Dress comfortably—shorts, T-shirt, boots.* Was I really seriously contemplating going hiking with a guy who accused me of cheating and then left me hanging on the cusp of an orgasm because there were too many of Will's things in my condo? As I pulled on the shorts and a pair of thick socks, I realized that I was. What better things did I have to do? Sit here and knit? Why not take my knitting needles on a little adventure?

I dug out a worn T-shirt that said, "I knit so I don't kill people." Gray might appreciate the humor of it. Wait, did I really care what Gray thought of my T-shirt slogans? I threw it back into the drawer and found a workout T-shirt that had no slogans and was a neon green. Looking at my reflection in the full-length mirror on the closet door, I saw that the neon green made my entire face look sickly. My eyes shot toward the knitting shirt and vanity won out. If sturdy boots and shorts were some kind of code for outdoors sex, then I didn't want to make Gray sick at the sight of me. Not that I was going to have sex with him. He'd turned me down twice.

I slid the knitting T-shirt over my head. I didn't own boots and wondered if tennis shoes would be okay. When I pulled out my phone, I was struck with the realization that I didn't have Gray's number. Even if I'd wanted to cancel, I'd have to do it in person. Was that an accident because he just hadn't thought to ask, or was it intentional?

I tried not to think too hard about what I was doing and instead just drove over to Adam's house. Gray was on the lawn, throwing a football with one of the guys from the house. I didn't know them all, only Adam and Finn. Drums and the sound of a guitar poured from the detached garage where Adam and his band must be practicing. There was a hive of activity here. I didn't know exactly how many people lived here, but the number of people milling about had to be close to twenty.

I slowed down so I didn't run over an errant footballer.

Gray came up to my window and I rolled it down. "Is the offer still good?"

He leaned against the windowsill and his forearm was inches away from me. The healthy sweat from his impromptu game smelled good and I felt a little nostalgic for the times that I'd hugged Will after his track practice when you could smell fresh cut grass mixed in with clean male testosterone. A sudden urge to run my tongue up the side of his veined neck rocked me.

When I looked straight into his gold-flecked eyes, there was a corresponding hunger. *But what about last night?* I wanted to cry. We could have explored all of this last night, but instead I was going somewhere on an "adventure." Well, this adventure better be damned good. Almost against my will, I swayed toward him, but my seatbelt saved me from utter humiliation. It caught me mid-swoon and held me back. Looking down at my hands, I thought about putting the vehicle in reverse and driving away.

"I'll get the gear," Gray said, voice low. I fought back a visible shiver. What was wrong with me? Or maybe the better question was what was with *him?* "Don't leave," he ordered as if somehow my trepidation was obvious. "Don't leave," he repeated.

I sat there in my idling truck and watched the guys and girls on the front lawn, some staring at me and others admiring Gray's form as he loped toward the garage. It was hard not to admire his powerful build. Had I once thought that he wasn't my type? That had been some kind of crazy talk.

SEVEN

Samantha

GRAY DIRECTED ME TOWARD THE RED ROCK CLIFFS, A SMALL area of bluffs that dropped into the city's river. I'd never been here before. Out of the back he pulled out a bunch of ropes and nylon things and metal hooks.

"Is that what I think it is?"

"If you're thinking it's extreme macramé, then no it isn't." Gray didn't look at me but instead was intent on winding rope around his elbow and shoulder. He shrugged off one coil and handed it to me. The weight of it was heavier than I'd anticipated. "Think you can handle that?" Gray gave a chin nod toward the rope. I hefted it.

"As long as we aren't doing a twelve-mile run."

"No worries."

"So rock climbing?" I guessed this was a real adventure and not sex. I gave a mental shrug. At least I could cross off one word as a sex euphemism. That was useful. It occurred to me that I was being friendzoned. Rocking climbing instead of sex? That's what you did with friends, not people you wanted to see naked. Even I knew that. Oh well, I'd lost a lot of friends in the two years since Will's death. I could use this time with Gray to learn how to be a better friend. Although it was weird that we were rock climbing, since Gray could have easily gone with his buddies.

"None of your friends rock climb?" I asked.

"Sure they do, although Noah goes a lot less now because his professional fighting contract prevents him from engaging in dangerous activities."

"Then why are *we* here?"

"Because I wanted to spend time with you. Where's your knitting?"

He wanted to spend time with me? That seemed like something you'd say to someone you wanted to have "coffee" with. I was so confused. I handed him a small bag and he stuck it into a larger pack which he slung over his shoulder along with another coil of rope, another small bag, and set of harnesses. We took off, not at a quick pace, but a steady one.

"What kind of adventure are you taking me on?" I called to Gray's back. Any faster and I'd be too winded to talk.

"A baby one, don't worry." He turned and winked at me over his shoulder. "I'll take good care of you."

His promise sounded a bit provocative. Maybe it *was* sex. God, I had to stop thinking about sex. As I followed him up the hiking trail, I stared at his physique. His legs looked powerful but not overly thick. He had muscles in his back that moved as he climbed up the hill. Gray looked like he could take care of a woman. He was a guy with strength and endurance, who clearly enjoyed physical things. The pang at the missed opportunity last night hit me harder. Him lifting me up and easily holding me as he kissed me or as he rubbed his thigh between my legs had felt incredible. I'd guess his penis was thick and heavy to match the rest of his build. His rock-hard pecs would be the perfect place for me to place my hands if I rode him. My imaginings made me breathless.

"Hey, are you okay? Do you need to take a break?" Gray stopped and turned to look at me.

Yes, I need to take a break and bash my head against the rocks until the image of the two of us naked is flushed from my mind. Out loud, I said, "Nope," and gave him the fakest smile in two counties.

He looked at me suspiciously but as he couldn't read my mind, thank God, he just turned around. Every time I started thinking of Gray in a sexual way, I stabbed myself with an imaginary knitting needle. Good thing it was imaginary because I would've bled out about a third of the way up.

Gray

THE HAIRS ON THE BACK of my neck were at attention again. Sam was staring holes through me but whenever I turned around she gave me this wide-eyed innocent look. She was hiding something but I didn't know if she was mad that I was taking her on a hike or upset that I'd left her swinging in the wind last night. I considered telling her that I'd been miserable after I'd left her. The erection that had been killed at the sight of her dead husband's things popped right back after she dropped me off. I tried jacking off in the bathroom but when I did come it was unsatisfactory. My stupid dick wanted to be inside Sam instead of my hand.

The entire night I alternated between fantasizing about what it felt like being inside her and reliving the moment in the hallway when she came from just the pressure of my wood against her. The longer the night wore on, the more I wanted to punch myself in the face for stopping. Who cared about boots and empty backpacks? Her husband was gone. Neither of us was cheating on anyone. I'd been so close to sinking into her sweetness and I'd cockblocked myself. I wanted to hit myself even harder when I woke up this morning with the realization I hadn't gotten her phone number. Then she'd shown up, and I didn't waste time regretting yesterday or asking her whether she changed her mind because I could read the uncertainty in every line of her body from the tense set of her shoulders to the way her hand hovered over the gear shift. She looked ready to throw the Rover in reverse at any moment.

"Don't leave," I'd told her in my best command voice and she hadn't. Now we were hiking on an unfamiliar bluff, and I was going to use Noah's equipment to teach Sam how to rappel down the side of a cliff. In the Corps, this might be called a trust exercise. I wasn't sure what I was trying to prove with her.

Despite her labored breathing, she kept walking. I suggested stopping but I could tell that if I asked whether she was okay one more time she might push me over the cliff. That wasn't really the response I was angling for but she'd not entirely forgotten last night because we were walking single file. The path was definitely wide enough for two people but every time I slowed up, she slowed up. So what if she didn't want to walk beside me? She was *here* which meant she wanted to spend time with me and I'd take whatever crumbs she was willing to throw my way at this point.

"Noah told me to go up to the two mile marker and that there would be anchors for us there," I explained.

"What will I be doing?"

"Well, that's the adventure part," I joked, but when she didn't respond, I hurried to assure her. "That's why I have all this safety equipment." I held up the gear. "When we get to the marker, I'll test the anchors and then we'll rappel down to the one mile marker. Then while you knit, I'm going to rappel to the bottom and then climb back up to meet you. Sound okay?"

"Sure, so a baby fall for me and a big boy climb for you?"

"It's not a fall." Making sure she could see me, see that I was serious, I said carefully, "I'd never hurt you or put you in a position to be hurt. I thought, you know, based on what you said, that this would be kind of interesting."

She gave me a small quirk of smile, not quite a full one but like she found something funny. "It's not what I'd expected, but it does sound kind of fun, like I'll be starring in my own little action movie. What do I need to know about rappelling?"

"Go slow."

"That sounds boring. I thought we were going to do something exciting." She looked into the ravine below like anything short of jumping without a chute was going to be a sore disappointment.

I closed the short distance between us and looked down at her. The incline of the path made her tip her head back and exposed the long slender column of her throat. "Slow doesn't need to be boring if you're doing it right." I ran my hand down the outside of her arm over her small biceps, her soft elbow, and her thin wrist until I reached her fingers. This close I could hear the slight increase in the rhythm of her breathing. She wasn't unaffected after all. I threaded my fingers through hers and when she didn't draw away, I turned to finish the rest of the hike with her hand in mine.

When we reached the second mile marker, I spotted the anchors that Noah had mentioned this morning. "Give me a sec," I said, squeezing her hand as I let it go. I busied myself clipping our safety harnesses to the anchors and double-checking the bolts for surety. There was precious cargo with me today and I wanted to make sure we were extra safe.

A rustling of dirt and rock behind me made me look up. Sam was standing very close to the edge and peering over. The memory of the sad widow who'd overdosed flitted through my mind. Sam wouldn't be standing so close to the edge intentionally, right?

"You okay?" I called out softly so as not to surprise her. When she turned to face me, she had a queasy look on her face.

"I don't know about this," she admitted. "The idea was nice but maybe I should just wait up here." She squeezed her hands together and then pointed to a tall tree that provided some nice afternoon shade. "How about I just sit over there and knit? I can occupy myself for a few hours that way with no problem."

No, not trying to jump off, simply a little frightened. That I could deal with. I walked to the edge with her and put an arm lightly around her shoulders. She shivered a bit and I wasn't sure whether it was fear or anticipation. I drew her closer to my side where she fit perfectly, her shoulder under my arm. When I felt her head rest lightly against me, I resisted the urge to pull her even tighter, to conform her body against mine and kiss her until she forgot about being afraid or being mad.

"I'm being a baby," she muttered.

"Trust me, I don't think of you as a baby at all." I wondered if her husband had taken her out and not allowed her to be afraid. "Everyone is afraid the first time," I lied. "I promise this is a safe adventure." Pulling her back to the ropes, I shook out the harness and gestured for her to step into the web of nylon straps. She looked skeptically at me and then the harness.

"Hey, you got this."

She took a deep breath and stepped into the harness, grabbing my arm to steady herself. I slid the straps up her legs, over her slim calves and the tender skin of the backs of her knees, up past the golden skin of her thighs. Was that her trembling or was that me. As I slipped the nylon harness into place, I talked—more to distract myself than her because I was getting a little light headed after even that small caress. "This is Grace's harness, and you can bet your house that Noah checks this regularly for safety." I pulled the harness up a little higher so the webbing was over her shorts and not on her sensitive skin. "Okay for me to tighten them?" I asked, pointing at the straps.

She had that wide-eyed look again, the one that I thought signaled flight but she just nodded. With my face level with her waistband, I could only imagine doing one thing and that was learning forward and burying my face between her legs. I was feeling winded, and not because of the altitude or the hike but because kneeling between this girl's legs felt a lot more intimate than some of the things I'd done with other women—women whose faces have somehow faded from my memory. Pressing a knee into a stray rock on the path, I started reciting the Marines' hymn. That was a boner killer if there ever was one.

I hadn't invited Sam out for a public quickie in the woods. I'd tossed out the invitation because…the realization struck me. Because I wanted to spend more time with her. I enjoyed the hell out of just talking with her and that weirded me out more than the hard-on I'd just gotten kitting her out in safety gear. I finished as quickly as I could and stood up. Sam's face was flushed and her breathing was uneven. Ignoring those telling signs and praying my own erection wouldn't spring up again, I stepped back and busied myself testing all the connections. Satisfied that everything was in order, I hooked us to the anchor and then came back and went through some internal safety checklist a second time.

"Do all adventures require safety checks and harnesses?" she asked.

"Only the good ones." Over her hands, I pulled short fingerless gloves that would protect most of her palm and fingers from a rope burn. "I'm going to go first. You'll follow right behind me. Don't grip the rope too tightly, but let it flow through your fingers. You're going to walk the wall, and I'll be right underneath you, so if you let go too fast, I'll catch you."

Samantha

I'LL CATCH YOU. I LIKED that promise. In fact, I liked a lot about Gray this afternoon. His calm demeanor. His patience with me. His refusal to mock me for my little fears. I did feel secure in the harness he so carefully buckled me into although I almost passed out when he knelt between my knees. Eve's recounting of her favorite up-against-the-wall position had flooded my mind. *"If you haven't tried that position then I'm really sorry because up against the wall or door while he's between your knees, one leg slung over his shoulder is un-friggin-believable."*

I believed her because I felt ready to orgasm just looking down at him in that position as he was trying to put me in the safety harness. But my own feelings of lust were clearly not returned because, when he stood up, it was like he couldn't get away from me fast enough. I wasn't going to be sad about that. I was going to hang off a cliff holding on to a rope. That was pretty damn big for me.

Gray took hold of his rope and stepped over the side of the cliff like it was nothing. My heart climbed back into my body once I saw him braced against the side of the cliff with his feet, just below the edge.

"Ready?" he called.

I gave him a short nod and turned around. Slowly I let out the rope between my fingers and then started edging down over the cliff's edge. It was freaky and I almost let go. He must've climbed with amateurs before because he called out a warning.

"Don't let go of the rope. The rappel is all about the rope. Let it do the work." I slowly let the rope release through my hands, the friction miraculously allowing me to slide down slowly. I imagined I could feel Gray's body beneath mine and the thought steadied me. We slid down the rock wall and I felt like the action hero I'd thought about earlier. I wanted to throw up my arms and yell out but refrained, figuring Gray would bark at me to keep hold of the rope.

The mile-long distance between the top where we started and the rappel station below us sped by and before long, Gray was unhooking my harness and pulling the rope through the anchor. "Step back, I don't want the end of the rope to catch you in the eye."

Obediently, I stood off the trail. There was a smooth flat rock situated under a big canopy of trees. I guessed this was where Gray thought I could knit. It was a pretty perfect place. Gray was a conundrum. He'd turned me down last night but taken me out on an...outing, excursion—maybe even a date. Everything had been planned down to the last detail, and so thoughtfully. Even if I wanted to be mad at him for turning me down, I couldn't be. So he didn't want to have sex with me. He had taken me out and encouraged me to do something I'd never done before. Rappelling was incredibly fun and how many people could say that they'd done this?

After the rope fell down, I flew at Gray and gave him a big hug. "Thank you," I said, and then drew back, feeling a bit embarrassed at my exuberance.

"Fun huh?"

"Yes, very." The smile I was sporting actually hurt my cheeks. "Super fun."

Gray grinned back. "I'm glad." His eyes were warm and affectionate, like he was proud of his kid sister. I grabbed the backpack that Gray had discarded and tried not to be bummed out by the idea of Gray thinking of me like a little girl. He'd turned my advances down but was apparently willing to have me tag along for a little fun. The fact that he was sexy, nice, and thoughtful were things I should admire about him instead of objectifying him as a hook up. "I'll just sit here, then, while you rappel down and back up?" Given the quickness of our descent, I figured I wouldn't have a super long time to myself.

"I won't be long." He gave me a quick smile and jumped off to rappel down to the bottom. I sat down to knit under the shade but didn't even pull out the project. Instead, I stretched out on the rock and let the heat bake into me. It felt great. *I* felt great. I had been in a state of hibernation—and not just about guys. I'd shut myself off, and now I needed to work on being more social, enjoying interaction with others beyond my family and a few coworkers. Bitsy was right. I needed to start hanging out with other people my age, not just the over-fifty widows in my knitting support group.

I opened the backpack that Gray had shoved my knitting in and found sandwiches, chips, protein bars, and bottles of water. And napkins! My god, a girl could only be so strong. Mentally I prepared my police station confession. *I'm sorry, Officer, but he held my hand, smelled amazing, and then provided me food. I had no recourse but to attack him. Go easy on me.* Pushing to my feet, I decided to check on Gray. I stood and stared down at him—past the jutting rocks and the branches of trees growing out of the side of the cliff and long stretch of space until there was land. I leaned forward and felt the vastness take hold of me. And I laughed. It was more like a scream or a cry outside of my body but inside I felt relief and exhilaration. I didn't hear him at first because I was caught up in my own feelings. His voice was just an echo, like a free bird cawing to its flight formation in the wind.

"Get back!"

The sound was closer now, and when I looked down, my toes were poking into the space of the blue sky, and for a moment I tottered forward, startled by his shouts.

"Get the fuck back!" Gray roared. He was waving his arm at me. I wasn't sure if he was coming or going, but I stepped back obediently, my pleasure fading quickly. He clearly had a thing with people standing close to the edge. I didn't want to him to freak out anymore, so I lay down on my belly and dangled my arms over the edge as I watched his body get bigger and bigger as he closed the distance between us.

He was fuming mad when he got to the top. Even though he didn't say much, the jerky way he coiled the ropes and stuffed things into the backpack were pretty telling. Anxiety took hold of me. I hated when people were angry with me and when I disappointed them. It's why I kept having lunch with Will's mother once a month, even though it was more painful than a root canal as she tried to reminisce about the good old days when Will was still alive. Looking down at my shoes, I tried to shut out Gray's movements.

"Do you want to have something to eat?" he asked. Impatience rang out clearly in his voice even though he tried to pretend like he really wanted to sit on the nice rock under the nice shade and have a nice afternoon snack.

"No," I replied still looking down. "I think I need to get back."

His only response was to grunt and start walking down the hill. It didn't take long to get to my car and we hadn't exchanged more than two words on the hike back to the parking lot. When we were on the road, I ventured a thank you. "I had a good time today. Thanks for bringing me."

Gray sat in silence for most of the trip, but he obviously wanted to say something. He'd open his mouth, clear his throat, and then shut it again.

"What?" I asked, exasperated. "What is it that you want to say?"

He drummed the console between us with his finger tips for a moment and then gruffly asked, "Are you depressed? Do you need to see someone? There's nothing wrong with that."

"No! Why do you ask?" Where did this come from? I was so embarrassed.

"Because you were…" he paused, clearly fighting some stronger emotion, but I didn't let him finish. His unjust accusation fired my temper.

"I stood on the edge to see if you wanted to eat something. Clearly you have lingering guilt over the widow in your unit. Maybe *you* should see someone," I shot back.

"It's a platoon," he said curtly.

"I don't really care, soldier," I replied sarcastically.

"I'm not a fucking soldier, and you know it."

"Don't curse at me."

"Don't call me a soldier."

"You Marines are neurotic about this, you know. You should see someone, just so you can get it through your head that not everyone is insulting you when they refer to you as a soldier."

"Only the Army has soldiers." Gray fumed.

The Rover came to a shuddering halt at the light at the top of the exit ramp. "See, neurotic." I pointed at him, not even paying attention to the lights. We were both breathing heavily, chests heaving. Quick as lightning, Gray reached across the console, and for a second, I thought he was going to kiss me. Maybe he was going to and he changed his mind at the last second. Instead, he pressed his forehead against mine.

"I'm sorry," he said.

I should've still been angry with him but his apology, his fear, his resignation wiped it away. "Me too," I whispered back. We might have stayed like that forever if not for the cars honking their horns at me because the light had turned green. I pulled back reluctantly and took Gray home. I helped him unload the ropes, and he gave me a quick hug.

"See you around, Sam." And then he was gone.

EIGHT

Gray

I WANTED TO FIX THINGS WITH HER BUT I WASN'T SURE HOW. IT occurred to me that I kind of sucked at interacting with women. When I wasn't wearing the uniform, when I didn't have the power of the Corps behind me, I was inept. The girls I'd been with didn't hang out with me because I was funny or interesting to talk to. They fucked me and left me. I'd told myself for years that the only connection I ever wanted with a woman was a physical one.

The weird hiccups in my heartbeat when I watched my boys interact with their girlfriends made it clear that that statement was a lie. I'd shoved the desire for something more with a female down so deep I believed it didn't exist, but here I was all worked up because I'd fucked up with a girl I barely knew. Although that was another lie.

I'd shared more meaningful conversation with Sam than anyone I could remember, in years. Her eyes held no judgment only understanding. Maybe it was because she'd been married to a soldier, but she *knew* me. She could see inside of me and that both scared the shit of me and excited me in a way that made me worried for my own sanity.

A wicked ugly sense of insecurity washed over me and suddenly I was angry. At myself in part but at Sam, too, for opening my eyes.

I'd never gone hiking with a girl before. I'd never just simply enjoyed hearing her wild laugh at the first step off the cliff. Shit, that was a sound of pure freaking joy and I'd ruined it. When she'd leaned over the edge, her arms out wide, the sound coming from her was enough to make the entire valley smile, but for me? Within me, the sound had turned sour, and I'd reacted without thinking. I needed her to stop laughing, and so I accused her of doing something I knew, deep down, wasn't going to happen.

My actions came from the protective sense of self-preservation I'd cultivated since my girlfriend Carrie had cheated on me during my second deployment. I was getting shot at, my friends were fucking dying in the field, and I spent every night dreaming about being home with her, in her bed. But while I was creating fantasies to keep me from going insane, she had been shacking up with the local Marine recruiter.

Only in the Marines did you love your brothers one minute and then hate them the next for sleeping with your girl, rifling through your mail, and stealing anything of worth that wasn't locked down. A true fucking dysfunctional family. I wasn't sure why I loved it, but I did.

But it had been there for me when Carrie wasn't. When I came home to find her shaking the tires off her car with the Marine officer, it had been my brothers who took me out and got me wasted. It was the Corps that had given me so much shit to do that I didn't have time to think of Carrie. I had been too tired to even stroke my wood if I had the urge—which I didn't for several months after I saw her pale ass bouncing in the window of the car. It had been the men in my platoon who found me hook up after hook up until I was lost in a sea of unfamiliar pussy and had forgotten my own name as well as Carrie's. It had been Hamilton, my battle buddy, who'd recommended doing the friends-with-benefits thing with a local first responder. And one thing led to another until all I had in my life was my family, my brothers from the Corp, and a few women who I called up at ten at night to ease my physical ache. Then I left them, because lying in bed with a woman for the entire night was more than I could stomach.

I never spent time with woman just casually unless it was my mother. No wonder Sam confused me. But even as she scared me, I was drawn to her. We weren't done yet. I just had to figure out how to convince her to give me another chance.

The next morning, I took Noah and Bo up on their offer to run around the neighborhood. I think I'd foolishly hoped I'd bump into Sam. At five in the morning. Hey, she'd fucked with my mind. What could I say?

"This is like physical training. You always were a gunner, Noah," I panted as we came off a sprint. I'd made the stupid mistake of asking Noah how he was training for an upcoming fight he had on television. Come and see, he'd said, which was the same as saying that he didn't think my post-deployment ass could make it more than a few miles. I couldn't stand down from a challenge. I was regretting it now. Rather than a sustained run for eight or nine miles, Noah had decided that Bo and I should run interval sprints. For an hour. The good thing was that I was too tired to think about the shittastic ending to yesterday's hike. My cheeks felt hot when I thought about the tantrum I'd pulled. Rivulets of sweat blurred my vision, and I grabbed the bottom of my shirt to wipe my eyes and cover my flush. "You two do this every morning?"

"Bo's too busy with AnnMarie to run every morning," Noah complained, before sucking down an electrolyte pack.

"Got one of those for me?"

Noah pulled out two more from the pocket of his running shorts and handed them out.

I pushed the entire contents of the pack in my mouth and slid the crumbled plastic into my pocket. "That true, Bo? You wimping out?"

"God didn't make a girl like AnnMarie so she could wake up alone," Bo replied, his mouth still around the opening of his energy supplement.

"So she's sleeping with some other guy this morning?"

"Fuck you. She's at the house, and I'll be showered and back in bed for some morning delight before she's even awake."

"Or she and Grace will be making breakfast with Finn," Noah suggested.

"Man, I hope it's peach French toast. That shit's the bomb." Bo and Noah knocked fists together.

"I'm surprised they allow you to eat French toast." I ruffled Noah's hair, which wasn't easy to do given we were about the same height.

He knocked my arm away. "I can have one piece."

"So this is the good life outside the Marines? Hot girls making you breakfast? Hook me up." I forced out a laugh because joking about casual encounters with girls was normal. Wanting Sam, regretting marring the connection we'd had was something I barely understood myself and wasn't ready to lay out in front of the guys.

"What am I? OKCupid? Close your own damn hook ups." Bo slapped his empty pack in my hand and ran off. Noah laughed like a loon and followed. Fisting the garbage, I gave chase and eventually ran Bo down close to the house and tackled him in the grass. I shoved the empty electrolyte pack down his shirt.

"I always knew you wanted me." He made kissy faces at me while I play-punched him in the face. Our fight was interrupted when the front door opened and Noah and Bo's girlfriends were standing there—awake far too early but dressed in tiny shorts and tank tops. Goddamn, summer was my favorite season. I must've stared too long because Bo slid a glancing blow across my chin.

"Stop staring at my girl, motherfucker."

"Can't. She's too hot," I said just to screw with him. Noah had sprinted up the steps and spirited Grace inside rather than expose her to my lecherous gaze, I guess.

"You gotta learn some manners," Bo growled.

I swung to face him and put up my fists. "Yeah, wanna try to teach me some?"

He crouched into a fighting stance and we started circling each other.

"You coming in to have breakfast, or would you rather piss all over each other in a show of real animal dominance?" AnnMarie called from the door.

"I'm going to knock this fucker on his ass and then I'm coming in for breakfast," he called back.

"You get hit in the mouth, Bo, and we can't do those things we talked about last night!" She stood on the front stoop, hands on her hips. I made the mistake of turning to look at her and Bo took the opportunity to smack me right in the chin. I let him have the blow though, because I wouldn't want anyone looking at my girl either. But so he didn't think I was going to let him hit me any time he wanted, I kicked his Achilles heel and when he stumbled, I jumped over him and ran up to her.

"Leave him and run away with me, sunshine."

She just laughed and pushed me away so she could run over to him. He lifted her up and she wrapped her legs around him and gave him a kiss so hot I felt the temperature rise about ten degrees. I frowned and turned to go inside because the sight of Bo and AnnMarie wrapped around each other turned on a different kind of hunger—one that French toast wasn't going to satisfy.

After some damn good French toast, I cornered Adam before he could take off to his music studio above the garage.

"So man, about Sam Anderson," I started.

Adam shook his head. "You outta be careful with her. She's fragile."

"Are you warning me off? Because I don't poach. Ever." Although for Sam—no, I didn't. I'd step aside if Adam had a thing for her.

He fiddled with the headphones around his neck, looking uncomfortable. "I like her but I don't think she's a good person to get involved with."

"Is that the nice way to say she's a bunny boiler and I should stay away or my dick may end up on the roadside?"

He snorted at this and gave me a reluctant smile. "No, it's a nice way of saying that I don't think Sam knows there are other men in this world. Lost her husband in Afghanistan a couple of years ago. In the three years she's worked at Gatsby's, she's never even looked twice at another guy. Not before Will died and not once after. Think she's still in love with her dead husband. That kind of fragile."

That wasn't what I wanted to hear, but then it also didn't really match up with my experience with Sam. Aside from the fact she still had a metric ton of shit of her husband's in the condo, she didn't seem like the poor, grieving widow. She'd certainly done more than look at me. I could still feel her hot mouth on mine and the flutters of her tongue as it tasted and explored. Those weren't the actions of a grieving widow. But Adam's warning put me off from contacting Sam, so I allowed myself to be pulled into a day of drinking and lounging by the pool, trying to pay attention to AnnMarie and Grace's girlfriends.

Later that evening, I settled at the far back lawn, trying to get away from the noise and crowd. Crickets chirped in the copse behind me and the sun had dropped down behind the horizon, reducing the heat of the day from muggy to slightly steamy. The crowd had thinned, and only a few hardcore folks were still drinking. One of the roommates had fired up a grill and Bo had directed me to sit on the opposite side of the pool, probably so he and Noah could lay into me. A little drowsy from the travel, sun, and liquor, I couldn't muster up any *I care* emotion at that point. A mosquito buzzed around my head and I nabbed it out of the air before it could settle on my skin for a snack.

"Nice move, Mr. Miyagi."

"That's Master Miyagi to you."

Bo dropped down in a chair next to me and handed me a hamburger hot off the grill. Noah followed with the beer.

"Not complaining, but are we having a private party because you're finally going to confess your love for me?" I took a bite of my hamburger. "Don't need to say it. I knew you had a thing for me since boot camp, when you kept staring at my shorts."

"You had a label on them."

"My mom did it to be a smart ass. How many times I gotta tell you that?" I cuffed Bo lightly across the back of the head.

"As many times as it still produces a rise, I'd guess." This pithy observation was from Noah.

"What happened to the Widow Sam? She drove up and you guys took off but you came home in a real snit. What gives?"

I just ate my burger and ignored the question.

Bo tried again. "Okay, Widow Sam is off limits. How about the real deal about you leaving the Corps?"

"Don't call her that," I said flatly.

"Huh?"

"Don't call her Widow Sam. She's a person, not a character."

Bo raised his eyebrows at me and then turned to Noah and said in a stage whisper, "Another one bites the dust."

Rather than rising to Bo's bait, as Noah called it, I tried changing the subject. "You've a nice place here. Think this is where you'll stay?"

"Nope. AM wants to go to grad school at the University of Chicago."

"How about you, Noah?"

"Dunno. Go to Chicago too. More opportunity there."

"That's a first, you following Bo instead of the other way around."

The crickets made more noise than the three of us as Bo, Noah and I ate in silence. Finally, because he had less patience than a three-year-old at Christmas, Bo blurted out again, "Are you in trouble?"

"No," I sighed. "I just have a lot on my mind." And I didn't want to talk about it even with Bo and Noah, two of my oldest friends. I cast about for something to tell them, something that they would believe so I wouldn't have to put into words feelings that I didn't really understand myself. "My ex is sniffing around and I didn't want to spend my entire leave dodging her."

"Your ex isn't still with the LT?"

"No. They broke up after she had the syphilis scare."

"That was a janky thing to do." Bo reached for another burger from the stack Noah'd brought over. "You do know that she was an asshole, right, and not just for cheating?"

"Because she tried to pass on the syphilis without saying anything?" The talk of my cheating ex and her STI was making me lose my appetite. "What're you eating, Jackson?"

"Pork chop." Noah waggled the pale meat at me.

Drawing back, I shook my head. "Looks delicious. Not. Aren't you allowed to eat real food when training?"

"Not really. Conditioning is different. I have to last five rounds instead of all day."

"Bet it feels like all day after you get a dozen elbows to the chin."

"So what's this all about anyway?" Noah asked. I could put Bo off. He was never serious about anything except his new girlfriend. But Noah wasn't a bullshitting type of guy.

Stretching my legs out and tipping my chair, back, I sighed and gave in. "I'm twenty-five. I have an associate's degree in business admin that took me four years to get. From what I hear of other Marines, present company excepted, without a degree on the outside I'm pretty much fucked. Infantry Marines are good at following orders and breaking stuff. Other than being a cop or going to private contracting, I'm pretty much SOL. If I get out now, I'm on the wrong side of my twenties and just entering the work force. Then there's the whole female thing…" I trailed off. That was as much as I could get out without looking like I had a vagina.

"So this comes down to your philosophy that you can't have a serious relationship in the service because your girlfriend slept with the local recruiter while you were deployed," Noah surmised.

I shifted guiltily in my chair. "Not just. It's about leading men, being responsible for their mental wellbeing and their physical health. It's about having women like Sam waiting on tenterhooks to hear that their man is home safe and then, when they can't bear it anymore, getting their fears dispelled by some guy at home. Nearly every guy I know has been cheated on or has cheated or is divorced or is on their second or third marriages, and those are just the guys enlisted underneath me. One thing just leads to another." Noah opened his mouth but I didn't stop talking. "I get it, Noah. You wanted to slap a ring on Grace's finger when you guys finally got together. Instead you waited two whole years."

"Seemed like a motherfucking eternity," he grunted.

"Yeah, it was a miracle she waited for you. The immaculate conception was only slightly less amazing than that."

Bo coughed to cover a laugh and Noah looked like he wanted to reach across Bo and hit me—but only because I was right.

"So what are your options?" Noah asked.

"Go back to school. Get a full bachelor's degree in something. Hell if I know what. My brothers say to come work for them. They've got a waiting list about two years long." My older brothers run an auto body and custom chopper place in Orange County specializing in custom-made rides and 70s muscle cars. They were kind of famous for it and had always told me there was a wrench and a toolbox just waiting for me.

"But?"

"But." I let the chair slam down. "I always thought I'd retire, not separate from the military. How do you know that Grace or AnnMarie aren't gonna cheat on you two if you aren't around?" I gestured toward where the girls were sitting with the other guys who lived at Woodlands, soaking up the warmth around the fire pit, drinking something pink and fruity one of the roommates had concocted for them. "Your roommates could be buttering them up and screwing them blind when you're off at one of your fights or too busy doing stupid shit with your old pal from the Marines."

"You don't. You have to trust them," Noah said.

I barked out a bitter laugh. "I didn't think my girl of four years would either but she wasted almost zero time jumping into the LT's bed while I was gone."

"Your biggest problem is that you're not hanging around the right women," Bo explained. Noah nodded as Bo Randolph, the biggest skirt chaser in my platoon tried to give me advice on hanging with the wrong kind of women. I couldn't believe what I was hearing. Obviously Bo either missed my amazement or didn't care because he barreled on. "If you're worried about your girl running off with another guy and all you've got is your friend with benefits who isn't cranking your chain all that much then you should be looking elsewhere. Base bunnies are on you because your salary is so much sweeter now. In your dad's circle, everyone is trying to garner for favors. So you gotta put yourself in a place where you don't have those inside pressures." Bo dusted off his second hamburger and drained a beer. "Besides, we didn't like Carrie for a long time before she cheated on you."

"Since when," I scoffed unbelievingly but at Noah's steady stare I started believing. "Really?"

Noah nodded but Bo was the one who explained. "She was always trying to make you jealous. Chatting up some new Marine, placing him in jeopardy and getting you riled up."

"She was just insecure, is all." I didn't know why I was defending Carrie. She did like to make me jealous. In high school, when we'd first started dating, I hadn't been a jealous guy at all. I didn't mind when she had other stuff going on because I was busy. I liked that she went her own way. That's why I thought we'd make it when other Marine couples didn't. She was independent. But, eventually, I found out that she really wasn't. When I was busy and she deemed I wasn't paying enough attention to her, Carrie got her attention fix with someone else. At first, when she started flirting with other guys at the enlisted club, it made me feel good because while she may have gotten them worked up, the only fire she was putting out was the one in *my* pants. And the sex after those nights in the bar were scorching hot. As time wore on, though, the plays for other people's attention became tiresome. Like Bo said, she invariably picked on a new guy who I couldn't bring myself to punch out because I was superior to him in rank. It wouldn't be fair.

It was almost a relief to go on deployment. I didn't have to see her making eyes at anyone else and in my imagination, she never ever flirted with another man. Her eyes were only for me. My vision of Carrie and the reality of Carrie were two really different things. Yeah, getting cheated on sucked hard, but there was a welcome lack of anxiety there too. I needed to chew on that for a while.

"Whatever, just saying that her only flaw wasn't cheating on you so maybe you can believe that not all women are cheaters. Maybe it was just Carrie," Bo said.

"Maybe." I'd spent a long time running from anything even remotely resembling a relationship. I'd had sex with a couple girls who had been too busy with their own lives to want something steady, and I'd gotten the physical release I wanted without any emotional entanglements. But it seemed like everyone around me was settling down, even someone like Bo, and I couldn't help but wonder if I was missing out on something—something important.

The next few days passed in a blur as I tried to drink away my attraction to Sam and those unsettling feelings she roused. It was the only way I could keep myself from knocking on every door in the neighborhood to find her. I knew that if I sought her out, I'd be asking for more than forgiveness, and given my past behavior, I needed to work that all out before I saw her again. Could I take her to bed without her taking off her ring first? Maybe. Could I have sex with her in her condo with her dead husband's stuff all around us? Possibly. Could I stay here for forty some days and not see her again? No.

Amy, the small, slightly-dimwitted blonde, had tried to lay a claim on me. She'd rubbed up against me like a cat the other night, and I'd had to pry her off when I went to bed. I tried to tell her that neither of us was ready for anything like that but that alcohol and loneliness could drive you toward people that you ordinarily wouldn't hook up with. And it wasn't like I didn't understand. We were surrounded by couples, really happy couples, and seeing them together made you believe you could start something up and have it be just as meaningful.

Unfortunately my hard-on would not go away no matter how many times I tried to jerk it in the shower. After a week had passed since we went hiking, I asked Adam for her house number and her phone number. He gave them over with a warning. "You're Bo and Noah's friend and we like you but fuck her over and you'll never be welcome here again."

I didn't take offense. It was the same type of warning I'd give out if I had female friends to be protective of. I tucked the information in my pocket and made for the driveway. I was almost out to the street before Bo and Noah ran me down with Noah's truck. "Climb in, we're going to make a slip and slide today."

"I've got other plans for the morning," I said and turned up the street where the map app on my phone indicated Sam's house sat. Or at least her parents' house. Her condo was somewhere downtown but I'd start close to home and move on. Good recon took time and given my major fuckups with Sam, I figured the more insider information I could gather the better.

Bo frowned. "Dude. We need you to help build the slip and slide. This is about upholding the honor of the Corps. We build stuff. We get shit done. What else you got going on that's more important than showing civilians how awesome Marines are?"

"You serious?" Bo was never much of a motivator, as we liked to call super-eager Marines.

"Nah, but we do need you. Besides, it'll be a nice pick-up line for Sam." He grinned knowingly and said in a fake falsetto voice. "Hey Sam, I built you a slip and slide. Go put on your bikini and come down to Adam's house."

"You sound like a choking chicken." But his idea actually made some kind of weird sense. It'd give me an excuse to go and see her and she'd be nearly naked and doused in baby oil if she accepted the invitation. That was worth a short delay. "Shotgun," I said, opening the passenger-side door.

"You can't call shotgun when I'm sitting in the shotgun seat," Bo protested. I ignored this and pulled on his arm.

"I'm the guest." And with Noah giving Bo a shove, I managed to pull him out of the truck and then clamored over his body to get into the passenger seat. "Let's get this rust bucket moving." I slammed my fist on the dash of Noah's truck, which was still so new it smelled like it had just rolled off the lot. Nearly naked and oiled Sam. Now if that wasn't worth getting going for in the morning, nothing was.

NINE

Samantha

A WEEK AFTER THE HIKING TRIP, I STILL HADN'T HEARD FROM Gray. He'd mentioned that he'd see me later as he exited the Rover, but it had been a brush-off, which I hadn't figured out right away. I kept waiting for another invitation to do something but it never came. Somehow I had made him think I was trying to jump off the cliff. He must have been pretty traumatized by the experience with the widow and, looking back, I guess I could kind of, *sort of* see where he was coming from. I told Eve about it while we were bartending together but she thought he was the one who needed therapy.

"Randy was right on when he pegged soldier boy for being weird. You should stay away."

"I thought you said he was perfect because he was just here temporarily."

"You want temporary? Summer league semi-pro baseball is gearing up. A new visiting team will likely show up in the bar this week. You can't get any more temporary than a one-night stand with a player who won't be on the roster the next time the team rolls into town."

"That sounds super enticing."

"I'm sure that there are summer hobos you could try out. Do a little service project."

"Your ideas are terrible, Eve."

I kept looking over at Adam's table, but it stood conspicuously empty. Tucker and his friends had come in one night and sat there; I stared at the table as if I could wish Gray into existence. That had never worked with Will and it didn't work with Gray either. It did, unfortunately, make Tucker think I was ready to forgive him for ignoring his family.

"Hey, sorry again about bailing on lunch the other day."

I started to say that it was okay but then stopped because it wasn't okay. "I think Carolyn really could use a visit from you."

Tucker shrugged. "She likes to see you better. You're Will's wife."

"Will's wife could've used the support," I said more sharply than I intended, and then I felt bad for making him feel guilty. But I'd said it because I needed him to be there. It was tough emotionally for me but Tucker would always be the guy who was running away from all of his problems and leaving them for other people to sort out. While I admired the fact that he had gone off and pursued his dreams, a big part of me was pissed off was he couldn't be more supportive of the grief his parents were suffering. It was hard to hold up Carolyn and myself at the same time. We both could've used a bit of his support to lean on. My biggest objection against Bitsy getting involved with Tucker had more to do with the fact that I thought he was a selfish bastard then the fact that he was ten years older than her.

"Sorry," he said blandly but we both knew that he wasn't.

"Besides," I said. "I'm not Will's wife anymore."

He reached out and tapped my diamond. "This says you are."

I fisted my hand. "Maybe it's time to take it off."

Tucker's eyes widened but a rush of customers cut off any opportunity to talk. By the time a lull hit, he was gone. He and his crew had vacated the patio and either headed inside or to some other bar. Tucker's feelings for me were entirely fabricated. He, like his mother, viewed me as an extension of Will. They kept me close because I was someone who loved him and, I suppose, because I answered Carolyn's phone calls and went to the monthly luncheons for the same reason. But I was only twenty-two and I couldn't be Will's widow forever. There was only a long life of loneliness if I hewed to that path.

For the last week I'd run errands for my mom's law firm and when I wasn't tending bar, I knitted, all the while staring at the unfinished flag I'd been working on for Will when he deployed. When I realized I'd made men's socks on the second night, I resolved to hunt Gray down and make him listen to me.

I'd never finished the afghan, but I hadn't taken it down either. It kind of paralleled my life. The act of living it had been interrupted, and I'd never quite gotten back into the swing of things. Taking down the flag wouldn't even be that hard, but it was just one of those things I'd never gotten around to. I'd dropped out of college, abandoned the flag, and kind of holed up with my family hoping that it was all a bad dream.

Gray obviously thought I was just an emotional mess he didn't want to take on for his temporary stay. I was lonely, but I wasn't a danger to myself. I wasn't going to kill myself, and I had never thought of it, even in some of the darkest hours of my grief. While I had wanted Will to come back to life, I guess I was too selfish to want to leave it. Being out with Gray had made me feel enervated. Hanging off the side of the cliff, feeling that weightlessness, was exhilarating. I wondered if that sensation was what Will had felt, what he chased after, and I wanted a deeper taste, a fuller understanding of it. I thought Gray could give that to me.

So I was done waiting for him. I was going to find him and ask him to spend another day with me. Yes, there were lots of guys I could pick up for one-night stands here at the bar. There was always someone at the last call who'd struck out all night and would gladly go home with me regardless of what I had in my apartment or how many rings I wore on my fingers, but I didn't want them. I wanted this golden-eyed man who told me he'd catch me if I fell. I was determined that he not see me as a sad widow who'd tried to hurl herself off the cliff. That was not going to be his last encounter with me. I was fun, dammit. He was going to see that if I had to hold him down and motorboat him. And if he was nice, I'd give him the men's socks that I'd started knitting the other evening.

"So you think you're ready to take off your ring, huh?" Eve asked as casually as she could when the band took a break.

"Maybe." I fiddled with the ring. It felt looser tonight, like I could push it off my finger with a light nudge.

Eve eyed me speculatively. "Randy's got this friend he works out with—"

I held up a hand. "Just because I'm ready to take off my ring doesn't mean I'm going to start dating."

"What does it mean?"

"It means that I can't live like Will's coming back anymore." I pushed the ring back down to the base of my finger. Not yet. With a shaky smile I said, "I'm not ready for a relationship but I think what Gray has in mind might be perfect for me right now."

The next morning I contemplated the ways that I could run into him casually. I could go to my parents' house since that was in the neighborhood where Gray was staying. He might walk by and I could pretend I was getting the mail and he could stop to talk to me. With a sigh, I realized I was going to have to go down to Adam's house, and I had no good excuse for it. Except maybe... A thought occurred to me as I stared at my condo walls. That green felt should come down. The half-finished afghan was the first thing that needed to be packed up. I wasn't in the mood to complete it, and the project only made me feel bad. I could wander down and see if I could borrow a ladder from Adam's roommate, Finn. Finn was in construction, and he had to have a lot of ladders. If Gray happened to be standing nearby and heard I needed help, well, I wouldn't refuse it if he offered.

I drove over to my parents' house and walked into the kitchen by way of the garage, ignoring the stepladder that leaned up against one of the garage walls. Too short, I told myself. Wouldn't reach to the top of the green felt. Adam's house had a pool and he'd invited the staff at Gatsby's to come several times but I'd always turned him down. I was going to pull out a swimsuit and take him up on that standing offer to swim.

Upstairs I looked at my sparsely populated closet. I had my sketchy overall shorts that Bitsy had decreed would make a farmer embarrassed, a few skirts, and a couple of pairs of jeans. I pulled out a skirt—the short circle skirt that Bitsy had wanted me to wear to lunch with Carolyn and David. I remembered wearing it during a summer festival when Will had come home from Basic and before he took off to Alaska to jump out of planes onto mountains. We'd stayed out downtown all night drinking surreptitiously from beverages Tucker had bought for us. Will and I'd gone out to the reservoir, where we'd made love in his car. It was one of the better sexual experiences I'd had with him. I was excited he was home, so excited that I didn't care what we sounded like or that we were doing it in a car and that there were other cars parked up there doing the same exact thing.

Of course that was before the cops came and told us all to go home. That's when Will said we should just get married and that I could move to Alaska with him and then we wouldn't have to "fuck in a goddamn car." Will's mouth had turned filthy at Basic. I told him that wasn't going to happen. I was going to Central in the fall and would stay with my parents. Will huffed and we'd argued and then he'd gone to Alaska. I visited him a couple of times and each time, he begged me to marry him. When he got the call to go to Afghanistan, I called him right away and told him to come home and that I'd marry him. I think I'd half hoped that if we got married he would magically not deploy, but that didn't happen. I'd waited too long and wasted so much time here, and for nothing. I'd dropped out of Central when he died, and all I've been doing since is marking time. Like knitting one never-ending chain and never tying off.

I'd never had to suffer the indignities of wondering if some guy liked me because Will had always liked me, so the feelings of uncertainty I had with Gray were new. In some weird way, I liked that. Besides, I wasn't going over to Adam's house to see Gray. No, I was going to see if I could borrow a ladder. And should Gray be there with his shirt off, looking sweaty and delicious, it was just a coincidence. I smiled mischievously to myself and pulled on the green skirt. It still fit perfectly. Underneath, I slid on the bottoms of an old red bikini. On top of the swimsuit top, I pulled on one of Bitsy's long tanks and a loose-fitting midriff shirt. I had the choice of some grungy flip flops or canvas sneakers. I choose the sneakers.

"What is going on?"

A sharp voice behind me made me jump as I was shoving my feet into the sneakers.

"Jesus, Bitsy, why are you skulking around like a burglar?"

"Why are you wearing my shirt?"

"I'm going for a walk."

"It's ninety degrees out, and you're going for a walk wearing a skirt—and is that mascara you have on?"

I fought the instinct to shield my face from her penetrating gaze.

"Oh my God. Does the guy Mom said you were crushing on live around here?" She ran to her bedroom and started rummaging through her closet. There were no secrets in my life. I threw up my hands.

Chasing after her I yelled, "You're not coming with me."

"Did you go out with him? Is that what you were doing the other day? You went out with a GUY?" Bitsy virtually screamed the last part.

"I'm right here." I tapped my ears to check that there was no damage to my hearing.

"You're avoiding the question," she yelled at me.

"Fine, yes, Gray is staying over at a friend's house."

Bitsy gaped at me and then pulled me in for a hug. "Gray? His name is a color? Wait, I don't care. I'm so happy for you."

"Why?" Bitsy's energy was making me smile, making me release my pent up hopes about this afternoon.

"Because, you've decided you haven't died along with Will."

I didn't have much of an answer to that so I just finished tying my shoes. "I love you, Bit by Bit," I said and let myself out of the house. Bitsy's groan echoed through the door and I couldn't stop smiling.

TEN

Gray

BUILDING THE SLIP AND SLIDE HAD TAKEN A COUPLE OF hours. The house had a long, fairly steep drive. We'd gone out this morning to the sporting goods store and bought seven king size air mattresses and several tent tarps, and a kid's bouncy house was in the process of being inflated at the bottom of the drive. The big motor required to inflate it was making it hard to hear, even at the top of the hill.

"You do this before?" I asked Bo as we surveyed our work. The mattresses had been laid end-to-end and covered much, but not all, of the drive. The pressure of one end of the mattress on the other was to keep them in place, like a stacked set of blocks. The tarps, which would ordinarily go beneath a tent, were stretched tautly across the top of the mattresses. Bo, Finn, Noah, and I had worked in pairs to drive in the stakes to hold down the tarps while Adam and Mal, the other two roommates, had made sure that the bouncy house was set up securely down at the base of the hill.

"Nope." Bo flipped the hammer in his hand. "Haul up the hoses." We'd also had to buy to extra hoses to make sure that we could hoist one to the top of the drive. The bill for all the supplies was astronomical, but Adam had paid without a blink. Bo told me in the car ride back that Adam's dad would think this was the best possible use of his money. I shrugged. Not my dime—and it did look fun as hell. We'd also bought a couple of gallons of baby oil.

Bo threw one at me. "Time to lube up. I'm sure you're familiar with this."

"Oh I am," I replied. "I always apply lube. It's the only way any chick can take my monster cock."

"Is that the pick-up line you're using now? Because it seems like you'd end up disappointing them when you get home."

"No girl has ever left my bed unsatisfied. That's probably something you don't know a lot about."

"If you have to use lube, then I'm worried you don't know what you're doing in bed."

"Don't worry about me. I'm using lube because I'm going places no man has gone before."

"You're fucking their earhole?"

"Bo, I thought for sure we'd taught you a few things when you were in the service, but now it seems like you don't know your earhole from your asshole."

"That's not what AnnMarie was saying last night," he said smugly.

"Actually, AnnMarie told me that she didn't realize dicks were longer than her hand and wondered if mine was bigger than average." I squirted more baby oil on the tarps. "I told her no, that you were just really small. Poor girl. Good thing she isn't required to do a lot of math."

Bo threw down his gallon container with a roar and dived across the mattresses and tarps to get at me, but I'd slicked the tarp with oil and he went sliding down. I bent over and laughed so hard I cried as he kept trying to climb up to get me and I kept squirting him with baby oil. Noah put an end to our fun when he came over with the hoses and sprayed us all down. I jumped onto the tarp belly first and rammed into Bo and gravity took us both to the bottom where we commenced wrestling.

Adam's shout to the top of the hill made me pause and look up. Bo took the opportunity to hit me. "Dammit, Bo, always when I'm not paying attention?"

"Pay attention then." He shoved my head down onto the tarp and got up. "One of these days you're going to fall hard for a girl and she's going to break your ever-loving heart."

"Been there, got the T-shirt. Never going back," I said as I popped up. Adam was hailing Sam. I ran up to the top of the hill, stripping off my oil-and-water-slicked T-shirt. I wasn't trying to look good for her—okay, maybe a little. I was panting and out of breath when I got to her, but I beat Adam by about ten feet.

"Sam, hey, long time," I said and rubbed the shirt on my oil-slicked hair. She reached up. I thought she was going to run her hands over my head, and I dipped my head forward in anticipation, but she didn't touch me. Instead, she drew back and showed me a blade of grass that must have stuck to my head when I was wrestling with Bo.

"Are you and Bo always fighting?" It wasn't really a question but an observation, as if she'd encountered this type of male friendship before, and I suspected she had with Will. Before I could answer, though, Adam and the rest of the crowd had drawn level with us.

"Sam," Adam said, drawing Sam in for an easy hug. "I'm glad you stopped by. Finally taking me up on one of my offers."

This sounded vaguely sexual and I frowned at Adam. He said he had no claim on Sam. Adam caught my stare and rolled his eyes. "Loosen up" he said silently. Rolling my shoulders, I tried to let go of the tension that had taken hold.

"How's Finn doing?" Sam asked. Finn's grandfather had died earlier in the spring.

"He's doing okay. He'll be glad to see you. I think you're the one person who gets what's going on in his head." Adam took Sam by the shoulder and started walking her down the incline. The rest of their conversation was hard to hear as they merged with the larger crowd of people who'd gathered for an impromptu Friday pool party. I guess it was summer and no one had to work.

"Turn that frown upside down, Princess." Bo crept up on me. "She turn you down?"

"No," I said curtly.

"I keep telling you to save the 'let's go out for blood tests' until after the second date."

"You're an asshole, you know that right?"

"But a hot one," he replied.

"If AnnMarie wasn't watching us right now looking like she'd stab me if I started whaling on you, I'd have my boot so far up your ass you'd be feeling it in your throat."

"I love it when you talk dirty to me."

"How is it that you screwed half the western seaboard and still came away clean?" I asked.

"Dunno, lucky, I guess?" Bo shrugged, unconcerned. Then he turned to me. "I was lucky. I know this. I should've been more careful and I admire that you take care of yourself and the girls you sleep with. It shows that you're far more decent than I am but I also think you use this whole STI and cheating thing as a way not to get involved. So you don't want to get involved right now? That's all good, but don't do stuff to shoot yourself in the foot. You're better than that."

A heart-to-heart from Bo. My screw ups must have been more obvious than I'd wanted. "Let's talk about Noah and what his chances of winning his upcoming match are."

"Sure, don't want to talk about your feelings, that's fine. Just know that I'm getting it regular because I know what I'm talking about."

"Bullshit, you fool." I shook my head in mock disgust. "You're getting it regular because AnnMarie didn't see me first."

Bo grunted but we were back to our regularly scheduled insults which meant all was right in our world. That Sam hung out with Adam and Finn and looked happy and relaxed didn't bother me at all. That she came by and made casual small talk with me like there wasn't an electrical current that passed between us didn't faze me. That she looked hotter than a *Sports Illustrated* model in her two-piece bikini that showed off a pretty impressive set of legs, a perfect gap between her thighs, and a small-but-juicy rack didn't cause me to have to go inside and jack off in the bathroom. I just did it because that's what guys do. They jerk it while fantasizing about girls that they couldn't have, but wanted so goddamned bad.

I leaned my head against the bathroom door and then carefully cleaned myself up. "Gray Phillips, you are a stupid son of a bitch," I declared to the mirror. Bo was right. I'd been fucked up bad by a girl and it was ruining me. After my impromptu bathroom session, I wasn't sure I was relieved or discouraged that Sam was still there. I found her in the kitchen and all the jerking in the world wasn't going to solve my problem because I could feel a semi rising in my shorts just looking at her.

"Sam." She jumped at my over-loud voice.

"God, you scared me." She gave a nervous little laugh. Everyone else was still outside and for once, we were alone.

"About earlier," I started but stopped when she raised her hand, palm facing me.

"You know what. It's fine. I can see by the crowd that you have plenty of coffee offers to choose from." She waved her hand, gesturing toward the front lawn where people were still making use of the makeshift slip and slide.

Coffee? Shit man, she was still upset about two fuckups ago, not the most recent one. I blew out a big breath. There was a mountain of apologies and explaining I was going to have to do to make this right.

"No, there was no rejection the other night," I said firmly. The only way to salvage this was to make sure she understood that I still wanted her. "It was a delay. The coffee wasn't in the right mug. I needed a different mug."

"A different mug?" She looked at me like I was crazy—and maybe I was.

I drew a hand through my shorn hair. "Yes, the one we'd used felt like someone else had drank out of it."

"Oh, so you need a perfectly new bed, or excuse me, mug for coffee every time you have it? Good luck with that." Sam turned and began throwing open kitchen cabinets and them slamming the doors shut. I knew she wanted me to leave, but I wasn't going anywhere. "I mean, how many new mugs do you offer to girls you invite over for coffee?"

"A lot fewer than you seem to think, but it just looked like you weren't ready to have coffee."

"Wasn't ready? I was climbing you like a pole in the hallway of the bar and even after you accused me of cheating, I stupidly issued you another invitation. I've never been so ready for coffee!" she shouted at me.

"I know. And I'm sorry. I want your coffee. Bad," I pleaded.

"Well," she huffed. "You aren't getting any." She slammed the last cupboard closed and stomped out.

When dusk had fallen and Adam and Finn had fired up the grill, I'd made up my mind. She needed to give me one more chance. I'd show her exactly what I was feeling. People surrounded us and there wasn't any good way for me to extricate her from Adam's side. But when everyone gathered around the fire pit, he couldn't sit in both chairs beside her so I sat on her right before anyone else could. I'd convince her somehow that I wanted her more than anything and that all the shit she had in her condo and the jewelry she wore didn't matter. Around the patio, the after-dinner conversation turned to zombie survivalist techniques.

"If we did live in a post-apocalyptic world, people who worked with their hands would have a better chance of survival," Bo said. "So Noah, Gray, and I are going to be around." I think that was Bo's weak wingman attempt. Hook up with Gray, he'll save you if the zombies come after you. I wasn't sure that was helpful since we weren't even close to needing to jump someone's bones for survival's sake.

"Hey, I can kill a few with my instruments. Drumsticks or the broken throat of the guitar is going to do some damage," Adam protested.

Sam offered her up her own viability. "Then I'd be a valuable asset. I could skewer people with my needles and knit clothes out of fibers."

"Okay, you're in," I said immediately. She cocked her head and gave it a shake like she couldn't figure me out. I was going to make it clear to her that I was interested even if I couldn't get her alone.

"What about the repopulation of the human race?" a dark-haired girl with a ruffly swimsuit that barely covered her impressive knockers said coyly.

"Do you need some instruction? I can help out," another guy joked. I kept my eyes on Sam to see if she was interested in anyone else in the group. Her eyes were pinned on a square patch of concrete between her feet.

The girl scoffed. "I don't need instruction. I'm already amazing." She stretched her arms and the move showcased her admittedly perfect form to all those around.

"That's what they all say," muttered the guy who'd been rejected.

"Oh yeah? What makes a girl good in bed then?"

This time Sam spoke up. "Yeah, Gray, what makes a girl good in bed?"

Her eyes held a glittering challenge and everything, including the meat between my legs, rose up to meet it. I jumped in, feet first, without a chute. I'd either catch the wind or smash to the ground, but she was giving me an opening whether she knew it or not. "Enthusiasm," I responded without delay.

"She's there, doesn't that mean she wants it?" Sam said softly.

I shook my head, staring at her hard. "It's not the same thing. When you're going down on her, she lets you know how good it feels by telling you, grabbing your head, squeezing her legs together. When you're inside of her, she's squeezing the shit out of your piece and milking every last orgasm out of you. Guys want to see and hear and feel how hot she is for you."

"Sounds exhausting," said someone else. "What makes a guy good in bed?"

"Someone who's paying attention." My gaze was fixed on Sam.

"That's it?" she asked.

"Yup. Every time I touch a girl, I'm cataloguing the sounds she makes, the clenching of her muscles, how wet she is getting. It's my responsibility to make sure that she is wetter than an April shower and I do that by paying attention."

"But you like your girls pure, right?" Sam asked sarcastically. "Virgins only?"

I shook my head. "No, absolutely not. I don't care how many partners she's had before me so long as I'm the only one in the bedroom with her at the moment. I gotta know she's with me every step."

"What's your favorite position?" someone called out.

"Reverse cowgirl, am I right, ladies?" Two girls across from us high-fived. Sam shifted next to me and I waited for her to jump in but she remained stubbornly silent. The only female I wanted to know about decided she wouldn't share her opinion.

"What about you?" one of them asked.

"I like 'em all." Was this working at all? Or was I just making a fool of myself, trying to look boss in front of Sam? We stared at each other but I saw nothing in her eyes but a reflection of the firelight.

"But a favorite."

Without looking away, I answered the question. "The ol' missionary is a good one. You can stare into her eyes the entire time and if you hold her legs in the right position, you can hit the A-spot."

"You mean G-spot."

"No, A-spot. It's a spot on the back wall of the vagina." *I'm going to make it good for you, Sam*, I told her silently. *It'll all be worth it. Give me another chance.*

Everyone around the fire was getting hot now, and it wasn't just because of the flames. People were shifting in their chairs and the breathing was becoming a bit more ragged. The sex talk was hardening dicks and wetting pussies, but the only one I wanted was sitting next to me as impassive as a stone.

"I'm happy to be your test subject," offered the big-chested brunette, sitting up and swinging her legs to the side. "I'll let you know if you're good in bed."

My desire had a name and no one else but Sam was going to sate it but this girl had put herself out there and I wasn't going to make her feel bad. I just told her the truth. "I'm out of commission now," I admitted. Sam tensed up beside me. "I belong to someone else."

"Really? Because I could have sworn this past weekend, you were telling another girl you didn't have anyone back home."

"I don't." To get my message across to her and everyone else, I widened my legs so that my thigh brushed up against Sam's. Out of the corner of my eyes I saw the brunette glower. Next to me, I heard Sam's breath catch but she didn't move away. *Everyone* had gotten the message.

Bo hauled AnnMarie to her feet. "Boy, I'm tired."

"Me too," AnnMarie chirped, and they both practically ran in to the house. Sam jumped up and followed them. I rose to follow but Adam put a hand on my chest.

"Just remember," he warned me. "Fragile."

When I got into the house, I didn't see her downstairs. "Where'd Sam go?" I asked Noah, who'd been sitting inside watching television with Grace.

He jerked his thumb toward the front door. "She headed out."

Fuck me. I ran out the door but Sam was halfway up the drive by then.

"Sam, wait," I called after her but she didn't slow. If anything, she sped up, almost running but not quite. Clearly my fuck talk by the fire only pissed her off instead of turning her on. Had I miscalculated or what? I could either chase her down—and there was no question I could—or go back and toss myself into the pool. To hell with it, if I was going down, I was going to do it hard. I sprinted and caught her in about ten strides.

"Why are you following me?" she cried.

"I thought you understood back there that I—"

She cut me off. "I understand that you can turn your heat on and off like a light switch but I'm not that way. What do you have to be confused about?"

The unfairness of it made me explode. "You think I've got it all together? Let me tell you, sister. You know why I'm struggling with the decision to stay in? Because if I do, I'll be in charge of people. People who could die. It's one thing to make sure that your armored vehicle works or your rifle but people, Sam! I need to make sure my team has got it all together upstairs," I pointed to my head, "and here," I pounded my chest.

"Because if one part of the platoon is weak, we could all be in danger. I have to make sure that everyone knows what they are doing and what they should do and how they'll react. I'm fucking terrified of that, and I'm completely disgusted at myself for even hesitating. Hesitating can get you dead outside the wire." I was yelling at her, but Sam didn't move away. Her gaze, well, I couldn't read it at that point;

I was too caught up in my own misery.

"And women? Shit. My girlfriend of four years cheated on me during my second deployment with the local Marine recruiter, an officer!" I threw out my arms. "And she was going to climb back in bed with me when I got home. If it hadn't been for the LT deciding that it's bros before hos, I could have slept with her when she had an STI."

Sam stood stock still as I yelled. Scrubbing my hand over my mouth, I looked around and gave a mirthless laugh, embarrassed at the shitstorm I just spewed all over her. "Sorry." Could I pass it off as drunken behavior? I cradled my head in my hands so I couldn't see her expression of disgust. "By the way, I'm clean," I mumbled through my hands.

Instead of running away, Sam came closer. Her hand fell on my shoulder and then trailed down to my elbow. Looking up, I saw that she'd lost her angry and hurt expression and replaced it with a tender smile. Her other hand came up to cup the back of my neck and pull my head down to hers. There was no logic to her behavior. She should have been sprinting away from me and my mess, but I didn't correct her. I wasn't so stupid or so inept that I didn't know how to seize opportunity when it presented itself. Still as a hunter lying in wait, I remained motionless as her lips brushed my cheek, her soft breath feathering across my skin. The streetlights made her skin luminous, and this close I could see her pale lashes fluttering over her eyes. Her hand pressed against my forearm for balance as she leaned in, moving her mouth from my cheek to my ear.

"I'm thirsty. You thirsty?" she whispered, and her breath traveled straight from my ear down to my groin.

For a moment I didn't get it, didn't get what she was trying to say to me but then I recalled her smile, the light touch on my arm, and the tender way she kissed me. The lights inside my dimwitted head turned on. "I've never been so thirsty my entire fucking life."

"Come on then." She threaded her fingers confidently through mine. Her taking control in this moment? So very hot. "Is my Rover okay?"

"I could care less the place, but why?"

"Because I don't think I can wait to get somewhere else." She gave me a tremulous smile, and I was instantly hard.

"Let's go."

Her truck was parked outside her parents' house. I climbed into the passenger seat and she drove me up the hill to a park at the end of the development. There were no lights here. I pushed my seat back and pulled her onto my lap. I was going to be inside her before the night was over, or I'd be dead because nothing short of a bullet in the chest was going to stop us tonight.

ELEVEN

Samantha

Gray's talk of his favorite positions and what he liked in a woman had dampened my swim bottoms and made my clothes feel too tight. He was a mess inside but I liked that. I understood it. Another guy who was more put together would make me feel anxious and inadequate. That Gray was confused about life and where he was going and how he felt about women suited me perfectly and strangely bolstered my own confidence. Tonight he was going to be mine, I'd decided. I wanted to have an orgasm that wasn't brought about by my own fingers or just rubbing against him. I wanted his fingers to touch me and I wanted to hold his head between my legs. I just wanted.

We fumbled with my top, pulling off my T-shirt and then my bikini top. The strings fell away with a few tugs of his fingers and then his breath caught as he stared at my bare breasts in the moonlight. I'd always been a little self-conscious of my nipples because they were rather large and had a tendency to poke out of every shirt I wore unless I wore a well-padded bra.

I moved to cover my breasts but he brushed my hands away, cupping one breast in each large hand. "Goddamn, Sam, my mouth is fucking watering. I can't wait until I've sucked on both your tits."

But instead of heading right to my breasts, he began kissing the hollow of my throat, running his tongue along the ridges of my collarbone. His hands circled the sides of my breasts, measured the weight of them, and plumped them together until a valley formed for his questing tongue, but he didn't touch the tips. And the longer that he ignored them the more sensitive they became. The night air was sultry and heavy but I still felt every slight movement.

My sex ached. Moaning, I tried to move closer, tried to get him to ease that ache, if not with his dick, then his fingers or even his thigh. "Oh please, Gray," I gasped.

"What is it that you want?" His mouth moved against the top of my breast, licking and nibbling, but leaving the nipples untouched. "Tell me," he ordered.

"I need you to suck me, touch me," I cried out in frustration.

"Here?" he asked, stroking the sides of my breasts. "Or is it here?" His hand drifted down toward the waistband of my skirt.

"Everywhere," I gasped.

It must've been enough because he latched on, practically sucking my whole breast into his mouth. The ache between my legs only intensified. With one hand he plucked and pinched the other nipple. His free hand undid the button on my skirt and we struggled to push it over my hips and then his fingers were inside my bikini bottom. We both groaned when his fingers slid between my labia, just slightly inside me.

"You're dripping for me," he groaned. "*I* made you hot. *My* words turned you on. This arousal is *mine,* and I want it." I was barely paying attention to his words because I just wanted his fingers farther inside me. I slid forward on his hand, rubbing my clit against his palm. God, I could come just from this. Then his two long fingers slid all the way in until I could feel his entire palm covering me. The slick heat of me was making *him* breathless. I could hear the harsh panting in my ear as he thrust into me with his fingers.

"Do you want to ride my cock?" he growled. "Does this pussy want my cock inside it because, baby, I'm so hard right now. I need to be inside you."

Gray's words worked me up harder, higher, hotter. I rode his fingers while he described how he was going to take me after I'd come all over him. He told me he'd lick his fingers then stroke his own cock with our combined moisture. He whispered that my hungry noises made him want to come in his shorts but that he wasn't going to because he wanted to save that for me. He whispered hotter and filthier things until I couldn't understand a word he was saying. All I could think of was how big his fingers were and how the pressure of the pad of his palm against my clit was perfect and how I wanted to come so hard. I gripped his shoulders and ground down and down until the sensation I'd been chasing exploded and I was gone.

It took me a minute to catch my breath. I barely noticed when Gray withdrew his fingers from me, but I did see him lick his fingers like he promised, and the hungry expression on his face started my engine again. He dragged my head down and the contact of our mouths against each other was heaven. My tangy flavor was on his tongue, mixing with his very own taste. It was addicting. *He* was addicting. His tongue plunged in and out of my mouth in a mimic of his fingers and a foreshadowing of his thick erection inside me.

"Fuck," he whispered against my mouth.

"What are you waiting for?" I could feel the outline of his arousal between my legs. "Is this about being the only man in the room?" If he was going to leave me after all this, I'd never speak to him again.

"We're not in a room and my dick is so hard I'm about to cry so say my name."

"Gray Phillips."

"Is there anyone else here?"

"Besides me?"

"You're a smartass but that's only making me harder. Yes, besides you."

"There's no one but the two of us."

"That's enough for me."

He reached behind him and with one hand pulled his shirt over his head. His shorts were next, and then there was nothing between us but the still evening air. I spread my fingers over the ridges of his chest and abdomen. One thing about the military was that it churned out some amazing physical specimens. Will had gone away a wiry boy and had returned to me, not an inch taller, but bigger and more muscular. Like Will, Gray didn't have one ounce of fat on him. His entire body looked like it had been carved from stone.

Had I once thought that Gray wasn't my type? He was the type of every female who had a working pulse. I threaded my fingers through the light smattering of hair on his chest and followed a thin line that led to his pubic hair and then his shaft, which jutted out between us. I wanted—no needed—all the promises he'd made to me and not just the ones he'd made tonight. The night in the bar and then later at the condo. He'd promised to make me scream with pleasure.

Circling his cock, I squeezed it and was rewarded with a hard groan. His arms were pressed against the roof of the car and his feet were braced on the floorboards. His whole body was stiff and tense with anticipation and I could tell he yearned for the same release he'd given me.

Sliding off his legs, I took his shaft in my mouth. We both moaned when I closed around him. God, I had forgotten how good a man tasted and how feminine and powerful I felt with a strong man's erection in my mouth. His hands swept the hair off my face so he could watch as he disappeared in and out of my mouth. One hand held the hair back like a makeshift ponytail and the other caressed my jaw and then my cheek, stroking his hardness through my skin.

His eyes looked feral in the night, and his chest bore the signs of a light sweat, evidence of the immense effort he was exerting from holding back his orgasm. The vein in his cock pulsed against my tongue and he made small, truncated jerking motions with his hips, making sure that I controlled how deep he went into my mouth. The flavor was earthy, and I couldn't get enough.

I took him all the way to the back of my throat, twisting my hand around the base as I sucked and tasted him. This was turning me on so much. I squeezed my thighs together to relieve the torment between my legs and when that didn't work, I reached down with one hand to rub myself.

"That's enough," he said, his voice guttural and low. When I didn't respond at first, he tugged lightly on the ponytail. "No more."

"Why not?" I pouted a bit, sitting back on my heels. My jaw was pleasantly sore but I felt cheated that I hadn't tasted his come and felt the hot jets of his seed wash over my tongue.

"Because," he growled, lifting me onto his lap again. He pressed a button and the seat motored backward until it was almost flat. My hair fell around us, forming a curtain. "I need to be inside you. I want to fuck you so hard that you'll remember it tomorrow and the next day and that the next time you have a fantasy you'll be thinking of this moment and how thick and hard I was inside you."

I nodded wordlessly. This was an okay alternative. Gray kicked up his shorts with a flick of his foot and caught them in one hand. In swift, economical motions, he was sheathed and ready for us. "Come here." He pushed my hips upward. "I need to taste you to see if you're ready."

"I'm ready," I pleaded.

"Let me see." He was implacable. I moved up the seat until I was nearly kneeling on the back bench. He pulled me down until I was almost sitting on his face. All thoughts of discomfort fled the minute his tongue was on me. "You taste so good, baby. So good." Copying his actions from before, I braced my arms against the roof of the Rover, trying to hold myself steady while he explored every inch of me between my legs with his talented tongue. He didn't just lick me. He sucked on my lower lips. His tongue formed a spear that he pressed inside me. He bit and nibbled and *lapped* me as if I was the most delicious thing he'd ever tasted and as if he could never get enough.

When my arms and legs couldn't hold me anymore, I collapsed, breaking the connection between his wicked mouth and my most sensitive parts. I slid down his body until I felt the broad head of his erection pushing against me. Gray took over then, placing one hand on my hips to steady me and fisting his cock in the other.

A low noise rumbled in the car but I wasn't sure if it was coming from him or me. The sensation of him pushing his stiff thick length inside me was almost too much.

"How long as it been?" Gray said behind gritted teeth.

"Twenty-six months," I whimpered, moving slightly.

He clamped down on both my hips. "Don't move."

But I had to. Inch by inch, I worked my hips over him until finally, finally he was fully seated. Every part of him was straining against the effort of thrusting into me, allowing me to adjust to his size. I hadn't remembered this at all, how full I'd feel, how connected I was. This wasn't temporary for me and as he stared at me, eyes glittering with a deep emotion, I guessed it wasn't just temporary for him either. But by unstated mutual decision, we let the moment pass without comment.

"Now," I told him and he let go. He pulled on my hips and it was all I could do to hold on because he was making good on all his promises. Bracing my hands on his chest, I rode him, slowly at first because it took some getting used to. It wasn't just that he was big and I was small but that I was unused to having a man between my legs. The feeling was so good, though, the strokes of his hard erection rubbed every inch of my inner flesh.

Gray's hands were everywhere. He stroked my back and pulled lightly on my hair so that my breasts thrust toward him and my head tipped back. Leaning forward, he captured a nipple in his mouth and then opened wider to mouth more of my breast.

He wasn't a quiet lover. He told me with groans and grunts and whispered sounds of approval exactly what he liked. His eyes rolled back when I squeezed him on a down thrust.

"Like that, baby," he grated out between clenched teeth. When my nails curled into his chest he encouraged me. "Make your mark, kitten." Our sex was noisy, messy and full of teeth and nails—and it made me wild. I rode him harder and he met my movements with hard thrusts of his own. Tension built until my toes were curled under my ass and my fingers were dug hard into his chest, but I wasn't getting the release I needed. I hadn't ever known I could ache like this.

Sensing my frustration, Gray flipped us around so that I was underneath him. With one forearm braced by my head, he lifted my whole body up with his other hand. His movements weren't as furious now. As he supported the weight of his body, the muscles in his arm flexed. It was an unconscious action, but the visible signs of his core strength was incredibly sexy. When he moved inside me, he was slower and deliberate, minutely readjusting as if he were searching for something. It felt good but not...*oh my God.* What. Was. That?

The plump head of his cock was rubbing against something deep within me and my whole body went tense at the shock of pleasure. I released a loud whimper, no words, just a conglomeration of letters. Maybe a vowel. If I could verbalize something coherent it would be nothing more than a litany of oh gods, ohmygod, ohmyfuckinglord.

Above me, still holding my lower body suspended off the car seat, Gray thrust over and over so that the head of his dick just kept rubbing over that one spot until I couldn't keep it in any longer. I turned my face to the side and latched on to his forearm, biting down to keep from screaming my head off.

His response was to laugh, a guttural ferocious thing. Sweat dripped off his forehead and onto my chest, running down between the valley of my breasts until it mingled with our combined juices. "You like that?" He sounded smug but I didn't care. I was lost in some other world.

Without waiting for a response, he started pounding me, thrusting in and out as hard as he could. The pace got faster and more frenzied and as he reached the end of his tether, his motions became jerky and without rhythm. With bared teeth and an animalistic shout, Gray came. I could feel the pulse of his come as it jetted into the condom, so strong was his release.

Not done with me yet, he braced his body with his knees. With one hand, he pushed my knee outward and with his other he began rubbing my clit. It was a position only someone with tremendous strength and balance could pull off. Even though he'd come, he was still hard as a rock and he plunged in and out of me, all the while rubbing my clit until I was mindless again, thrashing my head from side to side as his fingers and cock sent me over that cliff once again.

Collapsing on top of me, he began kissing my forehead, my cheeks, my lips in soothing gestures. I was too stunned by the force of what had just happened to move. Instead, I lay in the curve of his arm as he soothed me with long strokes of his hand over my sensitive body.

He left me only for a minute to remove the condom and tie it off, sticking it into the pocket of his shorts. I protested minutely. "Shush, these can be washed," he whispered, lying down on his side. Pulling me against him, he returned to petting me.

"That was…" I trailed off. I couldn't think of the right words to describe what had happened. "The best coffee I may have ever had."

"Maybe it's because it's been a long time," he said kindly.

"Mmm." Maybe. But maybe it was because we were so connected and in tune with each other right at this moment. It was hard to remember what sex with Will had been like. It had been so long ago, but I hadn't ever recalled feeling like this—where the orgasms still tingled at the ends of my fingertips. We were young and inexperienced. I was surprised at how good it was with Gray because the first few times I'd had sex with Will, I hadn't enjoyed it. I was too nervous and we both barely knew what we were doing.

But I didn't feel awkward with Gray as I'd imagined I would. It could have been because he was experienced, but I just think it was *him* and how I felt like I knew him. Gray knew what he was doing and his enthusiasm and watchful attention to my needs made it an incredible experience. "Has it been a long time for you?"

Gray hemmed and hawed and then turned a bit pink around his ears. I laughed low. I was too replete and satisfied to even be upset at the thought that he'd been with other women. Besides, I was the one in the car with his big hand stroking every inch of my body. Not anyone else.

"Why, Gray Phillips, are you a ho-bag?"

"No," he exclaimed. He rubbed a hand against the back of his neck, throwing his muscles into relief and making the cords of his neck stand out. It was a very sexy look on him but he seemed too agitated for it to be an affected pose. Perhaps everything looked sexy about Gray right now, from his vulnerability to his muscular body. "I have a couple friends with benefits," he finally admitted.

"A couple?" I raised an eyebrow.

This made Gray's flush travel from his ears down his neck. "Three," he mumbled.

I shot bolt upright. "You sleep with three different girls!"

"Not at the same time." He covered his eyes. "When you have FWBs it's all about the sex. I don't pick up girls at bars and take them home at night because, well, it's dangerous. Pregnancy. STIs. So I just have sex with three girls who are just as careful as I am."

"And none of these girls have feelings for you?" I asked skeptically. I couldn't imagine having sex with someone more than once and not having feelings for them but this was the world I was heading into. What a bleak future, I thought.

"Hell no. One of them is a resident at San Diego General. She barely has time to shit and eat so we hook up only when she remembers she's a sexual being, which is like once a month, if that. At most, I'm a live action dildo for her."

"And the others?"

"Why are we talking about this?"

"Dunno. I'm kind of intrigued." I was. I should be more appalled but he was like an introductory course in modern mating and I was obviously in need of an education.

He sighed heavily. "Okay, the one I see more regularly is an on-base nurse. She does all the blood tests. We got to talking one day and one thing led to another. She doesn't want to be tied down to a military guy but right now, we're all that's in her path."

"A nurse and a doctor. You going to want me to dress up in nursing costume?"

There was a prolonged silence as Gray appeared to contemplate this for far too long. "Gray!" I pretended to be shocked.

"Sorry, sorry," he finally said. "Not that I'm asking, but would you?"

I shook my head at him but didn't say no. The idea of dressing up in a costume to have sex with him wasn't a turn off. Not at all.

"So the other?" I prompted.

"EMT," he muttered through his fingers.

"What was that?"

"EMT," he said more clearly.

"You do have some kind of medical fetish," I declared. "What are you doing with me? I'm a knitter. Should I take you over to the osteopath school and find some nice student for you?"

"Shush, you." Gray pulled me down. "I don't know why they're all in the medical profession. Probably because they have the same hang-ups as I do about safety before sex. It doesn't matter. I don't have it all that often and it's meaningless."

"I don't think so." I reached down and stroked his chin. The stubble on his chin that had appeared in the afternoon and grown into the evening was prickly against my palm. I actually loved the feel of it, so different than the smoothness of my own. The contrast made me shiver. The roughness of his stubble against my breasts and my neck had been thrilling. Just the remembrance was sending tendrils of excitement through my bloodstream.

"Why's that?" he mumbled, sounding distracted. I drew my hand away slightly and his head followed me, seeking out my touch. I allowed myself a tiny private smile. We *were* connected.

"It seems to me you do have relationships. They're girls you have friendships with and then you have sex. Isn't that some kind of attachment?"

"No, because all we do is have sex. At times that are convenient to us. There are no preliminaries. I call her up or she calls me up, we meet, do the deed, and then go home. No sleepovers. No cuddling."

"That sounds really… Cold." I wanted to say awful.

"It's not," he replied curtly.

"But how can the sex be any good?"

"It's good if you know what you're doing." The sides of his lips quirked up. "And I do."

"I know you do." I traced a finger in and then out of the grooves on the sides of his mouth. The gold flecks in his eyes glowed. As if they were beckoning me, I leaned forward and placed my lips softly against the sides of his upturned lips. He didn't move but just allowed me to explore him. Bracing myself with my left arm, I ran my free hand over his chest, savoring each hard ridge. The curve of his shoulder flowed into a large muscled arm and lightly furred forearms. In contrast to the indolent ease of the rest of his body, his large hands were gripping the cushion. I was gratified by this show of both control and desire. I had no doubt that Gray could make my body feel good. It was the rest of me that I was worried about.

"You have a beautiful body," I told him, whispering soft kisses over the high cheekbones and the peak of his nose.

"I think that's my line," he choked out.

"It's not a line."

Gray reached for my wandering hand and pulled me down gently over him, repositioning me so I lay between the V of his legs.

"Maybe not." He cupped my face in his hands and kissed me. His lips were both soft and firm, and at first, it was just a plush meeting of flesh. When he parted his mouth and I felt the wetness of his tongue against the seam of my lips, I couldn't stop my own answer. The touch of his tongue against mine made me shudder. Collapsing against him, I clutched at his shoulder and ate at his mouth with a fervor matched by his own hunger.

He pushed his hips up, his groin pressing directly against my center. The sensation was so exquisite that I nearly came from just the pressure. _This is so much better than touching myself._

"My God," he whispered against my lips. "Say it again."

I hadn't realized I said it out loud. "This feels better than what I've been doing at home."

"Tell me," he asked, rocking his hips against me. Reaching down, he pulled my legs over his, switching our positions so that my legs were outside of his. I could control the contact better and I ground down. I let out a moan of frustration.

Gray was experienced enough to know what that sound meant. He reached between us, slipping his big hand down to cup me between my legs. "Tell me," he demanded again. "I'll get you off again." Rubbing the heel of one hand directly against my pubic bone, his other hand pulled at my hair so he could leave a trail of wet hot kisses along my throat. "You tell me what you think about when you touch yourself and I promise, I will bring you off, and it will be _good_."

I'd've promised anything to him at this point.

"I think about being licked between my legs." I bit my tongue and whimpered a little as Gray rubbed two fingers against me. My inner thighs felt damp and I squirmed at the thought of how wet I was, but Gray wouldn't let me move away, just kept up a relentless stroking rhythm. My toes curled as I felt a tightness seize body.

"What else?" he growled in my ear. "When you touch yourself, do you get your fingers wet or do you just rub on top?"

"Wet," I choked out. "I get wet."

"I'm going to see just how wet." His fingers dipped inside me. "Very wet," he said and his approving tone made me feel sexy instead of uncomfortable. The touch of his rough fingers against my sensitive skin was delicious. Reaching down, I pressed my hand against his although I wasn't sure if I wanted him to stop or touch me harder. Then he started talking again and I was done for.

"I can't wait until we're in a bed and the lights are on. I'll be staring at your pussy." He ran his tongue against my neck while his fingers were busy between my legs, stroking me with short, firm movements. "I bet you're pink and your honey will be dripping off of it. I'll prop your ass up on a couple of pillows and then I'll kneel between your legs. My first motion will be to lick you from right here," he curled both of his fingers close to my most sensitive area and then swept them forward, "to here. I'll suck your little clit into my mouth until it's hard and while I'm doing that, I'll slip my fingers inside you and pump you until your sweet come floods my hand." While he talked, his fingers pinched my clit and then he slipped first one finger and then another inside me. And that was all it took. I came all over him, the words, the touching, all of it sending me out of my mind. My hips came off the seat, meeting the thrusts of his fingers eagerly.

He stroked me all throughout my shudders and then when my body had quieted and my legs had collapsed, he withdrew his fingers and cupped me tenderly. His lips came down on mine again.

"*That* was beautiful. Jesus." He shook his head against my body. "Sam, I don't know what's going on between us, but this is too damn good not to explore, even temporarily."

Smoothing my hands over the planes of his shoulder blades and down his broad back, I reveled in the feel of his weight pressing me into me. "Yes." It was the only word that mattered now.

TWELVE

Samantha

WHAT WE'D SHARED IN THE CAR CHANGED SOMETHING between Gray and me. And it wasn't just sex. It was the connecting we did afterward. I wondered if he could hear how much he actually didn't enjoy his random soulless hook ups—calling himself a live action dildo wasn't much of a compliment. They weren't even his friends, even if he liked to use the label "friends with benefits." Obviously his cheating ex had affected him badly, and he'd not gotten over it. But guys that went into the military didn't like to admit that they were weak.

Will had come home after basic training and I'd asked him why his feet looked like they had been tortured. *Was it called boot camp because your feet took on the smell and look of a worn rubber boot?*

But he'd scoffed at my concern. His fucked-up feet were a sign of his achievements, I guess. I tried to get him to get a pedicure with me, but he'd said he wasn't going to spend any minute of his leave having some chick paint his toenails. He'd never hear the end of it. I suspected Gray was just the same way. Admitting that a girl hurt his heart so much that he was afraid to get close again wasn't in his DNA. But I recognized grief and loss and sorrow and pain. I'd lived with it for years. Those feelings were intimate friends of mine, and they dogged Gray too.

I drove him back to Adam's house. He invited me in, but I didn't want to wake up in a house full of guys and neither of us were ready for him to go back to the condo. Heck, even I went back to my parents' house. I told Gray I was too tired to drive anywhere but the truth was that I was scared to go back to my condo. Scared that Will would be there, looking at me with disapproval. He'd be able to smell Gray on me and see the lazy look of satisfaction in my eyes. I'd just had an orgasm with someone other than Will, and I wasn't ready to bring that home. Instead, I climbed into my Will-free bed and dreamt of another man between my legs.

When I woke up feeling guilty and turned on, I called Eve for some courage and advice.

"You aren't supposed to have feelings for the rebound guy, right?" I asked Eve the next morning.

"Right!" she exclaimed. "Tell me you aren't falling for soldier boy."

I didn't say anything.

"Are you there?" Eve asked.

"You told me not to tell you anything."

"Dammit, Sam." The gusty sigh whistled over the telephone line.

"I know but he's so vulnerable." I told Eve about his friends with benefits.

"So he's not over his ex?"

"No, he's over her, but he's still suffering from the negative side effects. I get it."

"He's not a widower." Eve tried to depress my mounting excitement.

"I know, but he's suffered. I feel, I don't know, like he's a kindred spirit or something."

"I think you're reading too much into this."

"I'm not," I protested. We'd even exchanged phone numbers before he'd kissed me sweetly good night. The memory of last night made my body tingle all over. "He's very sweet beneath his prickly exterior. He really longs for a special connection with someone but is too scared to reach for it."

Eve contemplated this for a moment. "That sounds like how *you* feel."

"Could be. Could be we both feel this way."

"Just be careful." Eve sighed.

"Thanks for the pep talk." I smiled and hung up at her blowing me a raspberry over the phone.

GRAY TEXTED ME MID-MORNING.

U around?

Yes.

A few seconds later my phone rang. It was Gray.

"How are you feeling this morning?"

"Good, you?"

"Felt…odd," he said and before any anxiety had set in, he continued. "I missed you." Then he laughed. "I think. Sleeping over isn't something I'm familiar with but I woke up thinking about you. When I jogged over to your parents' house your Rover was gone."

I felt warm all over. "I went back to the condo and now I'm sitting on my balcony knitting."

"I wish I could come over but the boys want to head to the Boundary Waters and do some portaging."

"That's what? Carrying your canoe around?"

"Yeah and eating uncooked beans and rice."

"Sounds really fabulous," I said, completely insincere.

Gray chuckled. "Anyway, I wanted to call and let you know that I'll have no cell phone service for a week. Can I see you when I get back?"

I covered the phone and let out a shaky breath. Until that moment I hadn't realized how much I wanted, maybe even needed, to see him again and for him to want to be with me. "I'd like that," I told him once I gathered my self-possession.

"I'll be thinking about you," he said and his low tone made me tremble.

I took a step off the cliff, hoping the safety rope was still there. "I'll be fantasizing about you." It was about as edgy and sexy as I felt like I could get.

A long pause followed my words and I grew concerned that I'd interpreted all of this incorrectly. Then I heard a cough, a rustle, and a slight groan. The sound was different when he spoke too. "Sorry, had to get some privacy here," he said. "I'm going to need you to go into greater detail."

"Ahhh," I stalled. I had very little practice in talking dirty to someone. "Um, sorry, I'm sitting out here on my balcony and I think I'm redder than my neighbor's peonies."

He burst out laughing and the sound of it made me want to float up in the air. "That's okay." A pounding on the door echoed down phone lines and I heard Gray's muffled voice yell, "I'll be out in sec." To me, he said in gruff voice, "I gotta go. I'll call you the minute I get back and we'll do something fun. I promise."

The time apart was smart for both of us. I think we were both caught off guard by the intensity our encounter. I spent the week thinking about him and Will. Whenever Will would come home for leave, he'd try to convince me to move to Alaska with him, but I'd always rebuffed him with a litany of reasons. I had too many friends here. I would miss my family. I hated the cold. I may have been hoping that he'd give up jumping out of airplanes for me and realize that our dream of going to college together was so much better. But he was stubborn and the fervor of being a soldier held more power over him than I did.

Gray was like Will in some aspects. They both loved the military. But Gray's love was a bittersweet one, tested by loss and experience. He spoke so passionately about the men he served with and made sure that they were ready and safe. His confusion about whether to reenlist or separate was one that would easily resolve when he sat down and accepted that responsibility he thought he couldn't handle. Deep down, he knew he could do it but while there was time to resist, he would. As for him not trusting a woman enough to have a relationship? That was a different story but what I'd said to Eve was true. I felt a kinship with Gray and no matter what happened to us, I hoped we would be friends.

He made me feel young and excited, and I loved those feelings. They were better than sitting around my virginal bedroom wondering why I should get out of bed the next day. I found myself excited to get up. I was looking forward to his return, and I didn't care if he had another adventure planned. I just wanted to spend time together.

During the week, I spent more time with Bitsy and realized how much I missed her company. Her crush on Tucker worried me. And Tucker worried me, with his strained relationship with his parents. They needed each other, or at least Carolyn and Tucker needed each other. I wasn't sure if Will's dad needed anything but golf and Scotch.

On the day before Gray came back from his trip, I packed Will's things away—all but the flag. If I was going to make room in my life for another person, then his Army assault pack and combat boots needed to be boxed up. Will was still taking up a lot of space in my mind and my condo. And it was time to let him go. All those future plans I had made with Will weren't ever going to come true. Not the two kids we talked about having, or the dogs. Not the places we were going to see or the trips we were going to take.

None of those things were going to happen now—and I couldn't foresee a future that I spent alone. I didn't want that, and I knew Will wouldn't have wanted that for me. He was always so full of life and the fact that I'd spent the last two years wandering around in the wilderness of my mind would have pissed him off. I didn't know if he would have wanted me to take up with another military guy. He might be saying right now that I should be looking for an accountant or—no, he would have wanted me to take those adventures. He'd have been proud of me, I think. Silent, hot tears started rolling down my face, but they weren't really tears of sadness. They were tears nonetheless—and I cried about all the things that I'd felt for Will. I was sorry to let him go, but it was time.

GRAY HAD CALLED ME THE evening they'd gotten home. I could hear the weariness in his voice.

"Hey, missed you," were the first words out of his mouth.

It was easy to return the sentiment. "I'm glad you're back."

"Me too. I'm bushed from the ride. Don't know why that wears me out, but it does. Can I take you somewhere tomorrow?"

"Can't wait."

And now we were together.

"I don't get it," I said finally. Gray was lying in the canoe, hat over his eyes, hands folded over his chest. His fishing rod was lying next to the wooden seat beside him.

"What's there to get?"

"I thought we were doing something adventurous."

"It's hot as hell out here, isn't it?"

It was. The humidity in the air hung down like a wet blanket. The heat was more bearable out on the water and the battered hat that was about two sizes too big for my head, which Gray had produced out of the back of a roommate's truck, gave me some shade. But yeah, it was hot as hell. I dipped my hand into the water and splashed myself a little.

"How does that make it dangerous?"

"You could die from heat. A fish could capsize the boat. A gator might eat you."

I looked around the placid water.

"We don't have alligators here. I think that's a southern thing."

Gray tipped his hat back slightly so I could see his eyes. "For real, no gators?"

"I've never seen one."

"You ever been here before?" He waved an expansive hand over the water.

"No, I've never been." This place, just an hour south of the city, wasn't known to me. I'd heard of it before, but I'd never been here. Water really wasn't Will's thing. The river was quiet and there were a few boats on it. A cluster of trees and long reeds lined the shore. The whole landscape was a picture of lazy calm. "Seems safe though."

"You didn't even know about the gators not to mention all the other pitfalls."

"If it's so dangerous, why are you lying back with your hat over your face? Shouldn't you be alert?"

I tapped the bottom of his foot with the toe of my sneaker.

"That's your job. You wanted the adventure."

"So you're just going to sleep?"

"Yeah, you protect me and let me know if I've caught anything."

"Will we stay in contact when you go back to San Diego?" I nudged his tennis shoe again.

"Sure. Friend me on Facebook."

"You have a Facebook account?"

"Have to. Only way I can keep track of everyone from my platoon who separated."

I stifled a giggle.

"What? Why is that funny?" he sounded indignant, or as indignant as a person can sound half asleep in a small boat.

"I just can't see you reading a Facebook feed." An image of Gray sitting next to me at the Central College coffee shop, flipping through Facebook feeds as we took a break from studying flashed through my mind. I chased it down and held onto the image for a moment. Longing tugged at my heart. I wasn't ready to let him go.

"Hey, I like stupid cat pictures as much as the next person."

Sticking my fishing rod under the seat, I started to shift toward him but my motion caused the boat to rock with some force.

"Trying to make your own adventure?" Gray's low voice broke through the silence.

"Whoops, sorry. I want to lie down next to you."

"Sure thing, baby." The way he said *baby* reminded me of how he'd growled it while we had sex, and it sent a tremor through me that had nothing to do with the rocking boat. Although when I stood up, the boat did tilt too far toward the water for me to feel comfortable.

"Stoop and do a sort of duck walk until you get to me or we'll be swimming, not boating," Gray instructed.

I slunk down to my haunches and shuffled awkwardly over to Gray. His long legs with their surprisingly soft hair rubbed against me and the tremor turned into a tingle. Our eyes caught, and his smile was naughty. He pulled me upright while his legs braced against the boat, again reminding me of his physical prowess. I settled against him, the space so small that I was almost lying half on top of him. His arm was under me and it felt very cozy and intimate. Closeness, not just sex, was another thing I'd missed.

Gray sat up and picked up his oar and placed it across the top of the boat. He did the same with mine. This time he lifted his legs up and placed them on top of the crossed oars. His long legs dangled off the other side and rested against the seat I was on. Then his hands picked up my legs and rested them against the oars. When he returned the reclining position, he pulled me down next to him and covered his face with his hat. I should have been uncomfortable. I was lying on a small wooden bench leaning against a plastic cooler and my legs were resting on crossed wooden oars. His arm was under my shoulders, cradling me.

I'd not been held like this in forever. "Just stop thinking," he said. His head was so close to mine, I could feel the small puffs of breath as he mouthed each word.

"How?"

"Pretend I'm a pillow. Close your eyes and count slowly."

I closed my eyes and began to count. One, two, three. Little by little, my body relaxed. Whether it was the sun, the heat, or the soothing touch of Gray's hand on my forearm, I let myself go and I drifted off into nothingness.

Gray smoothing lotion on my legs woke me an hour later. I fought waking because the dream had been so lovely. Big hands and long fingers rubbing up and down my legs. Those capable fingers squeezed my calves gently and palms followed the curve of my knees. Those questing hands paused above my knees. "Don't stop," I moaned. I wanted this massage to continue, right up my thighs. Those thumbs could brush the crease between my legs and hips.

When the hand didn't move like I wanted, I pulled it up and placed it right where I wanted it. The tip of the thumb pointing toward my private place between my legs. The rest of the fingers splayed across the top of my thigh and because the fingers were so long, they could wrap around the side. I sighed with pleasure and heard a masculine groan of appreciation in return. The thumb dug in for a moment and then the pressure receded. Instead, I felt the hand on my opposite leg and then my arms. I frowned but was too weak and tired to protest more. Instead, I allowed sleep to pull me under once again.

THIRTEEN

Gray

As Sam drifted off into another lazy rest, I took the opportunity to look her all over. Too bad she wasn't nude, but I knew no amount of cajoling would convince her to sit in this boat without any clothes on. Shame because then I could have inspected every inch of her in the sunlight. I'd have put sunscreen on more than just her legs.

When she awoke after a short nap, I gave her a sandwich and ate two before she finished half of hers. I liked providing Sam's meals. There was something intensely satisfying about that. Probably a feeling that harkened back to our cave-dwelling ancestors, not that spreading mayo on bread was the same thing as going out and killing a wooly mammoth for food. But I could totally do that if she needed it.

"Tell me about your husband," I said, surprising myself.

"Really? You want to know?"

"Why not?" He was, after all, dead. I wasn't jealous of a dead man.

Right? Right.

"The only person that really wants to talk about him anymore is his mother, Carolyn."

"Is that as horrible as your tone suggests?" I squeezed her a little closer to me.

"Pretty much. The Will she describes isn't like the real Will. He's like a boy who never grew up. All perfect and innocent."

"And he wasn't?"

"No. He was crazy and wild. There wasn't a challenge that he didn't like to accept. He never believed in turning the other cheek. He wanted to suck the life out of every moment like—" She stopped then and swallowed hard. "Like—"

"Like he thought he was going to die young?" I finished for her when she couldn't.

"I don't think he was actively pursuing it but living on the edge was a very real thing to him, not just words in a song. It's why he was so keen on the ROTC. Why he volunteered for pararescue training right out of Basic. Why he asked for deployment again and again until I feel like they sent him over just to shut him up."

I didn't say anything right away, just mulled over what she didn't say. How she was disappointed at being left behind and didn't understand what it was that drew Will away from her. "I knew guys like that. Bo is kind of like that. He never saw a fist that he didn't want to test."

"Bo?"

"Yeah, the big blond guy."

"He seems so laid back, like you. The other guy, Noah, is intense."

"And Will was intense?"

She thought for a moment. "He was focused."

"On things other than you," I said gently.

"He focused on me," she protested and then swayed a little, dizzy from the sun, maybe needing some sugar.

I didn't challenge her. Instead, I grabbed her arm and steadied her. Holding her with one hand, I fumbled in the cooler and pulled out an ice-cold Coke. Popping the tab, I held it up to her lips and tipped it back. She sipped a little and allowed the sweet syrup to coat her tongue.

"More," she commanded. She drank deeply, not realizing how thirsty she'd been until I'd forced the cold Coke down her throat.

Taking the can from her, I put the opening to my mouth, placing my lips right over the area she'd drunk from and swallowed the rest of the soda in one gulp. Crushing the can in my hand, I threw the empty aluminum toward the other end of the canoe.

"I'm sorry," I said finally, meeting her eyes. "I didn't mean to suggest that he didn't love you."

"I know," she sighed. "I'm just sensitive about it. My mom always said that he shouldn't have gone into the Army and that it was selfish of him to do so. Is that how your girlfriend felt?"

"No, she was excited."

"How come you joined?"

I lay back down and tugged her on top of me. Rubbing my thumb up under the hem of her thin cotton T-shirt that said, "I'd rather be knitting," I stroked that small piece of warm flesh, enjoying the shiver it caused.

"My pops was an enlisted. Retired from the Marines after thirty years of service. Highly decorated. My dad retired from the Marines after twenty years of service. Neither of my elder two brothers joined. They set up a custom chop shop in southern Cal. Pops would tell me how great the Corps was, what a fraternity it was. When I was seven, he gave me a knife that had *Semper Fidelis* engraved on it which is Latin for always faithful. When I was seventeen he took me to the recruiting station and pretended to be my father and got me signed up before my dad even knew what hit him. But for a while it was all good. My old man was proud of me and Pops was over the moon. Then a year into my contract with the Corps, my dad runs for and wins a congressional seat. After that the Corps isn't good enough for me. He drops hints there's something better out there for me. Says I should go to college. Be a lawyer."

"Son of a bailiff," she murmured.

"What's that?" I cocked my head because I wasn't sure I heard her right.

"Your name, it means son of a bailiff."

I grunted. "Didn't know that. I think my mom read a romance book and fell in love with the hero. We all have romance book hero names. Lucien is the oldest. Then James and then me. Grayson."

She gave me a tiny smile that made me want to lick her lips. "I like it." Her eyes went unfocused and then her smile turned almost sly.

"I don't know what you're thinking right now, but it started out dreamy and turned to naughty."

She laughed guiltily. "You can see all that?" She pressed her hands against her cheeks as if she could hide her blushes, and then I couldn't resist. Her lips were pink and a little shiny from the Coke or maybe her saliva. I dragged my tongue lightly over them until she parted her mouth and her small tongue met mine. This time our kiss wasn't fervent or grasping. It was slow and thoughtful like our conversations. Her flavor, mixed with sugar of the cola was the best thing I'd had on my tongue in forever.

I didn't know what I'd been hoping to find here, so many miles from home, but it wasn't Sam and her understanding smiles and sweet touches. I wasn't sure why Will had run from this, because maybe, if I'd had Sam, I wouldn't have wanted to enlist. Her hands brushed over my closely cropped hair and down my face. My muscles tensed as she ran her fingers over the planes of my chest and then lower. I held my breath in anticipation, hoping she wouldn't stop at my waistband. When she drew back, panting a bit, I whimpered like a disappointed baby.

"I want to hear the rest of the story."

I sighed but got the message. "So at Christmas time, Pops asked me if I'd signed my reenlistment papers, and I hadn't. 'What are you waiting for, boy? Your CO to come over here and give you an engraved invitation?'" I mimicked my Pops gravely voice. "My dad interrupted him. 'Speaking of your CO, I've heard talk that you should be going to Officer Candidate School.' Pops replied in his gravely voice, made so by all the yelling he did as a drill instructor, that OCS was for washed out enlisted and that a true Marine was a grunt. He reminded my dad that I could be NCO, a non commissioned officer. Then the two got into a yelling match about how I was going to uphold the Phillips family name the best."

"Sounds painful," she winced. Based on earlier conversations it was clear she knew all about painful family engagements.

"The worst thing is that they both love me so I know they want the best but they're engaged in this power struggle over what I should do next."

"Will's dad wanted him to be a lawyer. Our parents are law partners. I think Will was trying to escape that as much as anything. He wasn't cut out for the office and legal briefs."

"How about you?"

"No. But Bitsy, my sister, might be one. Heck, she might even be president someday. For sure a judge. She's so smart. So my parents don't hassle me about it. They do think I should go back to school. I dropped out after Will died."

"I can't imagine."

"You ever do it? Death duty?" she asked.

"No, and I never will. I think you suffer more PTSD delivering constant news of someone dying than you do by being there."

"It can't be fun. I wish I'd held it together better. The chaplain kept saying I was so young."

"Lots of young widows out there now."

We both stared at the water, thinking of the story I'd told that first night.

I spoke first. "Having her try to kill herself was like failing again. We couldn't save him and we almost lost her." My hands were fisted on my knees. Reaching over, she laid her palm over my balled hands. I had a very tough time processing grief but Sam understood. She got me in a way I don't think anyone had before. Not my pops or my parents or even my brothers. She rested her head against my shoulder and squeezed my hands tight.

This girl stirred some kind of tender emotion in me. Her observation the other day about the difference between wives and girlfriends was spot on. Carrie had been so hungry for the wife position but it was because she wanted a higher status. And she ended up with none

"You'd have made a good military wife," I told her. Sam thought about others. That was the mark of a good military wife. Military people had to be selfless. Both the people who served and those that stayed behind. It had to be a calling for both of them.

She gave a small laugh and shake of her head. "What makes you say that?"

"You care a lot about the other people, almost more than yourself. And that's not always a good thing. You keep downplaying your loss, saying somebody else's loss was greater or somebody else had it worse."

"I'm just really fortunate, you know? And I guess I'm tired of feeling sorry for myself. I've done that for two years. And I have a lot of regrets. I don't want to have any regrets anymore."

"What do you regret?"

"I regret not moving to Alaska when Will got shipped out." She plucked at her shorts. "He wanted me to. We could've gotten married then, or I could've just moved there. It's not like I wasn't without resources like some of the others." Sam turned a bit and shoved my sunglasses off my face, so she could look in my eyes. "Tell me about the girl who cheated on you?"

The question caught me off guard, and I stuttered my response. "Wh-what do you mean?"

"You don't do relationships. You have ultra-impersonal sex hook ups. And you flew off the handle when you thought I was cheating on someone. It's a big issue with you. Can you tell me what happened?"

No, not really. "I'd rather make love to you." I brushed my hand up her back and up to the base of her skull. She rolled her eyes but didn't pull away.

"I can't imagine how you ever survived deployment to the Middle East."

"You may be surprised to hear this, but I can go without for long periods of time."

"Is that right?" she mocked.

"That's right. I have a very active imagination." With a small movement of my hand, I had her face tilted at the perfect angle. I could kiss her lips or snake my tongue along the column of her throat. I choose the latter.

Against her skin, I told her what I envisioned. "You're taking your T-shirt off. You're braless and the fabric catches on the bottom of one your breasts so that it bounces when the shirt finally comes off. I catch it in my mouth, sucking on your nipple. You moan loudly when my mouth covers you." I reached between us and unzipped my shorts, pulling out my hungry, ready cock. Her hand wrapped around the tip and squeezed. Choking back my groan, I continued. "Your shorts come off and as you're standing in front of me, I can see by the wetness between your thighs that you're aroused."

Her hand paused mid stroke. "Um, don't stop," I choked out.

"How can I be standing in the boat? I barely made it over to your side without tipping us over," she asked.

"I bet you never fought dragons when you were a kid either, did you?"

"Oh right, we're imagining things." She smirked. "Go on, I'm naked and wet." The words sounded so dirty coming from her that I felt myself jerk in her direction. "You like that?"

I laughed hoarsely. "Yup." Hearing my partner tell me exactly what she wanted and how she wanted it has always excited me. Half the time I was talking to crank her chain but the side benefit was that it worked me up too. I moved my hand to cover hers. She picked up the motion again, and we covered my length together, rubbing it up and down. My head fell back and I returned to my fantasy.

"You're standing there naked, and you pull on your ti-nipples." She probably didn't like the word tits. "And with the other hand, you start stroking yourself. I'm watching carefully so I can make the same moves when it's my turn to touch you. Then you bend down and take me in your mouth."

"Am I still fondling myself?"

"Yes, you have great balance."

Sam bent over and placed my hard shaft inside her mouth. Our fingers were still entangled and I could feel her lips and tongue all over us. She sucked me hard, my dick popping out of her mouth with a loud noise. "What happens next?" she asked. Had she done that on purpose because she knew how much I enjoyed the sounds of our sex? I let out a shaky breath. I allowed my hand to fall away and she began to work me over. Her fingers couldn't quite fit all the way around the shaft but she kept making twisting motions and, combined with the suck of her mouth, I was pretty close to shooting my load. It was hard to think. "Yo-you're sucking me and I can hear how wet it's making you as you finger yourself." Gathering her hair up in my hand, I pulled her off my cock and up against my chest. I took her mouth in mine, bruisingly, but she only kissed me back harder. Somehow we managed to get her shorts off without falling into the lake. In another second, I tugged a condom on. Letting her set the pace, I focused on kissing her, exploring every inch of her mouth. Under her shirt, I rubbed her nipples until they were plump and erect.

My heart was pounding like I'd run a dozen miles as I waited for her to sheathe me with herself. When she did, I groaned, long and loud. I'd spent a week imagining Sam in all kinds of filthy positions. Initially she moved slowly, enjoying the feel of her inner flesh rubbing against my cock but we were both too worked up to be leisurely. Rocking against me, she clutched at my shoulders, her elbows digging into my chest as she used me for leverage. I loved it. I wanted to bottom out inside her, to get deeper into her than I'd ever been.

She looked powerful moving on top of me. Her eyes were squeezed shut and her face was flushed. We were moving in some kind of unworldly rhythm that I'd never achieved before. Passion was written on every surface of her body—in the tenseness of her arms, the tightness of her cunt around me, in the way she rode me with such abandon.

The tight, hot glove of her squeezed me hard, making the drag out of her body amazing. Was it possible to lose your mind fucking? Because I felt mine spiraling away from me with each downward drive of her hips. Did she know how much she affected me? How much I wanted this all of the time? How I could not wait to see her again after a week of absence? I'd missed her. I'd fucking missed *her*. And now that I was inside her, I didn't want to leave.

I moved my hands from inside of her shirt to grab her hip and plunged the other hand between us, using a thumb to rub against her engorged clit. We were both panting hard, and I could feel myself nearing the edge. I needed her to come. Tearing my mouth away from her, I began to whisper to her again. "You are so hot and tight. I love having you ride me. You feel fucking perfect."

"God, yes, talk to me," she cried, her eyes fluttering open.

I shoved up with my hips in a furious rhythm. "Your cunt is squeezing me like a vise. Your cheeks are flushed and your eyes are glassy and I've never seen a girl look so into this. I wish we had a mirror right now so you could see how fucking hot you are. Don't stop," I begged. "Christ, my balls..."

I couldn't talk anymore, but I didn't have to because she came apart in my arms. Her whole body tensed and she shuddered, crying out, "Oh God, Gray."

My balls felt like they'd nearly exploded when I came. "Almighty fucking...Sam." I clutched her to me as we both trembled in the aftermath. I could have fallen into the lake and drowned and never realized it because I was that senseless. I'd never had a fuck as good as Sam Anderson and was afraid I never would again.

I lay there against the hard bench and the cooler and hugged her close. There was no explanation I could think of—at least not one I was ready to accept—as to why our physical connection was so spectacular.

"It's so good with you," Sam muttered. She'd collapsed on top of me, tucking her arms between us, her warm nose in the crook of my neck. Not knowing how to respond, I just kept up rubbing her back in long strokes from the base of her neck to her spine. Then, when I was about to let the post orgasm stupor take me under again, she asked about Carrie.

This time I just vomited out the whole story. I suppose I could've blamed it on the timing but I think I wanted her to know. Sam seemed to understand everything else, maybe she'd get this too. And maybe I owed it to her. "When I was in high school, I was tall and gangly. I had no game, and the girls knew it. Like they sensed I was weak and ran far away." I grinned but it faded quickly as Sam looked at me knowingly.

Sighing, I snugged her up against my side and pressed her back onto the cooler so she couldn't look at me. Or I couldn't look at her. One of the two. With an exaggerated sigh, I pulled my sunglasses back down and continued the story. "We moved a lot up until my junior year, and then my dad got stationed at Pendleton. First day of school, Carrie walks right up to me, takes my hand and shows me around.

She eats lunch with me, has me drive her home, and that's it for me. It blew my mind that she wanted me, of all people."

"And then she broke your heart."

"Guys don't get heartbroken, honey. We just get pissed off."

She made a humming noise that could mean anything. I continued. "I'd always known that I was going to join the Corps, and I was up front about it. She loved the idea. Sometimes she'd squeeze my arm and say that the military was going to make me a man. Around Fallbrook, there are plenty of military, and not just Marines. I always felt like she was taking a step down to be with me. When I joined the Corps, it changed me a lot. Not just how I looked, but my whole attitude about things. I was way cockier after boot camp and even worse after I finished the school of infantry."

"Is that when you got this?" She tapped my arm where the bottom of my tattoo peeked out of my shirt sleeve. We were both bare-ass naked from the waist down but had kept our shirts on. That was kind of fucked up. Sitting up, I reached down and picked Sam's shorts and panties off the bottom of the boat. Thankfully they were dry. She pulled them on and then settled into the seat opposite me. I handed her another Coke and took one for myself. I needed the caffeine and sugar to get me through the story. I wished I'd brought some beer.

"Yup. All of us after we got out of SOI. We ran off to the first tattoo parlor we could find and got ourselves all tatted up. *Semper Fi*," I said mockingly. "And all of this thrilled Carrie. Her boyfriend had turned into something other girls wanted, but it also made her insecure. She flirted a lot with other guys to make me jealous. We fought a lot and had crazy make up sex. I didn't realize at the time that we were fucked up. Inside the bubble it felt normal. We got to see each other fairly regularly. She'd drive up to base and we'd stay at a hotel on the weekends if my battle buddy wasn't around.

"A few months into my deployment, I hear that she's been coming down regularly, every weekend, which at first seemed like she was just trying to be part of the network. I'd thought about proposing to her when I got back from my deployment. It was only going to be seven months. Then I hear she's been seen with a recruiting officer. The same goddamn 2nd Lieutenant that had signed me up. I got leave halfway through deployment, but I didn't tell her."

"I know the end of the story but already I don't like it."

"Yeah, me neither. Want me to stop now?"

"Nope." She tapped her can against mine and then took another sip. I downed the sugary sweet soda and then crumpled the can in my hand.

"I get back to base and I wait in my car outside the LT's recruiting office until it closes and then I follow him. LT can afford to live off base, and he's got an apartment in Oceanside with some other officer. I wait outside of his condo. If he doesn't meet up with her, then I've wasted a whole afternoon and evening of my tiny leave with this and that pissed me off but I had to know.

"He goes in, does whatever inside, and then an hour later, she shows up in the car her daddy bought her when she graduated from high school. She's wearing barely any clothes and fuck me heels. He comes outside and starts making out with her, playing grab ass on the street. I almost get out of my car then but something tells me to wait. He takes her keys and they get in and drive to a small private beach down along the coast, between San Diego and Oceanside and then…"

I stopped when Sam reached for the can in my hand. I saw that I'd been squeezing it so hard some of the metal had pierced my skin. With a sigh, I released the can so I wouldn't continue to make myself bleed, even though recounting this whole episode seemed like I'm reopening a scabbed-over wound. "Then they start fucking in the car. I didn't get it then. I thought maybe she saw me and was giving me the ultimate middle finger. I found out later that his roommate had told him that he either stopped screwing around with a deployed Marine's girlfriend or he'd report him to his superiors, so they had to resort to screwing in her car whenever they wanted to get off."

"I got out of the car and rapped on her window, staring at her ass gyrating like she's a stripper, until they finally heard me. She starts sniveling and crying and saying that he forced her. That didn't fly with me, so she changed her story. She was trying to help me get ahead. He just sat there like a dumbass, sitting on his thumb while he let her twist in the wind. I figured he was the kind of guy that if I decked him, he'd report me, and I wasn't going to fuck up my career for this bitch or that asshole."

"No touching the officers." Sam knew immediately why I couldn't have beaten the officer like I wanted to. Enlisted men don't ever touch officers. That was an automatic Article 15 or non-judicial punishment at the very least.

"Right. So I tell this girl that I dated for over three years, the girl I thought about proposing to, that I didn't want to see her cheating ass ever again. I left and got sick drunk and returned to A-stan."

"But that wasn't the end of it."

Stretching out my hand, I threaded a few strands of Sam's honey-blonde hair through my fingers. It felt like silk, finer than anything I'd touched before. The sunlight made her hair look a thousand different colors. I knew I could stare at it for weeks and not see the same thing. I could barely remember Carrie's hair, and I knew I hadn't ever been this fascinated with it. "Nope. The LT sends me an email while I'm deployed, telling me that I better get to the health center because my bitch gave him syph. And that he wasn't the only guy she was fucking while I was gone."

"Is that true?"

"Don't know, but I checked out fine."

We sat there as she took in my sad little tale. I kept sifting through her hair. She didn't try to tell me that I should've given Carrie another chance or that deployments were hard on everyone. She didn't try to offer any sympathy or, worse, pity. The wound I thought I had re-opened lacked the sharp pain that usually accompanied thoughts of her perfidy. Maybe I'd only had a little poison inside of me and we'd bled it out.

Her hand squeezed mine tight and then she turned and kissed my hand.

"I've never been to San Diego. I'd like to visit sometime."

"You can come and visit me," I joked but then I realized I was serious. I wanted her to visit me. I wanted to stay connected to her in some way.

"Maybe I will."

I wanted to change the subject and talk about something other than cheating girlfriends, dead husbands or the Corps. "Tell me about your knitting."

She told me about how a widow from the Yarn Over Knitting Club had reached out to her after Sam's story was told in their local newspaper, and how she hadn't wanted to go but her therapist thought it was a good idea.

"You still could have stayed home," I pointed out.

"I don't think my parents would have let me. I had moved out of my condo when Will and I got married but then after he died, I didn't do a very good job caring for myself so I had to move back home for a while."

The thought of a grieving Sam not feeding herself made me sick to my stomach and I curled an arm around her and brought her closer to me. It was strange but when she talked about how much she loved Will, that actually made me feel better. Like she was different and that she would've been faithful, unlike so many other women I knew. And men, too, I guess. The military didn't foster fidelity. Even though there were rules against it, adultery and cheating ran rampant through the Corps. It was almost expected that one of your comrades would sleep with your girl the first chance he got. If you didn't get cheated on, it was like you hadn't been tested in battle. I didn't know how other people started trusting enough to start up another relationship or maybe they just knew going in that they were going to cheat, that their partner was going to cheat and that they just lived with it.

I didn't want that. I wanted a relationship, but it could wait until I got out. Or when I was done deploying for long months. I just didn't believe that any relationship could survive long separations, but here was Sam. She'd stayed true to her husband while he was training in Alaska. She'd been true to his memory long after his death. If there was ever a girl that could be true, maybe it was Sam. I pulled Sam up from her seat and tucked her into my side.

I hadn't lied to her when I said that I didn't cuddle, so having her warm body snug against mine without the urge to flee, when we weren't enjoying some post coital glow, was weird. A good weird, but it was definitely hitting different nerves and neurosensors in my brain. I liked it. There was something really relaxing and almost comforting just holding her as the waves of the water slapped gently against the boat. It was so good that I just drifted off to sleep.

Samantha

"DID YOU SEE THE BIG piece of green felt in my condo? It hangs above my sofa."

"What's it for?" Gray's words sounded slurred and drowsy like the heat was lulling *him* to sleep this time.

"An afghan I was knitting. The felt holds the yarn pieces up so you can stare at the pattern. It's a flag but I'm supposed to do a technique called intarsia and I really suck at it so I haven't finished the star part." Gray fell asleep as I was explaining how intarsia knitting techniques had stymied my ability to finish my flag afghan, and I wasn't even the tiniest bit upset that he did. Gray often had a hard time relaxing. His eyes were always roaming around as if he was trying to identify all potential targets. His story about how he'd been cheated on hurt my heart. I wondered if he knew he was still grieving that.

Oh, he wasn't grieving the loss of his girlfriend so much as the betrayal of that trust he'd given her. And his sense of justice was offended too. He was over there in the dust and danger of Afghanistan making a huge sacrifice and she and an officer weren't even trying to match his sacrifice. He was so hurt he was holding himself apart. His friends with benefits situation sounded awful. The girl he slept with treated him like a human vibrator? That sounded too terrible for words. And yet, he not only pursued this setup, but was proud of it in some weird way.

That he wanted to have sex with me was out of character but in a good way, as if he and I were both stretching outside of our comfort zones because something we wanted was just out of reach.

Eve was right. I realized that now. Will's death had broken my heart. Actually, his death hadn't just broken it. For a while I thought my life had been buried with him. And like I told Gray, I only knew how to do serious relationships. Casual sex didn't sound appealing. It took me a while to get used to having sex with Will, which told me that based on my physical reaction to Gray, I must have a few feelings for him. When he was holding me and I could feel the deep rumble of his chest against my own body, I wanted to sink into that. And the body that I thought was too muscular when I first saw him in the bar had become a source of constant fascination. When he'd rowed us to the middle of the lake, I couldn't stop staring at the way the muscles under his skin undulated and flexed.

The light dusting of hair had felt wonderful against my breasts. Will hadn't had a lot of chest hair but Gray not only had hair around his chest but there was a lovely trail that bisected his stomach and led the eye downward. I'd heard Eve call it the treasure trail and it did beg for me to do some exploring.

And his erection. I smiled a little to myself, glorying in some heretofore unrealized feminine power, but Gray was erect around me a lot. His heavy cotton cargo shorts didn't hide it, and neither did the swim trunks he'd worn during the slip and slide party.

But it wasn't just his physical power that attracted me. It was fun to talk to him and to do things like going out on a boat and pretending to fish. Gray watched out for me, too, always making sure I had enough to eat or drink. There was a tenderness in his gestures, a sweetness too. Carrie had been a fool, but I wouldn't be.

FOURTEEN

Samantha

AFTER THE FISHING TRIP, GRAY AND I WERE INSEPARABLE. HE'D call or I would. May wound into June and each day brought us closer together. When I wasn't working or he wasn't off doing something with his friends, we'd meet up for a hike or just to play catch in the park. I wasn't very good at it, but he never complained. I started to get to know his friends and was excited to find out that some of them were currently enrolled at Central. All my high school friends had either graduated already or had never gone to college so it was a relief to know that I'd see at least a couple of familiar faces on campus in the fall.

I'd fielded one awkward phone call from Carolyn who asked sad questions about this guy I'd been seen spending a lot of time with. A friend, I'd told her.

"A male friend?" she'd asked plaintively.

"Yes." I'd packed up most of the stuff around the condo but the felt still hung on the wall. I needed a damn ladder but I wasn't about to ask Tucker for one. Maybe I'd hit up Adam for real this time, not just as an excuse to see Gray. *Besides,* I thought, a little giddy, I didn't need an excuse.

"I hope you're enjoying yourself." Her voice turned sharp. "I've been at home looking through Will's letters. I just can't believe it's only been two years since he's been gone."

My memories of Will were fading and I hadn't realized how much until I met Gray. Will had been such a big part of my life that at one time I felt like I was losing pieces of me. For so long I'd been a part of the unit that was Will and Samantha. I hadn't been able to move on because my future had always been as part of that unit. Everyone I knew identified me as Will's girlfriend, Will's wife and then Will's widow.

"I'll always miss him but…" Looking down at my ring, I started tugging and it slid off like my finger had been buttered. Palming it, I spoke more forcefully. "He's not here anymore."

Carolyn started crying and usually that set me off, but not this time. "I'm sorry. You should talk to Tucker." I'm not sure if she even noticed I hung up. I texted Tucker right after to call his mom and then I shut the phone off. I went upstairs and pulled out my jewelry case. I didn't have much. There was a pearl necklace my parents had given me when I was sixteen and a watch that my grandmother had gifted me on my graduation from high school. There were a few pairs of earrings and a couple of bracelets. I wore none of it other than a pair of gold hoops I never took out. I slid the ring inside, shut the lid and then kissed the box. I loved Will. Some part of me always would.

But it was time.

Out on my deck, I soaked in the sun and finished up the cap, sweater, and tiny booties, all in ivory alpaca yarn. Making baby items was one of my favorite crafts—and not just because the projects were a lot quicker to complete. I loved the soft yarns, the tiny booties, and the idea that some of my items were the first thing that a new human being ever wore.

I had started ticking off the days left in Gray's visit. My chest would get tight when I thought about him leaving. July was fast approaching. Ever since the fishing trip, I'd had different fantasies, imagining attending class with him. Holding hands as we walked across campus. Eating together in the cafeteria. We'd both be older students, and so we'd talk about how no one around us makes any sense, only we make sense together.

One night he appeared at the bar without Adam or any of the other guys. He just showed up.

"When are you on break?"

"Maybe ten minutes? The band has two more songs in the set list."

He leaned over and kissed me on the forehead and then spent the next ten minutes downing two waters. "Driving," he explained when I asked him.

Eve's eyes were wide but she didn't say a word. When the band finished its last song of the set, she pushed me out of the bar saying that she'd be fine. Gray took me by the hand and led me inside, down the hallway and into the storeroom.

"It occurred to me," he said as he knelt down between my legs, "that I'd made some promises I never delivered on." I was so glad I was leaning against the door because otherwise I would have fallen over.

His rough fingers and mine made swift work of my shorts. When I was nude from the waist down, he lifted one leg over his shoulder. "Lean against the door, baby. Your knees are going to get weak." He was smug when he said this, but why wouldn't he be? I was coming two minutes later.

"One more time," he said, kissing my inner thigh and rubbing the heel of his hand against me softly while I convulsed around his fingers.

This time both my legs were over his shoulders and he held me up with just one palm. He used his other hand to spread my lips and spear me repeatedly with his tongue. I felt the abrasiveness of his evening stubble against my super-sensitive skin. The only thing I could do was hang on. I dug my hands into his hair and clenched him tightly with my thighs, but he never complained that I hurt him. If anything, my eager response turned him on because he half growled, half laughed against my skin.

My heels thrummed against his back as my second orgasm swam through my bloodstream, setting fire to my nerves. It was sensory overload, and I sobbed out my release when I climaxed. Lowering me to the floor, he hugged me close, making sure that he didn't release me until my shaking had stopped and I could stand on my own, although I felt as wobbly as an infant.

"Shit hot in the bedroom, right?" He winked.

"And the storage room," I muttered weakly. Wickedly, he licked each of his fingers clean and I almost had another orgasm right there. When I reached for him, though, he danced away.

"You can return the favor later." Then he pressed me up against the door and kissed me so hard that I couldn't remember my own name. Drunk on the taste of him and in a fog from my orgasms, I couldn't come up with a decent counter argument so I just clung to his shoulders and kissed him back. I don't remember much about the rest of the night. I was in a sex daze.

I'm not sure where he went for the rest of the night but when the bar closed he was leaning against my Rover. I had a hard time not attacking him there but he made me drive to my condo and take him upstairs to the bedroom. Waiting could be foreplay according to Gray. Maybe he was right. I shot off like a rocket when he first entered me and came two more times before I went into my post sex coma.

I WANTED TO DO SOMETHING special for him, so with a little help from Adam, I took Gray out to Finn O'Malley's farm the next weekend.

"I'm excited about our excursion." Gray said. "I want ice cream to be included at some point."

Just the look of him made me feel good. "Not to worry. We'll get that on the way back."

"Sounds good." He made a big show of licking his lips. "Make sure it has whipped cream. In my sex dream about you last night, you were wearing a whipped cream bikini."

"You had enough energy for sex dreams?"

"Baby, every night after you wear me out, I'm dreaming about waking up and doing you again. And let me tell you, last night had me so horny this morning, I had a hard time getting out of bed. Good thing you'd gone down for breakfast because otherwise I'd have eaten you before the coffee and bagels."

I held up a hand to forestall any further description of his fantasies. "I only brought one pair of panties with me today, so you've gotta stop talking about sex right now."

"Does my talking turn you on, Samantha?" Just the tone of his voice could get my engine working.

"You know it does."

Taking pity on me, Gray started telling me about his friend Hamilton and Hamilton's sister, who was a dead ringer for some girl who posed in Playboy. "So you harass poor Hamilton about this, knowing that it's not his sister."

"Sure, we'd never do it if it was his sister."

"Why not?"

"Because we're assholes but not that big of assholes," Gray explained. Marine logic, I guess.

"So where we going?" he asked as we moved further west from the city center.

"Finn's farm. His dad owns—or I guess Finn, since his dad died, now owns about a hundred acres of land out west. His mom has horses."

"I don't know how to ride," Gray admitted.

"Me neither," I answered. "I want you to teach me to shoot a gun."

"For real?" There was surprise and excitement in that question.

"Yup."

"That's some hot shit, Samantha. Now I'm the one with wet panties."

Finn met us at the back lot of his property. There were wooden targets at various angles and then just a lot of empty space. A couple of collapsible tables holding cases, ammunition and protective ear gear were waiting for us.

"So some of this stuff is Noah's and Bo's and some is mine and Adam's. Mal doesn't believe in firearms so he sent this along for you to enjoy after you're done shooting." Finn held up a bottle of red wine that read The Prisoner on the label.

"Nice man, what do I owe you?" Gray stuck his hand in his back pocket to reach for his wallet.

Shaking his head, Finn replied, "Nothing. It's for Sam." He

slapped Gray on his back and kissed me on the cheek. There was grief in his eyes, still lingering from his father's death, and I followed my instincts by throwing my arms around his waist and squeezing him tight.

"It gets easier. I swear," I said.

Finn hugged me back and then pushed away to hold me by my shoulders. "I can see that."

Gray

INSTRUCTING A HOT GIRL HOW to shoot a gun was a lot different and more pleasurable than doing it with a recruit. I even found myself curling around her like some doofus in a chick flick, but I guess those doofuses knew what they were doing because it felt damn good. Holding Sam snug against my frame as we both held and shot guns was one of the best things I'd ever done with a girl before outside of the bedroom.

She shot the Ruger 357 revolver that had a barrel only a couple inches long. Her arm jerked up with every shot and not one of the bullets hit the mark that stood only fifteen feet away. I handed her the Magnum 45. It weighed over three pounds more than the little pistol but the longer barrel would have less of a kickback.

"You can do a two-handed stance or try the one-handed side stance." I reluctantly let her go but realized that the sight of her holding the big gun all on her own was just as hot. She shot all six of the bullets in quick succession and then laid it on the table.

Pulling her ear protection off, she said, "I kind of like that one. I'm surprised at the amount of recoil in the smaller guns."

The revolvers had to be Noah's because he was the more methodical and patient. He'd like spinning the cylinder and placing his bullets in the chamber one by one. Bo, on the other hand, would've wanted the ability to shove another magazine in as quickly as he'd emptied the one in the stock of the gun so the Glock and the Sig Sauer were probably his. I preferred my Colt 1911 Rail Gun. The .45 bullets it shot packed a big punch, and despite the fact that it took more maintenance, it had better accuracy. There was nothing quite like the toys that the Corps issued. Everything else may suck but the munitions were awesome.

"Yeah, you can get a lower recoil with a larger gun than a small gun. The accuracy of a small gun sucks. It's why in the movies when someone shoots ten rounds and misses with a small gun, it's kinda believable," I told her.

"Plus, it's hard to hit the ninja hero with his invisible hero force field around him."

I laughed. "That too."

We pulled our headgear back on and Sam tried out a few more of the handguns. Mentally I made a note that she gravitated toward the sub compact Beretta. If I was going to buy her a gun, that'd be a good one. After we'd torn through about sixty rounds and ten guns, Sam looked to be done in. Her hand was shaking from the unfamiliar exercise of holding five pound weights extended from her arm.

"I can't believe they feel so heavy. It's only a few pounds," she complained.

"When you're in boot, you have to hold a piece of paper in front of your face, both arms extended. After an hour, that's the heaviest fucking thing you've ever held." Sam giggled and we spent a few minutes of companionable silence picking up the brass casings around the target we'd set up fifteen feet away. Anything farther and Sam wouldn't have been able to hit even the outer edge of the paper. "Not that I'm complaining, but why'd you bring me out here?"

She didn't look up immediately but fingered one of the bullet holes that she'd made in the black area of the target, a hit but not a kill. "Do you know the seven stages of grief?"

Not the topic of conversation I would've picked, but if she needed to work through some issues, it didn't hurt to listen. "No, but are they real and not just made up?"

"Not everyone experiences them in steps. Sometimes they run together and sometimes they overlap but yeah, you do feel the seven stages at some point. Or at least I did."

"Where are you now?"

"I think I'm a mix of four and seven. Loneliness and wanting to move forward. What about you?"

"Me?" Surprised, I fumbled with some of the casings I had picked up, the brass making clinking sounds as I recaptured them and walked swiftly back to our prep area. Packing things up, I told her, "I'm not suffering any grief."

"Sure you are. Over the loss of your trust, your first love. Your belief in a happy ever after."

I stopped my busy tasks all together and leaned my hip against the table. Folding my arms, I gave her a repressive look, signaling the end of the conversation but Sam was undeterred.

"Didn't you at first refuse to believe that your girlfriend—what's her name?"

"Carrie." I said curtly.

"Didn't you try to convince yourself that Carrie wasn't doing anything wrong? That she was showing up around base to be part of the wives' support group? And at first, when you sat outside your lieutenant's apartment, you believed that it might be a waste of your time?"

"Yeah so?"

"And then you got sick drunk?"

I nodded cautiously. Feeling a little like I was being led down a dangerous path, I chose to just let Sam do the talking.

"So you have shock and denial, followed by pain. You probably had some thoughts that maybe if you didn't go on that second tour you'd still be together. That she wouldn't have cheated?"

Her spot-on analysis of my post-breakup thought process was unnerving. Quickly, I returned to packing up the firearm paraphernalia and took it all over to her SUV. She hadn't stopped talking, though, following me to the Rover and then back to the tables, which I swiftly dismantled.

"Don't look so surprised. After hours of actual therapy, I feel that I could be an expert. Also, I feel a lot of guilt about not moving to Alaska, so maybe I'm still working through stages two through seven," she mused.

Deciding she wasn't going to stop until she'd gotten everything out of her system, I shoved the two tables into the cargo space, shut the door, and leaned against the bumper. Crossed arms and a scowl on my face didn't faze her.

"And now you've got a lot of anger. You don't want to have relationships. You just want to have people you have sex with."

"Wanting to be safe and sensible isn't a product of anger. It's a product of good decision making."

Sam stepped in between my legs and placed her soft hands on my chest and her sweet scent mixed with gunpowder drained away any anger I'd felt toward the subject matter. Maybe Sam was feeling guilty about having sex with someone other than her husband. I'd noticed she'd taken her ring off, but I hadn't said anything. Sliding my hands up her arms, I wrapped my fingers around her shoulders and tugged her a little until she fell against me.

"I don't know if you really want to stay in or get out, but I suspect you want to stay in," she said. Everything about her was surprising me. "You'd make such a great officer, because you truly care about what happens to those you lead. You aren't in it for the power or the status."

I opened my mouth to protest but a single finger against my cheek shut me up. "I also think you'd be surprised at how the right girl would not only be true to you while you were gone but would make your time with her so amazing that it would last you both through those long, lonely nights."

When she opened her mouth to start talking again, I crushed her to me. Sliding my tongue between her surprised lips, I closed my eyes and savored the taste of her. I couldn't wait until I could fill myself at the buffet of Sam. Her fingers wrapped around my shoulders and when she kissed me back, I knew our conversation was over. I knew grief. I'd felt it when I'd lost friends outside the wire. What had happened between Carrie and I hadn't left me with grief but an education. Women and men couldn't stand long separations and the military was full of them. Temporary connections conducted in a safe manner was what I had going for me until I retired. If I felt a pang in the region where my heart sat, it wasn't because I longed for something deeper.

FIFTEEN

Sam

WE DIDN'T TALK ABOUT WHAT HAPPENED AT FINN'S FARM, BUT Gray came home with me that night. In the morning he was gone with a note that he was going to run with his boys. Noah liked to run at what Gray referred to as the ass crack of dawn. I thought it made more sense that it would be the crown of dawn, like the crown of a head, but he'd said no. It was definitely the ass crack. Later he texted me that he was filling in for Bo at a city league softball game and did I want to come? Was knitting the best hobby ever? Of course I did. Packing some dark blue yarn into a sling and my 16-inch circular needles, I headed out for the park.

AnnMarie waved me over, and I climbed up to join them on the bleachers. Out in the field, Gray was jumping from side to side. My heart flipped over. Oh no. I was falling so hard for him, and he was leaving. In less than two weeks, he'd be returning to San Diego. I cupped my hands in front of my face and tried to cover up my sudden distress.

"You look blue," Bo commented. One arm was slung around AnnMarie's shoulder and the other he held gingerly to his side. Maybe Bo could give me some insight. Perhaps Gray had talked to him about separating. Maybe they'd even talked about Gray staying here, going to Central with his friends.

"I'm just not sure—" Before I could get my whole sentence out, Bo held up his hands in a T formation.

"Hold on. I was just making conversation." He turned and let out a piercing whistle. Everyone to the left of us—and some to the right—stared in our direction. He waved to the beautiful blonde and yelled out, "Lana, you're needed."

She shook her head but he whistled again. I ducked my head and covered my ears. She came huffing up.

"What the hell?"

"She needs advice." Bo pointed to me. I kept my head between my hands so that I didn't wrap them around his neck and choke his brains out for embarrassing me like this.

"How many times do I have to tell you I'm just a fucking student?"

"No need to curse," he tutted. "But think of all the practice you're getting." He nudged me. "She's better at this than all of us but her bedside manner needs work."

She sighed and sat down next to me. AnnMarie mouthed "I'm sorry" as she was dragged away by Bo.

"What's up?"

"Psychology student?"

"Yeah."

"Well, I guess you're better than nothing since he's run off."

"I don't think he does feelings unless they involve AnnMarie." We looked down at them. He was now delicately probing AnnMarie's mouth with his tongue as they leaned against the back of Gray's team's dugout. Bo had claimed a gimpy arm, which is why Gray was filling in, but I think he just wanted to feel AnnMarie up.

"He's certainly exploring those feelings now," I remarked dryly.

"So you're the widow." Lana looked at me speculatively.

"Geez, is that how everyone knows me?"

"Pretty much."

"Thanks." I shook my head in disbelief. "Does everyone come to you for advice?"

"Not everyone." Her gaze drifted to Gray's team. "But if they do it's because I'm the most fucked-up person everyone knows."

"You say it with such pride and cheerfulness."

"Years of therapy and resignation. Lay it on me."

Oh why not.

"Gray's got me all confused."

"In a bad way?"

"Is confusion ever good?" I countered. Lana shrugged, the motion lifting one golden curl and settling it back on her shoulder. The crowd behind us sighed with appreciation. She was just so beautiful you couldn't help but stare.

"You ever been to therapy?" The jump in conversation topic made me blink but I just went with it.

"After Will died, my parents made me go."

"What'd you learn?"

"That grief is a process; everyone goes at a different pace; it's okay to move on; no feeling is wrong except if you want to kill yourself and in that case I should call the ER." I turned and looked at Lana. "I never felt like killing myself."

"And even that made you feel guilty."

Too surprised to be embarrassed by her insight, I said, "You get this, don't you?"

"Years of therapy myself, honey. Told you I was fucked up." Again her gaze strayed to the field. "Too fucked up for some, I guess. But enough about me. Why not just see where it takes you with Gray. Do you have to have answers?"

"No, I guess not. But he's leaving and I'm—I guess I'm afraid of losing something I value again."

"Because he's going back to San Diego?" Lana asked.

I nodded.

"So you'll bury yourself for love but you won't move a few states to pursue it?"

"I—ah—" I gaped at her like a beached fish. Snapping my mouth shut, I bit my lip. "I don't know."

"I guess that's the question you'll have to answer when the time comes. The answer you have to provide for yourself now is whether you're willing to open yourself up to the possibility of loving again. You, of all people, know how short actual life can be. What do you want to fit in before life is over?"

Lana patted my hand and left me stunned on the metal bleacher. That's what Will had tried to do—cram in as much living as possible. It wasn't that he didn't love me, but that he wasn't letting his fears hold him back from trying everything. If there was anything I should do to honor his memory it would be to start actually living.

I didn't share my discussion with Lana with Gray. We'd never talked about our future because our time had always been temporary. I just held her words of advice inside me and thought about it. Later that night, after he fell asleep, I let myself envision living in sunny San Diego and it didn't feel wrong at all.

"Get up, sleepyhead." A large hand I'd come to recognize as Gray's—just by the feel—cupped my cheek. Without opening my eyes, I traced that hand up the forearm to the biceps and tugged. I gave a sleepy smile when his weight came down to settle over my body and I burrowed more deeply into the covers, satisfied that all was perfect in the world.

A nose nuzzled my hair, and Gray molded the blankets around my body. After the long hours of sometimes tender, sometimes fierce loving, I ached pleasantly all over. My nipples were a little sore from being sucked and bitten, but the sensation only reminded me of how amazing it'd felt to have been brought to an orgasm by just the sucking alone. Well, the sucking and the pressure of his hard thigh between my legs. The memory of that made me tingle even more. "Don't want to. Snuggle up to me."

I felt the curve of his lips against my neck as he smiled. "No, I have a surprise for you."

"I have a surprise for you too," I replied. "Under the covers."

He let out of sound that was half moan, half laugh. "Keep that thought."

Realizing he wasn't going to allow me to continue to sleep, I flipped over on my back and peered up at him. He was already dressed in a form-fitting exercise shirt. Over the most impressive part of his body, he wore gym shorts. I pushed out my bottom lower lip in an extended pout. "I have a sad that you're already dressed."

"I've got plans." He slapped the side of my butt, but the comforter buffeted the hit. I stretched my arms above my head. The action made my breasts lift and the covers drop, which drew Gray's attention. I kicked the covers down a little lower, thinking to tempt him into removing his clothes.

This time the noise he made was clearly a moan. Reaching over, he lightly tongued one erect nipple and then the other but instead of reaching for his waistband, he pulled the sheet up over my breasts. "Can't think very well with those beauties staring at me."

"We don't have to do any thinking today." I patted the bed.

"You don't." He grinned. "But you'll be sore for a little bit and I thought you might enjoy this activity I had planned."

"What could be better than last night?" I said unthinkingly.

Gray's grin grew even wider. "Best ever, huh?"

"If you aren't going to do anything, then no, it was terrible." I pushed off the bed and flounced off to the bathroom.

Snickering, he called after me, "Oh, I'm totally rising to the challenge."

"What are we going to do?" I asked after we'd climbed into the Rover.

"What do you think?"

"Sky diving?" I still wanted to do that, and I figured Gray was the perfect person to take me up and push me out of a plane.

"That's not really very dangerous," he scoffed.

"It looks dangerous. Will liked it."

"Everything Will liked was dangerous?"

"It seemed that way."

"Like you?"

I rolled my eyes. "Yes, I'm very dangerous."

Gray reached over and tucked a piece of hair behind my neck. "The fact that you don't know makes you all the more lethal."

Embarrassed, I looked out the windshield. "I once got sick on a Ferris wheel."

Gray leaned against the corner of the car door and seat, settling in. "I can't wait to hear this."

"Our senior year, Will and a bunch of us went to Six Flags for senior skip day. We rode the Ferris wheel at the end of the day and the park looked beautiful at night." I swiped some stray hairs out of my eyes. "Will was anxious to leave for Basic. The closer it got to graduation and his leaving, the more frustrated he was. He and his friend, Trevor, started throwing a ball at each other. Trevor and his girlfriend were in the car in front of us. When our car was resting on the top, Will started crawling out of the car. He said he wanted to stand up on the rail. The operator saw him and started screaming at us. I begged Will to get inside and he did. When we got off the Ferris wheel, I threw up. I think it was from fear."

A sweatshirt landed on my lap. I hadn't even realized I was shivering. I could have just turned down the air conditioning but at the next stop light, I slipped it on and was immediately surrounded by the soft cotton and the smell—the spicy, ocean smell I'd come to associate with Gray. He directed me east of town toward the large expanse of land that was a farm back in the day but now held a small but functional airfield. Off in the distance I could see the major city airport. I swung into the small parking lot but made no move to get out of the Rover.

"Um, really?" I'd talked a big game about wanting to do this but now faced with the prospects I was frightened.

"If you don't want to go up, we won't," Gray said.

"But I did want to do something adventurous..." I leaned forward and looked at the small plane with the large side doors. Could I really jump out of it?

"Not all daring things occur up in the air. We could go whitewater rafting. Maybe play paintball. We could take a motorcycle out on the track." Gray shook my arm to get my attention. "You tell me what you want to do."

"I want to go up," I said truthfully.

"Okay, but if you feel uneasy at any time, let me know. I don't want to do things that scare you." I glanced at his fingers, which circled my wrist. I loved his hands. There were callouses on the palm and white scar marks on the backs. When I looked at them I felt safe, and when he put them on me, I felt excited. Those were good hands.

"I'll tell you if I'm scared," I said quietly.

He gave me a sideways smile, the one where only the left corner of his mouth rose. I was beginning to recognize that it meant he was not quite ready to tell me something but if I waited long enough it'd come out. We were getting to know each other in a lot of ways and that was about as scary and exciting as jumping out of a plane. When we were walking from the parking lot to the office, Gray's hand caught mine and he didn't let it go even after we'd signed our releases. We sat in the waiting room for the pilot and other jumpers to arrive. The plane could hold eight parachuters and there would be five today. Gray and me, an instructor named Jerry and two experienced jumpers.

Gray's finger rubbed over the empty spot where my ring used to sit. The skin was still paler than the rest of my finger, but he'd never said a word. Just like he never said anything the first time I took him to my condo other than to ask me where the bedroom was. I pointed up the steps, and he carried me up to the loft and made love to me, tender and sweet.

"Tell me the truth. Is this the scariest thing I'll ever do?"

He shook his head. "Nah, I wouldn't bring you if I thought you would hate it. But you've mentioned it a few times. The jump is about the descent. The free fall and the wind and the ground rushing up to meet you."

"Sounds terrifying."

"It's not really. Or if it is, the adrenaline is the product of a mind fake. You've got the parachute. If you were free falling without the parachute then I think the main feeling would be terror instead of exhilaration."

"But you like the rush, right? The excitement."

His response was slow, reluctant. "Yeah, but I'm not an adrenaline junkie."

"You like to do things that are dangerous," I pointed out.

"Within limits."

"Like Will." I sighed. "I must be an adrenaline junkie."

This admission caused Gray to laugh. "Why would you say that?"

"Because I keep falling for guys who are dangerous."

The words hung heavy between us and a part of me wanted to reach out and pull them back inside me. Gray pulled me around so I was facing him. His left hand was on my shoulder and his right hand pushed the hair out of my eyes. When his fingers drifted down to my chin, I raised my chin so he could read all the sincerity and emotion that had been building since the first time I met him. "You're falling for me?"

"Isn't it obvious?" I whispered. I didn't know how to play games or conceal my feelings. Living, even with its hurts, was so much better than hiding away.

"It's only temporary," Gray reminded me, his eyes searching.

"I know." And I didn't even care, not at that moment.

The descent of his mouth toward me was slow. My lips opened slightly in anticipation and my eyes fluttered closed.

"Samantha," Gray said, his breath tiny puffs of air against my lips. I slid infinitesimally closer to him. "Open your eyes." His voice was insistent.

I opened them. "Why?"

"I want you to know who's kissing you." His lips pressed against mine, firm and warm. He was always so warm. At first, he just pressed his lips against mine and then he began to move them. He softly nibbled against my lips, pulling my lower lip between his. I opened to him and his tongue slid inside my mouth, rubbing against my tongue and inviting me to play. He seemed to be saying that he could sit there and kiss me for hours as if nothing were more exciting than the feel of our lips against each other.

He might have said it was temporary, but we both knew it wasn't.

SIXTEEN

Gray

THIS WAS ONLY TEMPORARY, I REMINDED MYSELF, AS SAMANTHA so sweetly kissed me back. *I'm only here for a short time.* But as I felt her tongue stroke the side of my tongue, as she nipped her teeth against my lip, I wanted to just drown in the sensation. Her scent filled my head and the air around us shrank until all I knew was her small body sitting so close to mine. I moved my hand from her shoulder to cup her neck and angled her face for deeper penetration. I licked every inch inside of her mouth until the taste of her was all that I knew on my tongue.

And all that time I stared in to her green eyes and not once did she look like she was anywhere but right here with me. I saw *my* reflection there. Her heartbeat was made wild by *my* kisses. The ring on her finger was gone, and her condo was empty of most everything but yarn. It was a place I felt like I could be comfortable in.

And temporary was the farthest thing from my mind.

When we broke apart, our breath mingled together as we rested our foreheads together. Then I moved her to my side, tucked her under my arm. As we sat there waiting for the rest of the group to arrive, I asked her about safe things because I was feeling more on edge sitting next to her than I ever did right before leaping out of a plane or a helicopter. "Can you make me a hat?"

"Sure, that's not really challenging."

"What else do you make? I admit, despite what I told you the other night, I kind of do associate knitting with old ladies."

"Don't knock the old ladies. They've got skills." She elbowed me in the side. "I make sweaters although those are pretty challenging. My favorite thing is to knit baby stuff. It's quick and adorable."

When she tucked her hair behind her ear, I couldn't take my eyes off of it. I'd felt lust before. And desire. But this was something different. I felt hyper aware of every little thing she did. I noticed her fingers sometimes had nicks in them, as if she'd been inattentive too many times while slicing limes at the bar. And that her hair was always falling around her face.

The other night when we went out to eat, she told me she wanted Thai food and then took me to her favorite restaurant. With Carrie I'd run through a list of every restaurant in five-mile diameter and after she'd said she didn't care where we ate, she'd complain about whatever place we'd ended up at. She couldn't make a decision whereas Sam was pretty self-sufficient. She bought her own groceries, paid her bills, always had gas in her Rover. It was evident she'd lived on her own for a while. All that was incredibly attractive.

I ran my hand over my growing hair. By the end of my leave I should have a mop. And a beard. And my uniforms would still be pressed and perfect. Like I told Bo and Noah, I didn't have a good set of skills outside of the military. Would I even be good enough for someone like Sam? She came from a pretty nice life. Had her own condo, a nice truck, her mom was a lawyer. I wondered if my ability to iron would render me a good husband.

"Do you think ironing is an essential life skill?"

"Um, I have no idea. I don't think I've ironed one thing in my life." She snorted and held her hand over her mouth to cover the smile.

"That's such a random question."

"Will never had you iron his Alphas?"

"His class A uniforms? No way. He said I didn't know how to do it. He was very particular and I wasn't going to protest. Who likes ironing?"

"It can be a very soothing task," I declared but smiled at her arched eyebrow. "So I guess the answer is no?"

"I think it's one of the very first things you should put on your boyfriend resume. *'I iron.'* Right after, *'I am shit hot in the kitchen.'* You make a mean omelet."

"What about shit hot in the bedroom?" I asked quietly. Her smile died away, replaced by a long stare. So long and so heated I felt like she'd run her tongue all over me. Good thing I was already sitting down, because otherwise I would've dropped on my ass.

"You don't need to put that on your resume. Everything about you telegraphs that."

Talk about dangerous activities. "What exactly?"

A wisp of humor skipped across her face, and I reached out and brushed two fingers there. Maybe to catch the smile. Maybe just to feel her soft lips again.

"You want words?" she said low.

"You know I do." Her voice was still throaty with the early morning. Or it could have been something more that was making the words thick. I could listen to her all day. She glanced over at the counter attendant, who was busy with her phone. I leaned down so my mouth was close to her ear. "Whisper them to me."

For a moment I thought she'd comply but a noisy crowd entered the small waiting room. It must've been the other jumpers. Tension simmered between us.

As we sat through the instructional movie and then the live safety instruction, our legs brushed against each other, taking every chance to touch each other. I took the gear from the instructor and helped strap Sam in it, testing every buckle twice. We were both worked up, although some of it could have been anticipation for the jump. Her color was high, and I knew if I looked in the mirror I'd have that same heated look of lust in my eyes. I might only have a few weeks of leave left, but I wanted to spend a good portion of it with Sam.

Samantha

"I FORGIVE YOU FOR GETTING me up so early," I yelled at Gray. The plane we were on was specially designed for parachuters, Gray had told me. It rose quickly in the air and landed quickly. Every atom in my body felt enervated. I ran through the instructions. Gray and the other instructor would hold me when I jumped and then let go after my chute opened. We'd be the last ones out. Gray thought that was safer because I'd have less chance of getting tangled up in someone else's lines.

"Ready?" he mouthed. It was too loud for me to hear him with the door open and the jet sounds mixing with the wind. I gave him two thumbs up. He made me run through the motions of pulling the chute. Gray's worry was endearing and I would've kissed him if not for all our paraphernalia. Jerry, the instructor, gave me the five-finger countdown. Five. Four. Three. Two. One. They each grabbed an arm and we flew out of the plane. As instructed, I spread out my arms and legs like a bird. Gray still held on to one hand but Jerry had released me, which wasn't what had been planned but no matter.

I counted off in my head the seconds until I'd pull my chute. The wind picked me up and I felt almost weightless for a moment. All too soon Gray squeezed my hand. He motioned for me to pull my chute cord. Angling my feet downward as I'd been told, I pulled the cord and steeled my body against the jerk I'd feel when the chute would open. He'd told me that it was like someone pulling on my jacket if I was running, abrupt but not painful. Nothing. I pulled again.

Seconds ticked by and I was falling fast. Panicking, I jerked my hand free of his, ignoring his shout, and tugged frantically at my chute cord until I felt a release. But no jerk came. In my hand was just the toggle on the pull cord, which had come off. I turned to show Gray and then the wind took the cord and whipped it away.

The ground was rising fast, almost a blur through the tears that had formed. The tears from the wind, not fear, I told myself. And then, in an instant, I embraced it. So this was it. Perhaps my story was one of tragedy. Married young, widowed young, died young. I spread out my limbs again. When I fell and hit the earth, I figured the impact would be instantaneous. Death had to come to all of us.

The wind rushed by me and even with my goggles, I could feel the sting against my eyes. There was peace here. *But Gray.* I'd known him only for a little time. If I'd had one regret, I wished I had kissed him harder, held him longer. The sensation of regret caught me unexpectedly, invading my peace almost as if a physical reaction had occurred. Then I realized it wasn't regret that had hit me—it had been Gray. His body wrapped around mine, his arms coming up from behind me, holding me almost in a loose headlock with one arm. With the other, he must have pulled his chute cord, because it deployed immediately. He pulled his body back with it.

The ground still rose quickly, but he held me fast. The only thing that kept me from becoming part of the dirt was his strong, firm, and steady grip. I hugged his arms to me and wondered why I'd been so ready to give it all up. Sobbing, now with relief, I clung to him as we fell rapidly to earth.

The impact of the ground jolted me hard although I knew Gray had taken the brunt of it, landing on his legs first. He curled me into a ball and we rolled for several feet, tangled in chute cords and nylon until we were completely wrapped up. I ended up with my head tucked into his chest. Our legs were entwined.

His breath was harsh and wracked in my ear.

"Jesus. Jesus. Jesus Christ," he panted.

I said nothing, only clutched him closer to me. As I began to shake uncontrollably in his arms, he whispered consoling words in my ear. "It's going to be okay. We're safe now." But he wasn't immune either. I felt his body shudder against mine and we just clung to each other inside the cocoon of his parachute. His gloved hands smoothed up and down my body comforting both of us at the same time.

When he pushed my goggles off with one hand, I saw that his eyes looked wet. I'm sure mine were too. Pulling me against him, we began ravishing each other. He rolled us over until my body was covered with his. We kissed to make sure each other was alive. We kissed in celebration of our survival. We kissed because deep down, the emotions that we'd been trying to deny were overwhelming us.

He and I both knew that however temporary our relationship had been before, the fall had shaken loose our barriers and we were just raw nerves and emotion. I felt his erection heavy against me. I wrapped my legs around him and we pressed up against each other. We would've ditched our clothes and just fucked each other raw underneath the parachute if Jerry hadn't arrived and interrupted us.

"Hoolee shit," I heard him exclaim. "You two okay?"

Gray pulled away from me immediately and rested his forehead against mine, trying to gain some composure. The mood changed as I saw his emotions flip from desire to anger. He pulled loose of my embrace and untangled us quickly, although I'm not sure how. I was trussed up in enough strings and fabric to keep me immobilized for at least a month.

"Her goddamn chute didn't open, you motherfucker," Gray roared at Jerry. If it wasn't for the chute strings surrounding us, Gray would've been on him, beating the tar out of him. He began struggling with the harness.

"We check those chutes daily," Jerry protested.

"If you did, then you'd have seen it was defective, *Jerry*." Gray spit out his name like he couldn't stand the taste of it. Gray sat me up and pulled the chute off of me. I hadn't the first clue what had happened. I only knew that it should've released when I pulled on it. "And you shouldn't have let go of her. This was an accelerated free fall, and we both fucking hold her until the chute deploys."

He finally got the harness off of himself, and he turned to attack mine. He was spitting mad, but his hands were gentle as he handled me.

"What about the emergency cord?"

"Neither cord opened the chute," Gray bit out. I wondered if his jaw would crack from the effort of not yelling at Jerry. Gray knew— somehow just knew—that if he yelled right in my face, I'd lose it. I was so close the edge of a breakdown. He pulled both cords and the chute remained stubbornly closed, an innocuous backpack-looking thing. He yanked viciously again and the emergency cord pulled away, frayed at the end. He threw the entire thing at Jerry, who stumbled back at the weight.

"You better get your house in order because the FAA will be there by the end of the day to run an inspection on your entire equipment supply." Gray jabbed his finger at the guy's chest, his other hand fisted like he wanted to plant it in Jerry's face. "You're gonna be grounded. You could've fucking killed her."

The adrenaline rush, the fear, the passion had all drained away and I felt weak. "Gray." He was still raging at Jerry. "Gray," I said louder. His head whipped around. His eyes were wide and his nostrils were flaring. I wanted to touch him so I could get him to calm down. Instead I said the words that I knew would penetrate his fear and disgust and anger. "I need you."

Immediately he turned away from Jerry and dropped to his knees. "Baby, I'm here. What can I do?"

I wrapped my arms around his neck and nuzzled my nose against him. "Take me home."

Part of me wanted to rage too but mostly I wanted to go home and lie with Gray in my arms and revel in the fact that I was alive, no matter the faulty equipment. I'd done something very dangerous but I'd survived. I was glad to be alive.

Gray

I FELT SAM'S SLIGHT BODY against mine, her utter trust in me and felt a surge of something so strong that I almost fell backward. I firmed up the steel in my spine and picked her up into my arms. While I wanted desperately to beat Jerry bloody and then go inside SkyHopper and ransack the place, I wasn't going to leave Sam trembling and shocky. "Get me some OJ," I ordered Jerry. When he just stared at me like a dumb robot, I barked again in my best copy of my gunnery sergeant father. "Get me some goddamned orange juice or I'll cut off your nuts with your car keys." He got the message and took off toward the office building. One of the other jumpers came over.

"Need anything?" His hair was military short.

"Yeah, I need someone to file a complaint ASAP while I take care of my girl." Sam was silent, burrowing her head into my shirt. I wanted to get her home like she'd asked. As I reached the parking lot, I noticed a number of expensive foreign vehicles in the "owner" slots. The guy obviously had money or was wasting it on expensive toys rather than careful maintenance.

"On it." He gave me a smart salute and trotted off after Jerry.

I placed my girl tenderly into the passenger side of her Rover. I'd never driven it because Sam always seemed to enjoy being behind the wheel, but she was in no shape to pilot this vehicle back to her place. She curled up in the passenger seat, her big green eyes staring at me. The look in them, shit, made me feel like I was bigger than life. I knew some guys got into the military because they had a big old savior complex. They liked to be the hero, and going over and killing people that they were told were the enemy made them feel good inside. I'd never felt that way, but right now I got it. Sam was looking at me like I'd conquered King Kong as it was trying to devour the city

"Guess all those training jumps were good for something," I joked weakly, brushing the hair out of her face. Her color was still pretty pale. Fortunately for Jerry, he appeared within seconds with a bottle of orange juice. "Drink some of this," I commanded and then added, "please."

She must have felt a little better because she rolled her eyes but dutifully took a small sip.

"A little more." I winced as the request came out like another order. It worked though. The military guy came out with a form that he'd filled out. I signed it. "Thanks, man."

"No problem. That was scary as fuck just watching it so I can't imagine how you both feel."

Jerry was long gone by then, which was probably a good thing because now that Sam was feeling better I wanted to go beat the shit out of him.

"I've had better days," I admitted.

"Go home, get your girl into bed, and take a load off. I'll see this is filed. I'm going to make a call to the FAA too. This place should be closed down within the hour." The guy flipped open his ID and I saw it said "State Police."

I blew out a breath of relief. "Thanks, man." We shook hands and Trooper Jensen gave me his card so I could follow up.

By the time we got to the condo, Sam was getting back to her old self.

"That was certainly adventurous," she said drolly as I was pulling into the parking lot behind her building.

The thought of her crashing into the ground because the goddamn chute wouldn't release had me banging the steering wheel. I wanted to turn around and drive back and give Jerry a piece of my mind. "Good thing you stopped me from killing Jerry because there was a State Trooper who jumped before us."

"I can't say that I'm going to want to do that again anytime soon, but I'm not sorry that I went and I'm glad you were the one who took me." She rubbed her palm along my stiff forearm.

"If I'd just checked that damn chute—"

She cut me off. "*If onlys* are a fool's path. I know this from too many sleepless nights. Let's go upstairs and celebrate the fact that we're alive." She pulled my chin around and pressed her mouth against mine. "Take me upstairs and make love to me."

I can't remember how we got upstairs and into her bedroom. I only know that we did. In the bathroom, I turned on the hot water and undressed her while the shower heated up. She allowed it, passively standing there all the while watching me with burning eyes. Somehow she sensed that I needed to take care of her.

When we were both nude, I tested the water temperature and then pulled her inside. Sam's condo had no bathtub but the shower was incredible. There was a rainshower head recessed into the ceiling and another large spray head mounted on the side. I had turned them both on so that we could each be warmed by the streams of water. The one thing we were missing was a bench, but I'd make do.

I stood us under the rainshower head and let the soft drops of water fall onto our heads and shoulders and back. "Lean on me," I urged and she did, dropping her head against my left pectoral muscle.

She could probably hear it hammering but I didn't care much now. Any defenses I had against this girl were bashed against the ground. I'd seen her falling from the sky, and my heart had gone with her. There wasn't a calling higher than being with her, but I wasn't sure how to tell her. Now wasn't the right time, but *soon*.

I rubbed her head gently, kneading her skull and then her shoulders, keeping all of my touches above her waist and away from her breasts. That didn't keep my cock from being stiff as a pike and poking her in the stomach.

She made soft sounds of pleasure as I rubbed away any tension she had left. Turning her so her back was to my front, I grabbed the showerhead off the hook to rinse off the soap in her hair. "Tip back," I told her and directed the spray at the back of her head and then, cupping my hand protectively at her forehead so the soapy water wouldn't stream into her eyes, moved the spray around the crown of her head.

"You're really good at this," she mumbled. "Think you should put down 'I give good shower' right after 'I iron'."

That made me laugh. "I'm building quite the resume."

"You had the skills already. We're just itemizing them now." Turning around, she embraced me, and we stood like that for a moment, for maybe five or ten heartbeats, just holding each other as the water sluiced around us. My heart was about to burst when she raised her face to me.

"I love you," she said. "I know you said it's temporary, and this may send you screaming out of the shower, but I can't keep it in anymore." Reaching up, she brushed a thumb over my eyebrow and then traced a path to my temple, down my cheek to the other side of my mouth. When I opened it to tell her that I couldn't live without her, she shushed me. "Don't say anything. Not yet."

On her tiptoes, she kissed my neck and then the underside of my chin. Hoisting her in my arms, I met her lips head on. So she wouldn't let me say the words, but I could tell her how I felt with my kisses and my caresses. Twisting the knobs, I shut off the water. I draped a towel over her back but didn't let her go. I could care less about the water.

"We're wet," she half protested, but her heart wasn't in it. I tossed her down onto the comforter and crawled on top of her.

"Not wet enough," I said and spread her legs open for my mouth. I'd been down here before and loved it, but this time I went slow, savoring every scent and flavor her body exuded. My tongue lapped gently, caressing every sensitive inch. Her lips were pinker closer to her body, and they were flushed and plump with arousal. The droplets dotting her pussy weren't just water, but tasted of a special tang only her body could produce. The small offering only whetted my appetite.

"You taste so good, baby," I told her before plunging my tongue directly into her channel to gorge. Her hands threaded into my hair and pressed me closer.

"Don't stop," she panted.

"Won't. Ever."

Her thighs closed around my head, and I had to push one away so I could maintain my contact with her delicious cunt. As she climbed closer to her release, her body began to quiver, and her hips began undulating. I used both of my hands to keep her right against my mouth. I could spend hours down here, eating her, licking her, *savoring* her. Blood pounded in my groin as my body screamed for its own release, but I ignored it because there was nothing I wanted more in that moment than to have her come all over my tongue and face.

"Ohhh…God…please." Sam's body thrashed, her back arched like a bow off the bed. I bit her, gently, right on the clit and she started screaming. "Gray, Gray, Gray…" It was the best damn music I'd ever heard. I lapped all her juice as she quivered, her walls contracting rhythmically and then more sporadically as her orgasm shuddered on. Keeping my mouth over her cunt, I licked tenderly at her engorged flesh, trying to soothe her. Her screams turned to whimpers and then to sighs.

Sitting up, I wiped the back of my hand across my face and took my painfully erect cock in hand. "You ready, baby?"

Glassy-eyed, she nodded. Easing into her, we both gasped as I felt the bare flesh contract around the tip of my penis. Shit, I wanted to be inside her without anything between us. I'd never wanted that, not since Carrie. It was shocking but felt right.

"You on anything, Sam?" I heard the faint pleading note in my voice and shook my head in wonder.

Her face was crestfallen when she answered in the negative. "No, I'm so sorry. I'll get on it right away." Then she turned her face to the side as if she remembered that my time here was coming to an end. But it wasn't the end for us. I slid another inch inside her and nearly cried at the amazing sensation.

Turning her head back with one hand, I pinched her chin lightly. "Yes, go on the pill so that when we see each other, we can do this anytime, anywhere." I pushed all the way in, until I was seated up to my balls inside her hot, wet, tight cunt. The feel of her walls clenching around me made me want to shoot all I had inside of her until she was filled with nothing but my come. I wanted to experience her orgasm against my naked cock more than I wanted anything else at that moment. I had to restrain my lower body. Staring at the wall above her, I started counting the bricks until my head cleared enough to withdraw. It was painful coming out of that hot sheath and the urge to shove back in almost did me in. "We're not done yet," I told her. "We may not ever be done."

Her eyes widened in understanding and a smile broke out that lit up the entire room. I heaved myself off the bed while I still had an ounce of self-control left and went to find my shorts. Tucked in my buttoned back pocket, I had three condoms. I might need all of them before we were done here. It was, after all, only mid-afternoon.

"I'm sorry," I told my dick. "But hang in there, someday we're raw dogging her until we both can't see straight."

"Are you talking to your penis?" Sam called from the bed. She didn't sound nearly breathless enough. I hurried back and flopped down beside her, my erection hitting her on the hip.

"Yup, I'm consoling it and telling it to stay inside the condom."

She giggled and then reached down to squeeze me. It still felt good. Hell, any contact with her felt good at this point.

"So you're going to come back and see me?" Her eyes were serious, belying her light tone.

"I want to," I confessed. Smoothing her hair back, I told her what I'd been wanting to say since I caught her in the air and tumbled to the ground with her. "I love you, baby. I don't want this to be temporary.

I don't want it to end."

Her eyes became wet with tears, and before I could do anything, she was leaking all over the place. I swiped as many as I could with my fingers but they were falling fast so I leaned in and started kissing her. She pushed me away.

"These are happy tears." She laughed and then used the back of her hand to dry her face off.

"Women." I shook my head. "Don't understand you at all."

Sam's response was to take my hand and place it between her legs. She was wet there too. "Do you understand this?"

"Yeah, I'm a quick learner." I slid two fingers inside her and felt her readiness. Pulling her hips to mine, I pushed into her again. It was easier this time because she was so wet and I had prepared her well. And even with the condom on, being inside of her was like heaven. It was better than a free fall from the sky. Better than shooting a M249 Saw, one of the heaviest, most bad-ass guns in the Marine Corps arsenal. Better than sitting down after a twenty-mile ruck through the woods carrying a hundred pound pack. It was better than anything I've ever experienced. And I never wanted it to end.

Rolling her over onto her back, I glided inside of her, looking for the minutest change in her reaction so I could be sure I was hitting the best spots. When her breath hitched or her eyes widened or she gasped out loud, I'd stroke that flesh over and over again. Her mouth turned and latched on to my wrist, which was braced against the side of her head. Ordinarily I'd tell her to scream out her pleasure, but I liked the fierce bite of her teeth on my skin. It was like she was marking me, making me hers.

Plus it was one more way I could tell she was totally lost in the pleasure I was giving her. I leaned down and fused my mouth onto hers, trying to tell her how much she meant to me. Her hips rose to meet mine, and we were caught up in our own rhythm. She was so beautiful, her golden hair spread out on the pillow, the edges of it lit by the fingers of sunlight reaching the upper loft through her floor to ceiling windows. The orgasm I'd given her earlier and her current arousal painted her skin with a rosy hue. Her eyes were closed and a light sheen covered her forehead.

As I thrust into her, I felt the connection in every part of my body from the tip of my cock to the ends of my fingers and toes. I was electrified by the feel of her. As her teeth bit into my skin and her fingers clenched my ass, I could feel her orgasm closing all around me. I gritted my teeth and held the pace, knowing what brought her to the point would tip her over. Reaching between us, I rubbed her swollen clit and she broke away from my wrist to release a long, sustained wail as she convulsed around me.

"You're so fucking beautiful, Sam. I wish you could see yourself," I panted in her ear. "Your face looks so amazing, so fierce."

She sighed. "Your turn?"

"My turn," I growled. I slung both her legs over my shoulders and began thrusting into her, fast and hard. She pressed her palms flat against her headboard and pushed back. The wet sounds coming from her cunt and the slap of our flesh against each other all added to the sensory overload. My balls tightened and I could feel my orgasm tingling at the back of my spine. Then I lost all control and let go, pistoning my hips against her ass until I felt my come jetting out. Clutching her to me, I fell to the bed, muscle memory taking over and rolling us to the side so I wouldn't suffocate her with my chest. Still snug inside her, I ran my hand over her spine, feeling for the hole I was sure I'd made when I shot my load.

"What're you doing?" she asked drowsily.

"I came so hard, I'm sure I blew a hole out your back." It was, thankfully, still intact. She chuckled weakly.

"I'm so exhausted. I feel like I could sleep for a week." She snuggled into me and we lay like that for a while until I had to get up to take care of the condom. Sliding back into bed with her, I tucked her body close to mine and let the exhaustion of the day take us under.

Hunger woke us up a couple of hours later. Sam was still sleepy when I climbed out of bed and went down to scramble some eggs. The full extent of my skill in the kitchen was making omelets and sandwiches, but if she thought I was shit hot in the kitchen, then I wasn't going to correct her. The microwave was my bitch, though, and I could dial for delivery as good as anyone. But I'd take fucking cooking classes if it meant keeping her with me.

She stumbled down the stairs dressed in my T-shirt and looking so fine I wanted to carry her back up and make use of my second condom. *Fuel first, fuck second.*

"Where's your permanent duty station?" she asked between forkfuls of eggs, which she declared delicious. She must be in love because they weren't anything to write home about.

"Right now my duty station is Pendleton, but I think I might still have to do a two year unaccompanied in Okinawa." The eggs tasted like sawdust as I thought about being away from Sam for two years. There would be almost no way for me to come home for more than a few weeks during that two-year period. "Good thing we have Skype, right?"

Sam didn't answer, just stirred her eggs around her plate. Then she took a deep breath. "I've always wanted to travel."

"You have?" If an unmarried Marine went overseas, he usually went alone because few partners could take a couple years off and afford to live wherever he went but it wasn't unheard of. Some lucky bastards had girlfriends who would move over and teach English or other shit. I held my breath.

"Yup. I don't have any debt. I've got the death benefit, and Will's life insurance. His dad bought it and half went to me and the other half is Tucker's. I could rent out the condo. I've always wanted to learn about other countries' fiber arts history. You know, needles were invented in China."

"What if it didn't work out?"

She took another bite of her eggs and chewed. "Well if I still had places to visit I would do that, and then I'd decide what to do. Maybe I'd continue to travel to New Zealand to get my hands on their Merino wool. Merino is some of the softest wool yarn around. Then maybe I'd come back here and sell my baby stuff at craft fairs or online. Set up an Etsy shop."

"You wouldn't regret it? Like not going to college and shit like that?" My heart was beating faster than a rabbit's. Any faster and I might have a heart attack. It never occurred to me that Sam would move with me. That she would give up her home and family and college dreams and move across the country or even across the world to be with me. I hadn't ever had anyone say that they would make that kind of commitment—not even Carrie. My throat closed up and I had a hard time swallowing my eggs.

"No. Not for a minute." She gave me a sad smile, and I knew instantly she was thinking of Will. But this time it didn't bother me one bit. "I don't ever want to stay home again. Be left behind. That's what I regret. If I went and the relationship failed, I'd enjoy the experience and the new friends I'd made. I can always come home."

I set down my fork then and picked her up. "I'm going to take you upstairs now and we're going to fuck—no, we're going to make love so hard neither of us will be able to walk tomorrow."

Sam patted my chest. "You talk a good game."

"Don't challenge me, baby, or you'll be too sore to walk for a week."

"Can't wait," she whispered and then bit my ear.

LATER I GOT A TEXT to go over to Bo's place.

"You want to go?"

"No, I'm too tired." She moved her legs experimentally and then groaned. "And sore."

I tried not to look too pleased about that. We'd used all three condoms and then I wished we had another one but since we didn't, we pleasured each other orally. Best sixty-nine ever. I took *a lot* of mental pictures of her ass in my face as I ate her out and fingered her to a couple of orgasms. I'd be pulling those out regular when I was away from her. I wondered what I'd be able to convince her to show me on Skype. God, the dirty stuff we could do was getting me worked up again.

"No, no, no." She held off a warding hand as I found myself leaning down toward her. "I'm done in for at least another twelve hours. Let my girl parts revive."

"All right," I said reluctantly. "I haven't seen the boys in a couple of days so I'll go have some beers while you recover."

"Fine."

I tucked her under the covers and gave her a deep kiss before heading off to The Woodlands.

SEVENTEEN

Gray

THE FARTHER AWAY FROM SAM I GOT, THE EASIER IT WAS FOR second thoughts to creep in. Years of having sex with women I didn't care about had left me unprepared for the emotional wave of fulfillment, the complete sense of belonging. The rightness of it all. Oh and the motherfucking fear of loss. This time my heart was pounding, not out of excitement, but of fucking fear. Just what had I agreed to back there in Sam's condo?

I was totally not in the mood to see one Ethan Drake at Bo's place.

"What the hell is Drake doing here?" I muttered to Bo as I stomped in the house.

He rolled his eyes. "Chasing down Noah, I guess."

Ethan Drake barely made it through boot and got kicked out in his third year, dishonorably discharged because he was snorting his measly enlisted paycheck up his nose.

Worse, Drake was a dog. He fucked anything in his path and

didn't hesitate to offer a shoulder to a deployed Marine's girlfriend. But women seemed to be blind to his smarmy ways. I'd once seen him come out of a bar's bathroom with a girl he'd obviously just screwed. She actually fucking giggled when he said he was just doing his patriotic duty by seeing to her needs. I almost tossed my cookies right there, and the fact that she didn't made me wonder about whether she'd been snorting coke along with him.

But as Noah, Bo, and I stood with our arms crossed, glaring at his head, the girls nearly fought each other about who was going to bring his next beer.

"All the way from California, you drove?" Grace asked in wonder.

"Yes, ma'am. Couldn't wait to see Jackson again."

"That's so sweet, isn't it, honey?" She glanced toward Noah but didn't really see him because if she had, she would have seen her man looking like he was going to either barf or hit Drake, possibly both.

"I can't watch this shit," I muttered to Bo. Grabbing a few beers from the refrigerator, I headed to the patio. About ten minutes later, Bo came out with a bottle of whisky and two glasses.

"Why're you drinking alone in the dark?" he asked. I contemplated the bottom of my nearly empty bottle, debating whether I should say anything. What the hell, though, if you couldn't talk to your brothers, who could you talk to?

"Sam almost died today."

"Out of fear from her first jump?" He cackled.

"I wish. Her chute wouldn't open."

"What the fuck? Over at SkyHopper?" Bo sobered up quick and looked properly outraged.

I nodded and took one of the glasses. "Fill her up." Bo poured me three fingers. "Don't be stingy."

He filled me up.

"I've jumped there before. What happened?"

"Faulty equipment. I pulled the chute cord when we landed and it didn't open. Pulled the emergency cord, and it came off in my hand." I clenched my hand again, wishing I'd decked the SkyHopper guy.

"Mother fucker," Bo cursed.

"That's putting it mildly."

"You fix that?"

"One of the other folks there was a state trooper. He filed a complaint and said it'd be shut down within the hour."

"So that why you're drinking in the dark by your lonesome?"

I wish. "I was terrified today. Actually terrified. Like if I was the type to shit in my pants, I would've been soiled by the time I hit the ground." I leaned my elbows on my knees and stared out at the dark water of the pool, now almost black without the underground lights turned on. I was afraid to close my eyes because I feared I'd see Sam sprawled on the ground with her head split open like a melon. "I don't think I've come so close to touching mortality. Even over in the desert, I figured we could all take care of ourselves. But this time..." I trailed off. I remembered that first night I saw Sam and how my heart had stopped beating for a moment. This time my heart had stopped for enough counts for me to be pronounced dead.

"Life is short and precious?"

"Something like that. What am I doing with this girl, Bo? I'm here on leave to have a good time and now I'm fucking around with a widow. She says..." I paused. Did I want to tell Bo? Why not, I thought. "She says she'll follow me, come with me wherever I'm deployed."

"And you can't wait to shake her off?"

"No, that's the weird thing. It felt good."

"And that terrifies you?"

"Yeah, still shitting in my pants terrified."

"Good thing you aren't the type to soil yourself."

"No kidding." I sighed and drained half the glass.

"You may want to slow down there."

"No, I don't think so. If anything I'm drinking too slow."

"Alcohol isn't going to change the way you feel."

"Can I find clarity in my drunkenness? Because I need some answers. I've only got, what?" I held up my fingers and tried to count. "Ten days to figure out what I should do. Ten days left with Sam? I swore I wasn't ever going to get involved while I was in the Corps."

"Twenty years of solitude seems like a pretty big reach. Don't know any FWBs that work out that long."

"So instead I get married, cheat, get divorced. Get remarried. Rinse and repeat?"

"Not everyone is like that."

"Name one relationship that has survived boot, deployment, or constant movement around the world."

"The statistic is like sixty-five percent or something that fail, so one out of three succeed, buddy."

I snorted. "Those are great odds. You betting on those odds?"

"You don't know that Sam is a cheater. She married an Army guy."

"I don't know that she's not a cheater. Maybe if I had a way to test her. Try her out." There was some thought forming at the back of my mind. I tried to reach for it, draw it forward so I could examine it.

"Whoa, I don't know if I like the sound of this." Bo took my now-empty glass and moved it away from me but I didn't care. I didn't need the alcohol now. I was on to something. "You might want to stop that thought train right there."

"No, this is actually a great idea. Maybe one of you can hit on her. Or no, she knows you guys. We need a stranger." The idea was taking shape and form and seemed brilliant.

"This idea is alcohol fueled. No good comes from alcohol-fueled ideas." Bo cautioned. What did he know? Like he said, he never let AnnMarie more than two steps from his side. That wasn't an option for me.

"It's like boot camp. BC for couples. For relationships. If it could weather a hard test, then we could make it." I tried to explain it to Bo but clearly he'd drunk too much because he wasn't getting how amazing this plan was.

"Don't test her. You'll lose her."

"That's the whole point, Bo." I tried to make him see the sense of it. "If testing her makes her do a runner, she's not good for the long haul anyway."

Bo rubbed a hand over his head. He'd allowed his hair to grow long since he'd separated. "I don't think I can talk any sense into you tonight but trust me when I say that this is the worst idea in a box of bad ideas."

"I'll do it." A voice came from the left. Ethan fucking Drake. Had he been listening to our conversation the whole time? As I peered up at him in my drunken fog, taking in his black hair that swooped down over his eyes, I was struck with the clarity I told Bo I'd been searching for in the bottom of the liquor bottle. There were always going to be guys like Ethan Drake out there sniffing around someone's girl. And some girls who were lonely and lacked confidence or backbone were going to fall for his line. And the rest weren't. I could live the rest of my life alone because I was too afraid to take a chance, or I could borrow a leaf from Sam's book and just hang it all out there.

She'd loved and lost and no matter how she said that she never compared losses, losing her husband had to be a helluva a lot harder than getting cheated on. Yet, she allowed me inside her life, her body, her *heart*. She told me she loved me without any certainty about my response. She was out there living and I was cowering the dark like a five-year-old convinced there were monsters in my closet.

"Nah, no need, man," I stood up, swaying a little at the alcohol rush. "I got this. Bo is right. Sam's a keeper. She doesn't need any test."

I left them both behind. I wished Sam were here with me now. Inside, I sat down on the sofa in the living room and texted Sam.

Where RU?

LOL. You drunk, baby?

No, horny. Really horny.

She sent me a smiley face. I wondered what that meant.

Come over and hump me.

Still recovering but I'll be ready for some morning action. Luv you, babe.

Luv U2.

Typing those words out came easily. My momentary panic washed away as quickly as it had come. Yeah, letting someone into my life was scary but I wasn't better off without Sam. I lay down on the sofa. When I slept off some of the liquor, I'd drive over to the condo and tell her how much I loved her and how stupid I was for doubting us for a second. She'd understand. I knew she would.

The next thing I knew I woke up in a puddle of my own drool face down on the leather sofa. I wiped it up with the bottom of my T-shirt. The sunlight coming in through the windows wasn't early morning sun, it was late morning sun—I couldn't see the orb on the horizon. And it was bright. Really fucking bright.

Shit. I must have drank too much and overslept. As I sat up, my head started pounding. I needed water, aspirin, and a shower in exactly that order. My whole pity party seemed stupid in the light of day. I needed to get back to Sam. Picking up my phone, I was relieved to see that I'd texted Sam last night before passing out. My messages were slightly cringeworthy, but hell, I'd been drunk. At least I wasn't spouting poetry or something. She'd have real concerns then. My phone showed she called twice this morning. Once at nine and again ten minutes later. Then nothing. I'd call her as soon as I showered.

The front door opened and Adam and Finn came in. They stopped near the sofa and Adam gave me a weird look.

"What's up?" I jerked my chin upward in acknowledgment and then winced when the motion sent a spike through my temple. Ugh. Water. I needed rehydrating.

"Left your friend over at Sam's this morning."

"My friend?" I pushed off the sofa and headed for the kitchen. Hand on one hip, I surveyed the room. If I were aspirin, where would I be? Next to the sink. Wait, I'd just ask Adam. "Aspirin."

He pointed to the cupboard next to the sink, just as I'd guessed. Smart man. Inside I found glasses, aspirin, mints, and a big box of condoms. This was definitely a house full of men.

"Ethan Drake," he said as I swallowed four aspirin dry and then filled up a glass.

"Yeah, not my friend. Freeloader that came to see if Noah had room in his entourage."

"Huh." Adam swirled his keys around his finger.

There was loads unstated in that sound. A sense of foreboding settled over me. I glanced at the clock on the microwave. It was close to eleven in the morning. A lot of time had passed since I'd texted Sam and since she'd tried to call me.

"What?" I asked almost afraid to hear the answer.

"Sam called and asked for you this morning."

"I saw that," I replied impatiently.

"She wanted some help taking something down, so I told her Finn and I would do it. Your pal Drake said that he needed to come along because he was delivering a message from you."

"Oh fuck me, no."

I got up, ignoring the stabbing pain in my head. "I need to get over to Sam's right away."

Adam threw me the keys. "Have it at. Don't like that guy and didn't like leaving him there, but he insisted and Sam, well, she seemed eager to talk to him."

I didn't like the sound of that either and for a moment, I wondered whether Drake would succeed in seducing her. And then I woke up from my stupid hangover stupor and mentally punched myself. The likelihood of Sam cheating was matched by the likelihood that Drake would stop being a fuckhead. Meaning no likelihood at all.

EIGHTEEN

Samantha

"So you're old friends with Gray?" I asked after Adam and Finn had left. Ethan Drake made me feel uncomfortable and I wished they hadn't left. I called Gray again but he wasn't answering his phone. I didn't want to be here alone with Drake so while Ethan was looking at every corner of my small condo with an appraising eye, I texted Tucker. He was probably on his way into his shop. Maybe he could stop by.

Ethan whistled as he looked around the small place. "Nice setup you've got here." He stretched out his arms as if measuring the square footage of the place. "So you're Gray's new lady."

He sounded like he knew Gray, sounded like they were friends but there was something off about him. His eyes were really bright and he looked flushed, like he'd just got done exercising or something. Oh, who knows. I was being far too judgmental.

"Can I get you something to drink?"

"Beer'd be great." He sat down and raised his feet to rest them on my coffee table and then thought better for it. I was relieved. I didn't really like when strangers touched my things. But beer in the morning? That seemed…weird but again, who was I to judge?

"You served with Gray and his friends?" I handed him the beer and it felt like he deliberately brushed his fingers over mine. He gave me a lazy grin and sat back, one arm stretched across the sofa, looking like he owned the place. Ethan Drake sure had a lot of confidence.

"Yes, ma'am. We were all part of the 101st and I got out about the same time Noah and Bo did. Noah asked me to come up and help him train for his next fight."

"That's nice." *This is a friend of Gray's,* I reminded myself. *Be nice to him.* After a few moments of uncomfortable silence, I asked, "Were you deployed with them? I know Gray went to both Iraq and Afghanistan." He was clearly agitated. His leg bounced up and down and then he stood up and walked over to the window and then back again.

"A-stan."

I scratched my head as I watched him pace back and forth. "Are you okay, um, Drake?"

He flashed me a big smile, a smile that affected a lot of girls positively. It was very charming. He had dimples that made him look roughish and endearing at the same time, but for some reason his smile bothered me, probably because he'd crossed the room and was standing so close to me that if I took a deep breath, my breasts would brush against his chest. I slid backward as unobtrusively as possible, but he followed me until my back was pinned against the counter that separated the kitchen from the rest of the main living space of the condo. "Call me Ethan." Then he did the move that Gray always did, which was to tuck some of the strands of my hair behind my ear.

I pressed a hand against his chest and pushed but there was no budging him. "Ethan, I'm sorry to say this but you're making me feel really uncomfortable." For a second, I felt him push forward and I felt frightened, almost more frightened than when I feared the chute wouldn't open. Where was Gray?

Then Ethan laughed and took a step back. "You're a little high strung, aren't you?" He slugged down about half the bottle and then sauntered back into the living room. "I can see why Gray's into you. Own your own place. A lot of nice cars in the lot out back. Got rich friends. This what you spend your death benefit on?"

I gasped. You never asked a widow what she spent her death benefit on. Even on the Internet forums where women shared everything from how they shaved their pubic hairs to where they could shop if the PX got shut down, no one ever talked about the death benefit but in the vaguest terms. It was the height of rudeness to come out and just bluntly put that forth. Not to mention he was making me feel unsafe in my own home.

"Look, Ethan Drake, I don't know why you came here but you can just leave now." I stalked to the door and threw it open.

Drake did get up off the sofa and lazily walked toward me. He set his bottle on the granite counter. "You know why I'm here? Cuz your man asked me to come and try to seduce you. I told him I wasn't into that kind of thing, but he begged me. It wasn't pretty. And you know us Marines got to stick together. So I did it for him but I can't really guess why he'd want into your dried-up cunt."

I slapped him. I just up and hit him with my open palm across his face. It was instinctual, like my whole body revolted and wanted to push back. Drake didn't hesitate to return the favor. The blow from his hand was swift and hard. Maybe I deserved it. I hadn't ever hit anyone before in my life. My head hit the back of the door and I felt something warm trickle down the side of my face. For a moment we stood staring at each other, as if neither of us could believe what'd just happened.

Shaking, I pointed. "Get out. Get the fuck out of here and never come back."

"I wonder what I'll tell old Gray. Should I tell him how easy it was, how you didn't hesitate to drop your panties on the ground for me?"

I wanted to fly at him but was too afraid of being hit again. "You get out or I'll call the police on you."

"Fuck you, cunt." He spat at my feet and then walked out. Still trembling, I closed the door behind him and sunk to the floor.

It's funny how the mind allows you to forget the exquisite

feeling of pain but leaves behind the memory of it. Looking back, I remembered being so overwhelmed with anger and sadness and loss when Will died that it was hard to get out of bed. The cocoon inside the bedcovers made it easier to shut out all truth and make up my own reality—the one where he was still alive and I was living with him in Alaska. But each day had gotten a little better until I no longer fought to stay inside my dreams and I could get up and move around and while my chest still felt hollow, like I'd buried my beating heart somewhere with Will, I was upright and functioning.

The mind's ability to self-heal wasn't a boon, it was a nightmare. If I could still call up the exact, piercing, debilitating pain that I'd felt when I lost Will, I wouldn't have ever allowed myself to fall for Gray. I'd have protected myself. Maybe I could've had sex with him, or maybe I would've just stayed away because then I wouldn't be reduced to this cold, trembling, little girl thing on the floor of my condo. I wondered at my endless capacity to generate tears. Was salty water all that I was made of?

My face throbbed where Drake had hit me, but that blow was nothing compared to the knife in my gut. How could I not have foreseen the danger Gray presented? Why hadn't I done a better job of protecting myself? I curled up in fetal position and cried until I didn't have anything left in me.

I'd never felt so betrayed and misused in my entire life. If this was love, I was better off a widow for the rest of my life.

I don't know how much time passed. Maybe it was thirty minutes but it felt like hours. A pounding at the door startled me. Standing up, I looked out the peephole, afraid that Drake was back but the person on the other side was almost worse.

"I don't want to talk to you or see you ever again." I leaned my back against the door and started crying again. I'd told him I loved him. I said I'd move to Japan for him and he had to test me?

"Baby, forgive me." I heard him say and whatever hope I'd had that Drake had made it all up burnt to a crisp under the flame of his apology. If Gray was sorry then Drake hadn't been lying.

"Why?" I asked. My hands were trembling, and I was shaking all over. "How'd you ever get the idea that I would cheat on you? That I needed to be *tested?* Why'd you bring that awful person into my life?"

"I was drunk. I wasn't thinking right. I'm so, so sorry." He jiggled the doorknob. "Let me in," he pleaded.

"No, you knew exactly what you were thinking. This was cold and calculated. I'm a person. Not a thing. You don't test me. You either trust me or you don't."

"I trust you, baby. I swear it." A thudding against the door had me moving away. It was like he was…running and jumping against it.

"Stop it." I pounded on the door right back and the thudding stopped. "You take your tests and get the hell out of here. I never want to see you again."

"You don't mean it." He sounded anguished but it didn't touch me.

"I do. I'm done with you. I'm done with military men. You aren't good enough for me!" I cried, and then I left the door and ran upstairs to my bedroom. I heard him plead and knock on the door, but I buried my head under my pillows and curled into a tiny ball. I searched out that place I'd discovered back when Will died. That open cavernous place where I'd spent so many nights after Will's death, and I enfolded myself in the cold loneliness that I thought I'd left behind.

Gray was a bump in the road. I'd get over him, and I'd never fall in love again. There was no room for that anymore. My heart couldn't take it. I wrapped it up, surrounded it in concrete blankets. Safe, secure, and…dead.

From a distance I heard him call my name. And I thought I saw him. I ran toward him but he kept moving farther and farther away and I was so so tired. I'd forget him in time. That's what I'd spent the last two years learning. How to forget.

I closed my eyes. The voice that called my name was distant and indiscriminate and finally the thudding stopped.

It was done.

Deep down in somnolence I found peace. And I never wanted to wake up again.

NINETEEN

Gray

THE DRIVE BACK FROM SAM'S CONDO WAS A BLUR. I COULD HAVE hit five cars and four pedestrians and I wouldn't have realized it. I was just that numb. A few careless words had laid waste to my life. For a moment there, I'd had everything. A gorgeous girl who was loyal and loved me and was willing to see through my decision to stay in the Marines. She was experienced and knew what deployment felt like. She was self-sufficient and had her own hobbies and plans. She wasn't reliant on me to make her entire life, even though I was beginning to realize that I wanted her to be my sole focus. But because I had a moment of insanity, I'd ruined it. *Give her time,* I thought. I just needed to give her a few hours to cry it out. Then we'd talk and I'd make her see that I was over that moment of indecision.

I pulled in blindly to the driveway and into the car pads. The rain was making it hard to see. I switched on the wipers but the wet spots remained and I realized it wasn't rain but that I was crying. I swiped the back of my hands against my cheeks and they came away wet. The driver's door opened and I looked to see Noah and Bo looking down at me with concern.

"I fucked up, boys," I choked out. Bo nodded gravely and offered me a hand. I took it and he pulled me out. The two led me out to the far end of the pool. The place was quiet, an unusual state for the house. I dropped into a lounge chair and folded over, knees on my elbows, head in my hands. Finn liked to ask people what superpower they'd ask for. Right now, I needed to be Superman and turn back time so that I could stop myself from making the biggest mistake of my life. Bo and Noah didn't say anything. Just sat there in silent contemplation.

"Want to talk about it?" Bo asked.

I shook my head. "No. I just need to wait her out."

No judgment or sage words of wisdom came forth from either of them. An hour had passed when Tucker Anderson came charging into the backyard. I heard the squeal of tires and then the slam of a car door, but I paid no attention to it. I was mesmerized by the pool and by trying to count the number of blue tiles in the mosaic trim. It was hard because the blue tiles started morphing into white tiles and then into Sam's face. I had to close my eyes when that happened and start over.

My attention diverted, I didn't see Tucker barrel down the side of the pool and dive right at me. He knocked me right on my ass, my head thudding against the lawn. My sole thought in that moment was that it was a good thing I was sitting on grass because my head would have cracked like a spoiled melon if we'd been on the concrete pool deck. Dimly I heard shouts but Tucker had the right of it. I needed an ass kicking and as her brother-in-law, he probably should deliver the punishment. As I took one blow after another, I wondered if this penance was good enough to win her back. *Hit me all you want, Tucker, I deserve it.*

Perhaps it was my lack of response, but his blows died out after the first flurry. Tucker was fit, but he wasn't a Marine, and it was easy enough to dislodge him. I swiped at my mouth and looked at the blood left on my hand. No kissing then, not with a split lip, but then

I thought of Sam and her bruised heart and wished that Tucker could hit me again and again and again. But Bo and Noah were holding him back. I leaned back on my arms and shook my head. "Let him go. I deserve it."

Adam, the only other roommate present, looked disgusted and walked off. Maybe I could set up a punching booth instead of a kissing one and all these Woodlands guys and their pals could take a swing at me to make themselves feel better.

Bo and Noah let go, and Tucker shrugged off their hands.

"Why don't you give us a minute?" I asked my friends.

"We let you have those blows, man," Noah bit off, "because Gray seemed to think you had the right. But you don't get any more freebies. Got me?" Noah loomed over Tucker, a big black blot in front of the sun. Tucker gave a short nod but I could see his eyes burning with more retribution.

"Let it go, Noah. I can take care of myself."

Noah turned on me. "You haven't shown any signs of that so we'll just be at the other end. You want to right your wrong then get your head out of your ass." Then his voice softened. "I know what it's like to make bad decision after bad decision but the right girl will forgive you."

I hoped he was right. Bo and Noah took their own sweet time getting to the other end of the pool. In the meantime, I stood up, using the chair to steady me and offered one of the recently vacated seats to Tucker. He refused.

"I'd offer you a beer, but I'm not allowed to drink," I joked weakly.

"You take orders from Noah Jackson?" Tucker sneered.

I just shook my head. "You aren't riling me up with that so just sit down and let's get it out."

"I knew the minute I saw you that you were no good," Tucker spat.

I didn't care what Tucker thought of me, although maybe I should. He was her brother-in-law after all. "How is she?" That was the only important question in my mind. Tucker looked like he wanted to haul off and hit me. He actually raised his fist, but I grabbed it before it could make contact. "Noah was right. I let you have those. I deserved them but no more." I squeezed his fist until he grimaced. I could take him, and he needed to know it so that his first response to everything I said that he didn't like—which was probably every other word out of my mouth—wasn't to try to beat me up. At some point, I'd get tired of him trying and have to teach him a lesson. Then Sam would be mad at me. Again or more. Whatever. I was going to do everything I could to make sure my actions never angered her again.

Tucker's arm relaxed, and I let him go.

"She's got a bruised face and a broken heart. How do you think she is?"

A bruised face? "What the hell?" I stood up.

For a moment, Tucker looked confused and then his face hardened again. "She texted me before I went into work, but I ignored it. I knew she wanted that goddamn piece of felt down, and I knew exactly why. Because she was pushing Will out so you'd feel comfortable."

My heart sinking and my fury rising, I listened to Tucker fill in details I knew nothing about. I should've broken down that goddamned door.

"About lunchtime, I felt shitty because I've ignored a lot of requests from Sam to go to lunch with our family or do stuff because I don't want her to be over Will. I called and called but she didn't answer. I went over and pounded on her door and she didn't get up, so I use the key that was Will's—"

"You used her fucking dead husband's key to get into her house?" That was some sick shit, and I wanted to punch him hard for that. He looked slightly chagrined but not enough.

"Yeah, I used the goddamned key, and it's a good thing I did because she's got a shiner on her face the size of some man's fist."

I didn't let Tucker finish. I ran toward the house. Inside Ethan was laughing it up with a couple of the girls. I jerked him out of the chair and slammed my fist into his jaw. Ignoring the screams from the girls and the "what the hells" from the guys, I dragged him outside onto the lawn and pushed him down on the ground. "You like to hit girls, you bottom-sucking boot?" His flesh gave way under my fists but it wasn't satisfying. Hands pulled me back and I heard gasps behind me but my attention was focused on Drake. Struggling against the arms that held me, I shouted at him. "You don't deserve to breathe

the same air as her."

He wiped a hand across his mouth, displeased I guess because I made him bleed. "Shit, you are such a pussy, Gray. Left your balls on her counter, did ya? All this crying last night about how you were so worried about her cheating on you. Do you want to know what we did while you were passed out in your drool here?"

He laughed maniacally and I charged him, breaking away from the human bonds of my friends. He tried to fight back but he was slow and uncoordinated. Not even one of his fists came near my face. I had him on his back, repeatedly hitting him until I was dragged away. He lay still, knocked unconscious, but my blood lust hadn't abated. I spat on him and then turned away, looking for Tucker. He stood off to the side with a disgusted look on his face and his arms folded. "She need anything?"

"For you to leave her alone." He turned and walked toward the front of the house. I followed him. I wanted that key back. It should be mine, and I was going to give everything I had to convince Sam that I belonged in her life. I'd quit the Corps, move here, live in her little condo, and service her on my knees every day if that was what it took.

"Other than that because that isn't going to happen." I had ten— no nine—days left before I had to go back to San Diego and every minute of them was going to be spent convincing her that she should give me another chance.

"She doesn't want to see you ever again. She never wants to hear from you. She's going to wipe you out of her memory."

The verbal blows landed harder than the physical ones but like a stupid man, I stood back up and asked for more. "Did you talk to her about what happened?"

He snorted. "Only that she was done with military guys forever." He threw something up in the air—her key—the shiny metallic glinting in the sun. I wanted to grab it from him. I clenched my teeth together to prevent the yowl of pain that was rising up inside me. I hated to hear that I hurt her so. Tucker went on digging the knife even deeper, twisting it so every part of my heart felt like it was being scored by a dull knife. "I only remember seeing her that bad once before, and that was after my brother died. She was like a ghost for months. Didn't eat. Couldn't sleep. We had to force her to take sleeping pills and slip protein gunk in shakes so that she wouldn't die from just not caring for herself. We almost lost her after he died, and when she started coming around a few months ago, started smiling again and interacting with her family again, I thought it—" He broke off but I knew what he was thinking.

"You thought it was time for her to start loving again."

He fisted his hand but at my challenging look he placed it carefully on his thigh and nodded grimly. I would've loved to repay him with a fight right now. I was brimming with unspent rage. He turned his back on me and walked to his truck. Whatever he'd come to say was done. "But you aren't going to see her anymore. They're going to England tonight for ten days to see her dad. In fact, she's being driven to the airport right now. And Bitsy's confiscated her phone. They don't want her in contact with you." He said the word "you" like I was a terrorist.

Ten days. My heart sunk and the terror I was feeling must have shown on my face because Tucker laughed, a mean and ugly chuckle that had nothing to do with mirth and everything to do with his celebration of my pain. "Yup. You aren't going to be able to contact her for a good ten days, and by that time, it'll be over for you. You aren't Will. She'll be over you by the time the plane lands in London."

With the knockout blow delivered, Tucker turned and jogged to his truck. The implication was clear. He'd be here when she got back, and I wouldn't. But I wasn't leaving anything to chance. I sprinted to Bo's car and jumped in. Bo stood in front of the car, allowing Tucker to leave first.

"Goddammit, get out of my way," I screamed at Bo. He wrenched open the driver's door and shook his head. "Move over, I'm not letting you drive in that condition."

I didn't care who was driving as long as we got to Sam's condo in the next five minutes. It took twenty, and I cursed Bo the entire way. His patience was at an end because he bit out, "If you open your mouth one more time, I'm turning the car around and driving us both into the nearest lake." I shut up promptly after that.

At the condo complex, I jimmied the outdoor lock, not wasting time getting someone to buzz me in. Bo was following hot on my heels. I ran up the three flights of stairs and down to Sam's condo. "Sam, let me in." I pounded on the door. I hit it repeatedly, yelling her name. I kept pounding even after my hand started bleeding so I switched to my other hand. Finally a door opened but it wasn't Sam's door. It was her neighbor's door. I leaned against the metal door, and waited to for the words I didn't want to hear. "She's not here, asshole. She left about fifteen minutes ago with her family and a big suitcase."

I swallowed back the bile at those words, but I wasn't ready to give up yet.

"Back to the Woodlands. To her house."

We raced back to the Woodlands. I wisely kept my mouth shut and so did Bo. I cradled my bloody right hand in my lap, trying not to get blood all over the interior of Bo's sports car. We drove up to Sam's house but it was empty. The lights were off and the house looked still. I still got out and looked in every window and door I could, pounding on the door with my left hand and yelling for Sam. But she was gone. They'd taken her away from me. I sunk down on her back porch. I hadn't even had the opportunity to make it right, and by the time she'd be back, I'd have to be back at Pendleton.

"I'll stay here, then," I decided.

Bo knocked me on the back of the head. "So you'll be dishonorably discharged or thrown in the brig? That's going to win her back?" He hit me again. "Use your fucking head."

"All my ideas are shit." Bo opened his mouth and I threatened him, "Don't fucking say I told you so or it'll be on right now."

He closed his mouth then and then said, "I'm only standing down because I think the squirrel over there is stronger than you at the moment."

"I don't know how Sam got up and lived again after losing her husband because right now the pain is fucking unbearable," I choked out.

Bo drew me against his side, a hand on the top of my head and I allowed myself to lean into him, like we were out in the desert and too tired to stand up after a thirty-mile hike through the hills of Afghanistan. "You gotta go home, get your head together, and plan an assault. There is no citadel, human or natural, that can withstand a siege from a Marine."

"I hope you're right."

They took me to the airport the next day. Silence was our fourth companion, so heavy and weighty it could have been another passenger.

When we arrived at the gate, Noah and Bo both got out of Noah's truck. Bo had felt so sorry for me, he gave me shotgun even though I hadn't called it.

"You look like hell," Noah commented.

"Thanks, man." I shouldered my seabag and rucksack. "It was real fun."

Any moment the police would come and boot them out of the drop off lane but neither of them seemed to care. Noah grabbed me and pulled me in for a long hug. "You know we love you, man."

I nodded, the emotions of the last few days riding so close to the surface that I couldn't speak. He shoved me away then and grabbed me around my neck so I'd look straight at him. "You love her enough, you never stop fighting for her. Never stop showing her how much she matters. You give it your all, and even if she doesn't accept it, you lived up to your own standards and you can walk away with no regrets. But I'm telling you, Gray, that if you love her, she's going love you back. I know it."

I think it was the most words I'd ever heard Noah string together.

"Do you now?" I snorted.

"I do." He let go and said, "*Semper Fi,* Marine."

Always faithful.

Noah was right in one sense. I wondered a lot after Carrie had cheated on me if I'd given it my all. Maybe I hadn't. Probably I hadn't. I loved having sex with her, but I loved playtime with my boys just as much. And that had sat uncomfortably on my shoulders. Deployment had been a relief from the constant emotional upheaval.

In the airport, people shied away from me, the bruises on my face making me look like a dangerous man. The airline ticket agent didn't give me the upgrade that servicemen and women usually received and I was stuck in the back by the bathrooms in a tiny seat with no space. The woman beside me shrank to her side as if I was a monster. I was a monster, though. Only a monster would've done what I'd done to Sam.

When I arrived home, I threw away my enlistment papers and drove out to see my parents.

"I'm not reenlisting," I told my dad. His mouth quirked to the side in what looked like disappointment, but he didn't ask about my bruised face.

"What will you do?"

I wasn't going to say that I planned to return to the city to try to win over a girl, so I just mumbled, "Don't know."

"That doesn't sound like much of a plan." My dad had been a drill instructor when he retired, and you didn't get to that position without perfecting a stern look of reproof and disappointment. He laid a good one on me, but I was too numb to care.

I threw up my hands. "What do you want out of me? You said there were better things for me than just the Marines. You and Pops got in a fight about it at Christmas, and made Mom cry, so now I'm telling you I'm getting out. I'm going to get a degree, maybe go into law." Maybe I'd be the lawyer Sam didn't want to be. At this point I had no other plan but to win her back.

"I told you that because you were looking like you were at a crossroads. I wanted to make sure you thought long and hard about whatever decision you made."

I gaped at him. "I thought you wanted me to get out."

"Hell, no." He stood up and began to pace, his hands folded behind his back like he was barking orders to an unseasoned recruit, which is what I was acting like. "I wanted you to know that the Marines weren't your only option. That because we have a little more money now and I have a certain position, that you've got other choices. The Marines were good enough for your grandpa and me but we didn't have much. I know that there was a lot of pressure on you to enter the Corps because your older brothers decided against it. I wanted you to have an out."

I sank back in my chair. "I don't know what to say."

"Think about your service again," Dad recommended. "I don't want you making a hasty decision because you thought that's what I wanted, but you'll have to do it on your own time and you'd better hurry before the boat fills up."

Boat space—or space in the Corps—was limited, particularly with the troop drawdown and the government tightening its belt on the defense budget. Ponder too long about your future options, and they'd be decided for you.

At my sigh, Dad came over and squeezed my shoulder. "But no matter when you make your decision, there will always be room for a good Marine like you. I'm proud of you, son."

Oh man, if you only knew. I swallowed and stood up, saluting my dad. He knocked my arm down, and drew me in for a hug. "Looks like all that thinking took a lot out of you. Let your mom coddle you for a bit. It'll make her feel good."

I spent the day with my parents and then drove over to my brothers' garage and they took me in without question. Unlike my dad, my brothers knew immediately what was wrong with me and it wasn't that I'd been wrestling with a decision about my future. "Girl troubles, huh?" said Luke, my oldest brother, but that was it. I tooled around in the garage doing odd jobs, running errands and learning a bit about custom painting, silently stoking my pain into hardened determination. Then it was back to Camp Pendleton.

My bruises were mostly healed by the time I got back to base but my CO still called me in. "Am I gonna hear about some Marine breaking shit in bars and generally making the Corps look bad?"

"No, sir."

"I'd better not," he harrumphed. "Where's your reenlistment papers then?"

"I'm not reenlisting, sir."

CO Dailey looked alarmed and then narrowed his eyes at me. "You better tell me what happened out there."

"Nothing important, sir."

"If it ain't important, then why the hell aren't you reenlisting? If it's a tiny bar fight, then we give you an Article 15 and call it a day. With your record, that ain't gonna hamper you."

"No need for a non-judicial punishment, sir. Nothing will reflect poorly on the Corps, sir."

The CO stared at me for a long time hoping I'd cough up some details but I stood rigidly at attention, giving him nothing but the stony face I'd learned in boot camp.

"Go on then, get out of here."

TWENTY

Samantha

A DAM'S CREW CAME IN THE NIGHT I RETURNED FROM ENGLAND.
"You look good," Eve commented.

"Do I? Because I feel like shit."

"Okay, I was lying to make you feel better. You look like you went on a bender in Reno and are still hung over, rather than a ten-day vacation to jolly England."

"The Reno description is pretty close to how I feel. Besides England isn't very sunny. Lots of rain." It had mirrored my mood.

"Sorry I pushed you on soldier boy."

I didn't bother correcting her. Gray wasn't even around to appreciate it. Oh Gray. That stupid asshole. I hated and loved him at the same time.

One by one Gray's friends came up to the bar to tell me how much he missed me.

"How come he's not here saying it?" I said curtly.

"Because if he'd stayed around till you got back, he'd be absent without leave, court martialed, and kicked to the curb," Bo shot back just as curtly.

That shut me up, but I wasn't interested in hearing reasonable things about Gray Phillips so I made Eve serve them the rest of the night.

They were persistent, though. Bo and Noah showed up the rest of the week I worked, and while they didn't talk to me, I got the message. Gray missed me and he was showing me through his friends.

And it was working. Even Eve was impressed.

"He's got good friends. You can tell a lot about a guy by his friends."

It was true, but I wasn't ready to forgive him. Eve just wanted me to get over it. We hadn't made any extra tips because I didn't want to kiss anyone but Gray, not even Eve.

When Bitsy, Mom, and I came home from England, I went with them. I wasn't ready to go back to the condo, where now it was filled with my memories of Gray. At first my mom wanted to kill Gray—or at least file a police report—but then I explained that it wasn't him but some other dude who'd hit me and that I'd hit him first. She dropped it after that.

But she frowned whenever she saw me in her house, and unlike after Will died, she started making comments about how little birds pushed out of the nest should learn to survive on their own. Her most recent comment was about how older sisters were supposed to be good examples for their younger sisters.

"Am I screwing you up, Bitsy?" I asked, dragging myself out of my bedroom about noon one day, wearing hobo overalls and not bothering to brush my hair.

"Nope. I've accepted that you are pathetic and weak and I'm the stronger sister," Bitsy said airily. I winced but she wasn't wrong so I just shut up and ate my cereal. Tired of my moroseness, she jabbed me with her finger. "Why'd you guys break up?"

God, what to tell Bitsy. "I think he got scared and then I got scared back."

"Because you didn't want to move to San Diego? So you're making him choose between the career he loves and you? What is it that you're giving up here? A knitting group?" Bitsy gave me no quarter.

"My family." It was a weak argument, and I knew it.

"You'll always have us. It's not like Mom and Dad wouldn't pay for you to fly back every month if you wanted to."

"What are you going to do in three years?" Yes, I was changing the subject.

"Chicken," she said softly. "One thing I liked about Gray was that you smiled a lot when he was around. Anyway, be a sad sack. I don't care. I'm going to go to medical school and be a transplant surgeon. Save lives." She flexed her fingers.

"I thought you were going to law school?"

"No way!"

I reached across the table and patted her arm. "That's awesome, but does Mom know this?"

"Of course," Bitsy said, annoyed.

Then I laughed and couldn't stop. Bitsy stood up and stomped around the kitchen. "What's so funny?"

"Oh, Bitsy. I love you. You are the absolute best."

Whatever expectations people had of Bitsy, she didn't care. She made her own path. If my fifteen-year-old sister could do that, couldn't I be brave enough?

I MOVED BACK INTO THE condo. The sheets still smelled like Gray, and I cried the first time I washed them as if I were cleaning him out of my life. I couldn't forget about him; he wouldn't let me. At first, I received phone calls and then voice mail messages. I deleted his entry from my recent call list and binned the messages. After a week of silence from my end, he began texting me once a day, at the end of his day.

Initially, his texts made me angry and I deleted the messages without even reading them. In the second week, I began reading them and was surprised at how ordinary and conversational they were. It was like a diary entry of how he spent his days. And he ended each "conversation" all the same—late at night, right before he went to bed—he sent me a three word message.

I love you.

As July wound down, I started to prepare for classes at Central. When I thought about the fantasies I'd cooked up about Gray and me together on campus, my heart ached so much I actually had to rub my chest, but no amount of medicine was going to ease the pain. I attended two more painful lunches with Carolyn and David. Tucker came to both; he had been extra nice since the Gray incident. I was just glad he'd never brought it up.

When classes started, none of them interested me. I was both bored and extremely busy. Eighteen credit hours were too many for me, even though I'd quit bartending. Making friends with eighteen- and nineteen-year-olds was painful. The seniors were the only people my age, but I didn't have anything in common with them either. Rather than go drinking with them, I would find myself down at Gatsby's where Eve still worked. Sometimes I'd see AnnMarie or Grace or Bo or Noah around campus, but I avoided them as much as possible. I didn't want to be around reminders of Gray.

I missed him though, so much. I missed his body next to mine. I missed his smell. I missed just talking to him. I'd never really given him a chance to explain and the distance from it all made me reflect on how maybe I couldn't believe everything Ethan Drake had said to me. After all, he threatened to lie about what had happened between us, which had been a big old nothing up until I hit him and he returned the favor. But whenever I got to that point, I remembered Gray apologizing so profusely. What did he have to apologize for if he hadn't meant to test me? That was a question that would only be answered if I talked to him.

And as every day passed and I ached all over for him, I could feel my defenses weakening and lowering. His persistent contact in spite of my stubborn silence made my insides mush. I started looking forward to his texts and wished he'd message me more often. Like five or ten times a day. By the end of the third week of classes, I'd made up my mind.

"He's texted me again," I told Eve. "He has since I got back from London. Every night, two texts for over two months." I was a little awed by his dedication.

"What do they say? Like sexy stuff or I miss you stuff? Or I'm a huge dickhead and I'm sorry stuff."

I nodded. "All of it but mostly everyday texts. Today I received *'Hey got caught about two steps from commissary during colors. Sux.'*" I read it off my phone, then I tucked it away and played with the beer Eve had served me an hour ago. It was warm and tasted horrible.

"What's that mean?"

"If you're outside and they play this particular song, you can't move. You have to stand at attention, but if you're indoors then you can move about."

"So like Simon Says, only military style."

"Kind of. What do you think it means?"

"That the military likes to play games?"

"No, not colors, the texting," I said impatiently.

"Dunno. He's weird, remember? We told you to stay away from him."

"No, you told me to pursue him and then you high fived me after I told you I'd experienced the whole head-thrown-back, screaming orgasm thing, *then* you told me to stay away from him."

"Yeah I guess I did say all that, but I've always maintained he was weird. Your dates were like out of a *Field & Stream* magazine. Hunting, fishing?"

"Don't forget the skydiving."

"Yeah, the one date that ended with a near-death experience followed by a run in with a druggie who called you names and hit you."

"I think I share too much with you," I muttered.

"He's a rebound guy. It's easy to get over them." Eve hummed "Summer Lovin'."

"I don't think I can. I love him," I admitted. Tears were forming and I picked up the soggy beverage napkin to dab them away.

Her humming stopped short. "No."

"Yes."

"You're crazy. He's your rebound guy. Now you can hook up with someone more permanent!" she cried.

"Why does he have to be the rebound guy?"

"Because that's how it works. You always have one person in between relationships who hits the reset button."

"The reset button on what? My feelings? My vagina? I think after two years I've been officially reset."

Eve looked at me uncertainly for a moment and then rallied. "I've got this great guy—" I waved her off.

"I think I'm a one man kind of girl. I know what it feels like to be in true love. It's not just the longing for a body next to you, but his particular body. It's *his* smell and *his* touch you miss. It's his laughter and his sense of adventure."

"So you're just going to go back to him after he did that totally douchebag move?"

"It was a douchebag move. Like in the pantheon of douchebaggery, he would be at least on the royal court."

"So you recognize this but you're still going?"

"Eve, I've spent my short life playing it safe. And I still got burned. I lost my husband and my heart currently feels like it was trampled by a rhinoceros. I can't hurt like this any more. So I'm going to take a chance. It might be the stupidest thing I do, but at least I'm doing something. I'm not waiting for life to come to me. I'm going out and leaping across the cavern and hoping somebody is there to catch me on the other side."

"And if there isn't?"

"Then I fall and I get back up again. I go out to San Diego, and I tell him I'm going to give him another chance, and if he fucks up then I leave him. But at least I'm giving myself a chance at happiness."

Eve looked at me with sad eyes, and she shook her head.

"I know you don't agree with me, but what's the worst thing that can happen to me? The worst thing has already happened—I lost him. The best thing is that he realizes what a mistake he's made and he trusts me. But whatever it is, there's a connection between the two of us that I hadn't felt since I was with Will, and God, I know what a lucky bitch I am to get that feeling, to have that soul-deep connection with someone, not just once, but twice. I'm going to pursue that until it's dead and beaten into the ground. I could be a total fool for giving Gray another chance. But I'll be a fool who exhausted every avenue in front of her, and when I look back on this moment, I'll never wish I'd tried harder. I'll never say 'I wish I'd done something different,' which is what I've been saying since Will died. I wished I'd moved to Alaska with him. I wish I'd married him the first time he asked me, right out of high school. I wished I would've been more enthusiastic about his dreams instead of selfishly thinking about mine all the time. I'm going to do this, Eve."

Stunned in to silence by my monologue, she said nothing. Then she gave me a rueful smile and a small, one-armed hug. "Go get him, tiger."

TWENTY-ONE

Gray

Back at the base, my days simultaneously ran together and refused to end. Every night I went home and worked on the afghan, or BG as I called it, because I was a Marine and we only ever referred to anything by its initials. BG stood for Big Gesture but could've also stood for Big Garbage, since that piece of shit looked like yarn that had been chewed up and vomited out by some large animal. Hopefully when I showed it to her she would realize it meant that I was placing her first in my life and that I was trusting her with my damaged heart, the one that I realized I now wore outside of my body, exposed.

I slept, ate, exercised, trained, worked. Whatever calling I thought I had here was missing. I'd left all my ambition and my soul at the feet of one girl. But she hadn't stomped on it. I'd been the one to grind all that we could have had into the dust with my size thirteen boot. Ironically, I was better suited to serving now. The fear I'd once had watching over these guys was nothing compared to the fear I'd had watching Sam fall out of the sky or the fear that burrowed deep in the back recesses of my mind that I'd never win her back. Those were real fears. The fear of leadership wasn't even close.

"Marine, you are one sad sack." Captain Dailey looked up at me over his long, hawkish nose. The bushy, beetle-shaped eyebrows were furrowed together, forming one long, hairy snake over the tops of his eyes. I stared at the row of fur in fascination, waiting for it to crawl off. I was back in his office to hear yet another lecture on the glory of the Corps.

"Yessir." I snapped off a knife-sharp salute. You said, "Sir, yes sir," even if your commanding officer told you to suck his dick.

"I haven't seen your reenlistment papers." I guess he'd conveniently forgotten I'd already told him I wasn't reenlisting.

"No, sir."

"Why's that, Marine? You're too soft for us now?"

"No, sir." If anything I was more hardened and determined than ever. My goals had shifted but I wasn't revealing that to the captain.

He stared at me, trying to wait me out, but I'd learned a few things in my seven years of service and the mantra that they should never see you sweat was one of the important ones. Show a weakness and they'd needle you forever under the guise of making you a stronger warrior.

Maybe that was how you created a better Marine, but I wasn't convinced that trying to find someone's weakness and exploit it always made good sense—but I knew better than to tell the CO my thoughts on the matter. Instead I stood with my heels together so that I stood straight as a tree and as unmoving as a steel post. My arms were glued to my side, fingers pointed straight down. I could have been a plum line, my bearing was so perfectly erect and straight. I'd practiced this pose for years watching Dad and Pops. I'd stood in front of the mirror and saluted. I'd had the best salute in boot and was even praised for it, when they weren't busy spitting obscenities in my face and mocking me for being a hard charger.

My dad had never forced me into this. I had been happy I was going to fulfill the dreams he and Pops had of one of the Phillips boys carrying on the tradition. I'd even had those dreams myself. Of Carrie and I having a son who'd be in the Marines. And maybe he'd be an officer, and it'd be a proud moment for both of us where we'd choke back manly tears.

Being a Marine had been what I'd wanted to do for as long as I can remember and now I was going to give it up for a girl. But it all felt right to me.

Captain Dailey sighed and thrust his short fingers through his non-existent hair. "At ease, Marine."

I let my body relax, shoulders dropped, grateful for the rest. I folded my arms behind my back.

"I don't understand you, Phillips. You've an exemplary record, a high tolerance for bullshit, and a sterling family history in the Corps. You'll probably make gunnery sergeant in record time. What's out there in the civilian world that's worth throwing this away for?"

I hoped the question was rhetorical because I didn't have a good answer. If pressed, I was going to lie and say college but I was afraid my lack of enthusiasm for sitting in a lecture hall with a couple hundred snot-nosed teenagers who thought it would be funny to make pew pew pew sounds when I walked by would be all too evident.

Captain Dailey didn't need an answer. He paced in front of me for ten minutes, giving me a lecture on the glories of being a Marine.

"It is an honor to be a Marine. We have the smallest number of men compared to any other military branch but we are the first to be called out. We stand constantly ready and can be shipped out in twenty-four hour notice because the president knows that we are always ready. The Marines were called on first to lead the charge into battle. The Marines were the first to orbit the moon. John Glenn was a Marine. John Wayne wanted to be one. The Marines are first, ready, able. Our fighting force is so fierce that the Germans called us *Teufels Hunden*."

He was really worked up using the German word so I threw him a bone. "Devil Dogs, sir!"

"That's right. We're the Devil Dogs, the first to go…" His steam was running out. *Last to know.* I finished the saying in my head.

He walked around and dropped heavily into his chair. "We need men like you, Staff Sergeant Phillips. Not just because of your record or your family legacy. You care about what happens to the other men here. You wear your leadership lightly and those under you know it. Think about it. There's always going to be room in the boat for you."

"Yes sir." I saluted.

"Dismissed." He waved a weary hand at me.

I walked as fast as I could without making it seem like I was running. Captain Dailey's speech was one I'd heard before in a million variations but it still struck me hard. I did love the Marines. I loved, in a non-sappy, brotherly way, the guys I slept beside in the sand for days without a shower.

I'd still stay close to those men. I stayed in contact with Bo and Noah and they'd been out for two years. I'd keep coming back here to Camp Pendleton to check in with old buddies. I'd be a Marine for life, even after I got out. No one would think less of me. I just had to convince myself of that. It was all worth it. Letting this go so that I could be with Sam.

Later that night, I texted her as I did every night.

Almost bit my tongue to prevent from laughing when a poolie (new guy for you Army folks) got my rank wrong today. They're supposed to greet every individual higher in rank than them with a salute and acknowledgement of rank. A lot just use "good morning, sir" no matter what time of day it is but this one said "Good morning, Gunnery Sergeant." It was dusk. I patted him on the shoulder but I could hear a Lance Corporal chewing him out. I haven't heard back from you about my flying up to see you. I'm still working on getting some days off.

I debated telling her I was coming regardless but figured that sounded too threatening. I'd been texting her so that I was constantly in her thoughts, not so that I could creep her out. Of course, it was possible that she deleted my texts before even reading them. Or that she'd blocked me and I didn't know it. Could she do that?

I grilled myself a hamburger and washed it down with a bottle of Miller, and then took another bottle into my small living room. I flicked on the television to ESPN, picked up the instructional book I'd bought a week ago and the mess of yarn and needles. I was trying to knit the blue section of the flag with the white stars—the part that had stumped Sam—only doing it so that the stars were knitted into the pattern instead of added later. Intarsia was what Sam had called it. Fucking impossible is what it was.

I'd started and ripped out the section what seemed like a thousand times. It'd taken me a week just to figure out the basic stitches and how to get the tension right. I'd had to remind myself that I could do amazing things with weapons and tanks and even excelled at fine motor skill dexterity tasks, but holding two needles in one hand while threading yarn in and out was about the most complicated fucking thing I'd ever had to do.

What I currently had going was a lumpy mess with loose stitches creating a misshapen thing that looked like a geometry test gone wrong. There were no right angles, only waves of misstitched edges. But at this point, I wasn't ever going to finish if I started over, so I just went forward. It'd be the ugliest part of the flag, but somehow I'd gotten it into my head that if I presented this to Sam, she'd fall on her knees in joy.

In fact, I'd dreamed of that moment more than once. In my dreams, the stupid thing was perfectly created, but that didn't matter as much as Sam hugging it to her chest and then stripping down to her birthday suit and begging me to take her hard. Or sometimes I imagined that our reunion would start with my face between her legs. Either way, it ended with me doing her for hours as she gasped out my name in time to my thrusts. Unfortunately, since it was only a goddamn dream, I woke up with messed-up sheets, a hard-on, and an aching heart.

Weirdly, knitting actually made me feel closer to Sam. I imagined she was knitting at the same time that I was. Although given our two-hour time difference she was probably sleeping. Still, I felt some kind of kinship. I can't say that I understood why she liked knitting, but I hoped the effort would make her understand how much I loved her.

A knock interrupted both the Padres game and my futile struggles with the yarn and wooden poles. I stuck those under the sofa cushion. I didn't need that kind of hazing out on a training mission.

"What's up—" My greeting died in my throat as I gazed at the figure of my ex-girlfriend. The one who'd cheated on me with the local Marine recruiter. The one who nearly passed on her STI, had I not caught her in the act. Yeah, I had zero to say to her, and I let the door close.

Too quick for me, Carrie shot through a narrow opening and into my apartment. I needed to get into one of those condo units that had a security door in the front, like Sam's place. I grabbed the door and held it open so she was clear about where I wanted her to be. Outside.

"Scuttlebutt around base is that you met someone."

"Get out."

She ignored me and started to walk around the room. I could see a stray bit of yarn peeking out from the bottom of the cushion and panicked. Slamming the door shut, I strode over to the couch and sat on top of the cushion, hoping one of the wooden needles didn't stab me in the ass.

"What do you want?"

Carrie wandered around, putting her hands on my things. I wanted to get up and shove her out the door. It was like she was touching things and trying to put her stamp of ownership on it. Made me angry and annoyed. The only females I'd ever want in this place were Sam and my mom.

"Just wondered what you were up to. You haven't been out with the guys."

"Don't know why you're keeping tabs on me." I crossed my arms and hooked one ankle over the opposite knee. It was weird that she knew what I was doing.

"I still care about you." Carrie sat down next to me, so close I could smell the perfume and feel the heat off her body. She looked rail thin. I tried to move away but was stymied by the arm of the couch.

That horrifying statement and her placement right next to me made me jump up. I went over to the door. What if Sam came and saw her here? It was an irrational though, but still.

"Okay," I said, and then grimaced when I saw the tip of a knitting needle sticking out from beneath the cushion. If Carrie shifted just to her right, she might scrape her leg and then—oh fuck it. I walked back over and sat down next to her and pressed my bare calf against the needle in hopes of shoving it back. No go. The weight of my ass was preventing the needle from shifting and all I got was a sharp stab in the calf muscle.

Carrie had watched my gallop from the couch to the door back to the couch again in wide-eyed amazement but I couldn't look away from the door, praying Sam wouldn't suddenly show up. I checked my phone. Nothing.

I didn't know if I was relieved or pissed that the silence from her end continued. But that didn't stop the quickening of my heartbeat.

Carrie took my resettling by her side as an invitation and pressed one hand behind my neck and slid the other across my chest. It was an embrace, and she was marking me with her stupid perfume. I'd have to shower and then wash these clothes. I wanted to pick her up and carry her to the door but I wasn't ever going to touch her again.

"I don't know why you're here or what you want but you need to leave." I held myself stiff in her embrace so she could tell I did not want her touching me, much like I didn't want her touching anything in my home.

"Baby," she whispered in my ear, her minty breath wafting by my nose. "I miss you so much."

That was it. I stood up, uncaring about the knitting needle and only wanting her to leave.

"I don't miss you and I haven't for some time. Yes, I am seeing someone else and I care about her a lot. You need to leave now," I repeated.

She moved and then, as anticipated, scraped her leg along the needle. "Ouch, what is that?" She stood and lifted the cushion and found my mess of dark blue yarn under the couch.

"Oh my God." She crushed the mess against her chest. Shit, could I wash yarn? I strode over and yanked it out of her hands and threw it on a nearby chair.

"Get out," I repeated and pointed at the door.

"Did I turn you gay?" she cried.

"What?" Following her train of thought was like trying to keep track of a jumping bean.

"Did I turn you gay?" she asked again, trying to look sad but secretive pleasure flirted at the corners of her mouth. God, what did I ever find attractive about this woman? "When I had that fling with

Lieutenant Maritz, did you turn to guys? Oh my God, Gray, tell me it isn't so!"

As if she could turn me gay. Was she fucking nuts? I shook my head at her presumptuousness. "You're a dumb woman, Carrie. It doesn't work that way. And guess what? I don't care what you think my sexual preference is as long as you understand it isn't you."

Carrie swayed over to me, swinging her skinny hips in an action that might've turned me on four years ago but now just looked like she had a weird hitch in her step. I swung the door open so she could take that hitch right on outside but she paused in front of me. The courtyard was occupied by a few people, but no one that looked like Sam. It was probably the first time in months that I'd been relieved I hadn't had a Sam sighting. Every other night I'd glance out there, hoping I'd see her come up the walk. No dice. But with Carrie standing far too close to me, I was glad that Sam was thousands of miles away.

"I'm glad I stopped by, Gray. I had this feeling that you needed me. You've been on my mind, and when I went down to the Enlisted Club and didn't see you, I was concerned. I'm glad I followed my instincts and came here." Carrie reached out a manicured finger and ran the tip down the front of my T-shirt.

The sad fact was that I *had* allowed Carrie to turn me off of women. I started mistrusting all of them because of her stupid behavior. I'd stopped thinking in terms of relationships. I'd only thought they were good for fucking and not much more. If the med student treated me like a human dildo it was because that's about how much emotion I'd put into it.

Sam was right. I had grieved and I was bitter. And I needed to let it all go.

"Thanks for your offer, but I'm not interested." How many times did I have to say that before she left? Carrie stepped even closer and the scent of her perfume made my stomach churn. I really needed her out of there and she clearly wasn't going on her own accord. Placing a hand on her chest, I stalled her progress and started sliding her out the door, slowly so not as to cause injury. I held both her biceps and easily lifted her over the threshold. The shock of it made her immobile for a minute and I was able to shut and then lock the door.

The yarn, needles, and mangled blue material looked like a nasty collection of fibers. I didn't have the time or patience tonight. Carrie knocked on the door but I ignored her, turning up the television louder to drown out her profanities. I left the TV and the knitting and went into the bedroom. Two beers and five instructional knitting videos on the iPad later, I went to sleep with renewed hope. One day closer to my End of Active Service date and one day closer to being with Sam.

"I REALLY NEED TO SEE you. Can you fit me in?" I begged. There was the sound of flipping pages as Dorothy looked through her appointment book.

"Can you be here in thirty minutes?" Dorothy asked.

"Yes." I jumped up and started stuffing my paraphernalia in my pack.

"I'll only have a little time for you in between my class," she warned.

"I'll take whatever you have. I just need to see you." I hung up before she could tell me no. Grabbing my pack, I looked twice to see if there was anyone I knew outside, and then sprinted to my truck. The drive to the shop was thirty minutes. I made it in twenty-five.

"Sergeant Phillips," a delighted squeal greeted me from Dorothy's mother. I leaned down and hugged the tiny German woman, placing a kiss on her parchment-thin skin.

"Hey, Mrs. Bend, good to see you."

Mrs. Bend dragged me over to the sofa in the back corner and tugged at my pack. I let her have it. The expression on her face was one of dismay as she pulled out the mess I'd made of the yarn I'd bought two weeks ago at her daughter's yarn shop. "What've you done, my dear boy?"

"Mrs. B, pardon my language, but this shit is hard." I tugged at one of the stray yarn threads that dangled off the needles. "I can sew on a patch or a button or even darn a hole in my sock if necessary, but this is beyond me."

Mrs. B flipped the knitted mess over a couple of times. Her purple fingernail pointed at a small white splotch in the middle. "And this is?" she asked.

"It's the star, Mrs. B." I leaned back and drew a hand over my face in frustration. "I'm never going to figure this out."

"Now, now, no need for that." She laid the yarn mess in my lap. "You'll have to take it apart though and restart. Let me watch you for a while to see if I can pinpoint where you're going wrong."

As I unraveled the yarn Mrs. B asked, "Are you sure you want to start with the intarsia technique? It's quite difficult."

I nodded grimly. "You know the story, Mrs. B." I'd told Mrs. B and her daughter Dorothy the whole sad saga of my relationship with Sam and how I'd fucked it all up. Mrs. B patted my arm. This was my grand gesture. I was going to knit Sam an afghan and take it to her the next time I had a three-day leave, which might not be before my contract ran out if my CO had anything to say about it.

"Well, I think this is very sweet and if it doesn't win her back, then I have a wonderful grandniece over in Sausilito. She's a nurse and you two would get along great."

"Thanks, Mrs. B." *Never going to happen,* I thought, but I just gave Mrs. B a smile and tried to figure out when I was supposed to bring in the opposite colored yarn. Because I was paying such close attention to her, I almost missed the commotion at the front of the store that stirred up when Hamilton and Ruiz from my platoon burst in.

"What're you guys doing here?" I asked suspiciously. Quickly, I moved the yarn stuff to the side and pretended like I was just relaxing. On a sofa in a yarn shop. With Mrs. B sitting right next to me.

"What are *you* doing here?" Hamilton scanned the shop in disbelief. "Is this a store for old ladies?"

"No, you dumbass, it's a yarn store." Given that everyone else in the shop was likely over fifty, I could see how Hamilton made that error. "What're you doing here?" I repeated. Standing up, I glowered at both of them.

"We followed you."

"What the hell!" I practically shouted it out. Mrs. B made a clucking sound of disappointment. "Sorry, Mrs. B."

"We heard a rumor." Hamilton lowered his voice but he was a drill instructor and the low voice of a DI is pretty much normal tone for anyone else. "You leaving the Corps because you want to knit? How come you can't do both?"

"I'm guessing that Carrie's saying I'm not re-upping for another contract because being near one of you and not having you is too painful for me. Which of you is the lucky guy?"

Ruiz jerked this thumb toward Hamilton.

"I'm a pretty tempting package." Hamilton smoothed a hand down his shirt. "I do tend to drive the ladies wild. Good to know my animal magnetism affects the lads in equal measure."

Ruiz looked upset and near bursting with something to say.

"What is it, Ruiz?"

"Why not me instead of Hamilton? Don't you think I'm attractive? Fun to be with?"

We both stared open mouthed at Ruiz. Hamilton recovered first. "Dude, what?"

Ruiz looked offended. "Just wondering why Hamilton?"

"Oh Jesus H. Ruiz, really?" I ran my hand over my recently shorn head.

"Yeah, I mean he's not better looking than me."

"That's not what your mom said last night, Ruiz," Hamilton shot back, offended that Ruiz thought that he was better looking.

I shook my head. Of all the comments Ruiz could make. Throwing my arm around the smaller guy, I said, "Ruiz, you're just too short for me." And then I thought about Sam and her small frame, which fit me just fine. "Plus." I dropped my voice low enough so just Ruiz and Hamilton could hear. "Hamilton's got a small dick and I'm the only one who doesn't care about that."

"Fuck you, Phillips. My dick is just fine. Your sister…"

"I don't have a sister, fuckwad," I cut in, forgetting about where we were. "You assholes. Knitting has fuck all to do with sex."

Dorothy came over with a big-ass frown on her face and I felt horrible. "Sorry, Dorothy, forgot where we were."

She shook her head and gestured toward the door. "Why don't you go outside and finish your profanity-laced sex discussion there?"

"Sorry." Abashed, I started out the door. I'd have to bring a big arrangement of flowers or something next time so that Dorothy and her mom would let me back into the store. Ruiz and Hamilton shuffled behind me, mumbling, "Sorry ma'am" to everyone as we walked out.

"No, don't let them leave," another lady cried out.

"God, no. Who cares what they're saying? We haven't had such eye candy in here since the last Lion trunk show."

"Oh, honey, if you're comparing yarn to this, you need to get out more."

"You're right. Hot young Marines just don't measure up to Lion yarn," the other woman shot back sarcastically.

Once outside I realized I'd forgotten my knitting. Thankfully Mrs. B stuck her head out the door and handed me my pack. "You're improving. Come back next week and I'll help you again."

"Thanks, Mrs. B." I took the bag.

"Don't forget, the color switch happens in the back. Trap the yarn, dear, in the back."

Hamilton and Ruiz started snickering. Mrs. B gave us a cheery wave and I stomped off to my truck without looking back. I could hear the dickwads clumping behind me like they were going on a march.

"In the back." Hamilton and Ruiz roared.

Later that evening, Hamilton came over.

"You think this is the most girlie thing ever?" I gestured with my needles. Hamilton took a long swig of his beer and then watched me fumble with the yarn for a few rows.

"Maybe if you were any good at it."

"I think my fingers are too big."

"That's what the ladies tell me too."

Shaking my head, I eyed the pattern Mrs. B had drawn for me to see how crappy the next few inches should look.

Hamilton offered his own assessment. "Looks like a piece of dog crap if he ate the yarn, got the runs and then shit it out."

"Thanks, man." I threw it down. "Fuck. What am I doing?"

"Don't know. What are you doing?"

"Why do we fight, Hamilton?"

"To protect our country, preserve freedoms, uphold the honor of the Corps."

"But what's the point of all that?"

"Regular access to prime pussy?"

"God. No." I rubbed my head. But truthfully I had gotten it into my head that Sam would forgive me if she could see how much effort I was expending on her behalf. Did it make sense? In my confused, fucked-up mind it did. Sighing, I said, "Close enough." I picked up the needles again.

"So knitting is the same as being in the Corps?"

"Close enough," I mumbled again and set to work once more.

Samantha

I PULLED UP TO THE Anderson house. It was a large brick monstrosity. I think about five families could have fit into the Anderson home but it housed only two people now—David and Carolyn. I guess that's why it was so easy for them to remain married despite the fact that they didn't really care about each other. They spent weeks without seeing each other. I walked around to the side door, the one I'd always used, and let myself in. Donna, the Anderson's housekeeper, was sitting at the gleaming marble island, a coffee cup by her side, flipping through a magazine. "Hey, Sam," she greeted me as I snuck in.

"Carolyn around?"

"In the sunroom." Donna started to rise and get me something to eat but I waved her off.

"I don't need anything, Donna. I'm not even sure how long I'll be." Even though I'd planned my speech to Carolyn all night, I was feeling nervous and sick to my stomach. I wished Tucker was here or that David was better at comforting his wife. Worried that Carolyn was going to need someone, I planned to talk to Tucker directly after.

Donna gave me a concerned look, but I was halfway through the kitchen and out the door before she could ask me what was wrong. The sunroom was a long, screened-in porch that overlooked the pool. When we were younger, Tucker, Will, and I all played out here, but when my parents moved out west of town and installed a pool, we started gravitating toward my house.

The Anderson house was oppressive. Even though Carolyn tried to decorate it in bright, sunny tones, the unhappiness of her marriage and the disapproval that Tucker and Will suffered under because they never lived up to their father's expectations made the house gloomy and unlivable. The sunroom, however, had been a place of noisy games and laughter when it had been the three of us kids here. Now Carolyn sat there almost every day with a book and a cup of tea. I didn't know if she read the book or drank the tea or if they were just props to make her look like she was occupied and not reliving scenes from the past.

"Hey, Carolyn," I called from the doorway, not wanting to startle her. A big smile wreathed her face as she took me in.

"Samantha, what a nice surprise." She walked over and grabbed my hands, pulling me in for a hug and kiss on the cheek. "I was just thinking about the graduation party we'd held for Will and you here." Leading me over to the settee, Carolyn sat me down and poured me a cup of steaming hot tea. It was always hot no matter what time of day or what the temperature was outside. I took a careful sip and tucked a slip of my hair behind my head. I didn't correct her. The graduation party had been held at a nearby park because we'd co-hosted it with my family. Maybe Carolyn was thinking of Tucker's graduation, which had been held here and which had been kind of crazy because it ended up with a lot of fully-clothed people in the pool.

Later that night, Will had snuck some weed from his brother's stash and we'd smoked it in the pool house and made out. But I didn't want to share that with Carolyn so I kept my mouth shut.

"We had some good times here," I said. It was true. While we didn't come here a ton and we were mostly at my house, as long as Will and I were together it had been a good time. I lifted up the box I'd brought with me.

"Carolyn, I want you to have these things." I held out the big white box to her. She made no move to take it. It was heavy so I couldn't keep holding it. I dropped the box to my lap.

Refusing to look at me, Carolyn continued as if I hadn't said a word to her. "It's good that he left, your friend," she clarified. "He didn't seem to fit in with us." Who knew what Tucker had told her.

"Carolyn," I started again, but she just talked right over me.

"How is that afghan going? I was over at the condo the other day and saw you'd taken it down. Did you finish it? I think it would make a great Christmas gift for Tucker. Something you made in remembrance for Will."

I'd forgotten she had keys to the condo and it was a little weird that she'd gone in there without telling me. But this too was part of my own weakness. I'd relied on my family too long, not picking up the reins of my own life. This was going to be so hard. Rubbing my forehead, I thought about the best way to make it clear to her that whatever dreams she had for me and Will or me and Tucker weren't ever going to come true. "I'm in love with him," I finally said.

"Oh, I know. We all love him." she said, deliberately misunderstanding. "I guess that's why it's so hard to have his things in your home?" She nodded toward the box on my lap. "I just know you'll regret it if you give them away."

"I'm not giving them away." I told her softly. "I'm returning them to you. I know you'll treasure them, but it just isn't right for me to have all these things."

The flags, the medals, his uniforms. I couldn't keep those things and go to Gray with an open heart. He was a good man and an understanding one, but these things were better off with Will's family. I knew it and I think Carolyn knew it too even if she didn't want to acknowledge it. I had my own Will treasures. The stuffed animal he'd won for me at the school carnival. The tickets to our senior prom. Pictures. Those were the mementos of our life together. The medals and honors represented Will's life in the Army and I felt like they were better off with his mother than with me.

"I love you, Carolyn. I loved Will. He'll always be with me but I'm ready to love again. I hope you understand that."

Silent tears dripped down her face but she acted like it was nothing. "Tucker's been making noise about going back to law school. Wouldn't that be nice?"

He'd done no such thing, but I lied again. "Yeah, that would be nice." It wasn't ever going to happen.

"I was thinking of the time that you and Will handed out candy at

Halloween. You dressed up like Gomez and Morticia Addams."

I laughed a little. "And Tucker was Lurch. And all the kids said I was too short to be Morticia."

"You looked so beautiful on your wedding day."

Carolyn's unhappiness was breaking my heart and I did love her, like a second mother. For a moment, I felt myself weaken. Would it be so wrong to stay here and sit in this sunroom and talk about Will for the rest of my life? But my heart was pulling me in the direction of California. Will was my past and Gray was my future.

I stood up then, leaving the box on the table. She didn't even look at me, and the guilt of loving someone other than Will threatened to sweep me under. If I stayed another minute, my resolve might break. "I'm sorry, Carolyn. I loved being an Anderson. I loved being Will's girl. But it's time for all of us to move forward."

I waited for a response but got nothing. Sighing I turned and started to leave. Her whispered words barely reached me. "I want you to be happy too."

"Thank you," I choked out. She didn't say another word, didn't turn toward me, so I left her in the sunroom, the sunlight not quite reaching her sofa, her tea untouched.

I wiped away my tears with the pads of my hands and walked toward the kitchen. Donna was standing up, either by some sixth sense recognizing something was wrong or because she'd been eavesdropping. I didn't care which. "She's gonna need something."

"I know just the thing," Donna said and then patted me on the shoulder. Pulling me in for a hug, Donna whispered. "You're doing the right thing. This family's going to be all right."

Maybe it would and maybe it wouldn't but as my mom had said to me, the Anderson family's emotional health wasn't my responsibility.

The next conversation was with Tucker, and that was going to be a hundred times more difficult.

I'd texted Tucker the night before, asking him to meet me for lunch. He'd told me to come by the shop. I'd picked up his favorite sandwich—apple and ham on a hoagie—and two cups of fresh-squeezed orange juice. His hair was messed up and he smelled of fresh sweat. Sometimes Tucker's smell had confused me because it was so close to Will's, but now I realized it was the smell of a friend. A good friend and one that I'd miss.

He gave me a wary glance but said nothing as I spread out the goods on one of the silver tool trays.

"You'll have to wash this when we're done," I teased gently. "No one wants sandwich crumbs in their tattoo."

Tucker shrugged and ate half the hoagie in one bite. "Maybe it will be a new thing. Like food tattoos instead of a memorial one."

I made a face. Memorial tattoos were made by tattooing ashes of people's loved ones into their skin.

"What's so important that it couldn't wait?"

"I'm leaving for San Diego today," I admitted.

Tucker took a deep breath and gripped the edges of the tray between us. "Sam, I never told you this because the time wasn't right—" Tucker began. I held up my hand and gave him a sad smile.

"Don't say it, Tucker."

"You don't even know what I was going to say."

"Maybe I don't, but I want you to know that I love you like the brother I never had and I hope you'll always feel the same way toward me," I replied. Tucker looked at me and then glanced down. I blinked away a few tears that had crept into my eyes. "Don't say anything that would mar that," I whispered. I did love Tucker, and I always would, but he was Will's brother and mine too. I'd never view him any other way, and it broke my heart that I had to hurt him.

"So Gray, huh?" Tucker was fiddling with the food and refusing to look at me.

"Yes, it'll be Gray for as long as he'll have me."

"Being a soldier isn't very safe."

I didn't take the time to correct his use of "soldier." I responded, "Gray loves it. It's in his blood. If he stayed here, part of him would shrivel up. He'd suck it up and he'd fill those spaces, but he wouldn't be the same Gray that I love."

"It's not real love if he resents you for decisions he made for himself," Tucker argued.

"Maybe not, but I have real love for Gray which means letting him go pursue his dreams."

"I don't want to lose you." Tucker was still avoiding my eyes. This time the tears wouldn't be stemmed by a few blinks. I let them roll out because they were part of the process of saying goodbye as much as the words.

"I'll always be part of the Anderson family for as long as you all will have me."

Tucker breathed through his nose and grabbed me. "We'll always want you."

I hugged him tight, this man who would always be a brother in my heart even though the line that connected us was broken.

His hands clutched me, and for a moment, I reveled in the embrace, remembering what it was like to be with Will. But I pulled away from his arms and he reluctantly let me go. I dug into my pocket and pulled out the gold-and-diamond solitaire ring that had sat on my left finger for over two years. Tucker gasped when I held it out to him and backed away. His hands came up as if to ward me off.

"No way, no fucking way. That is *yours.*" He glared at me.

"No, Tuck, this is your mother's. She gave this to Will, and yeah, she got a beautiful ring in exchange from your dad, but this belongs in the Anderson family. Not with me. Not anymore." I advanced on him, and Tucker turned away. I could see he was struggling with this but I pried open his hand and place the ring inside of it.

It wasn't the loss of me that he was struggling with. I'd become Will's avatar to his family and his friends. Through me, Will was still alive in some small measure. But that was over now. It had taken me a long time to come to terms with this, but it was time to move on.

MY ENTIRE FAMILY DROVE ME to the airport. Bitsy held my hand in the backseat the entire drive. Hugs were given all around and everyone was teary. It was like I wasn't ever going to come back.

"I might be back before the week is out," I joked weakly.

"Nah, as many times as he's texted, he won't let you out of his sight for a good month," Mom said.

"You'll have to come back and visit soon. It seems like I just got off the plane." This was from my dad.

"Love you." I gave them all another round of hugs. I'd return soon, for a visit.

And then I was off. The flight to San Diego required a stop in Denver, where I considered for the hundredth time texting Gray. But I didn't want to text him. I wanted to explain to him face to face why I was taking a chance on him, and I wanted to read every emotion on his face so I could reassure myself it was the right decision.

Instead, I spent the time finishing up the skull caps I was making for donation to the Warmth for Warriors group. At the San Diego airport, I ducked into the bathroom and changed out of my shorts and T-shirt and sneakers. I wanted to knock Gray's socks off. I pulled out the red polka-dotted dress with the sweetheart neckline that Bitsy had helped me find. Its flared skirt made my waist look tiny and the three-inch cork wedge heels made me tall enough that I didn't feel like I was going to be trampled.

"Pendleton," I told the cabbie. I'd packed only a carry-on with this dress and one other change of clothing. Bitsy and my dad said they'd ship everything out to me if I needed it. I had some cash to buy some new clothes if I was going to stay longer. Hopefully I'd be calling home to send the stuff right away. Even though I'd had nightly texts from Gray, seeing me there might be too much for him.

I just didn't know so I'd made a reservation at a nearby hotel. I also had a list of knitting shops that I'd make application to and if I didn't get into one of them, then I'd try something else. My application to FIDM was sent in and hopefully I could start in the winter semester since it was too late for fall admission. I was going to be in San Diego for a while. If it didn't work out with Gray, then the city would be big enough that I wouldn't have to see him and I'd be having an adventure, all on my own.

The ride to Camp Pendleton wasn't long, and as we stopped at the gate, I paused for a moment, wondering why the heck I thought it was a good idea to come to the base. But the cab had left before I could call it back, and there I was looking at the gate station. Two young Marines manning the gate watched me. Crud. For all my planning, it hadn't occurred to me until right that moment that I should've waited until Gray got off of work, whenever that was. But I didn't even know where he lived. Only that he was stationed here. I had been too chicken to ask Bo or Noah, but that was quickly becoming a more attractive idea. I pulled out my phone when a Marine driving up in a Jeep stopped beside me.

"You lost, miss?" he questioned.

I ran a light hand over the side of my lightly curled hair, not wanting to mess it up but feeling agitated. "We both know I'm not."

"You have a tour planned?"

A tour? I pulled up the Camp Pendleton website on my phone and checked out the visitor information. A tour could be pre-arranged. "Um, maybe?" Was this guy going to help me out?

"Who was it with?"

"Sergeant Grayson Phillips?"

The Marine's eyes widened in recognition. Then he looked me over thoroughly, so thoroughly I felt like I was going through the airport security line again. "Wait here, ma'am."

TWENTY TWO

Gray

"THERE'S A SWEET HONEY OUT AT THE GATE LOOKING FOR Sergeant Phillips. She looks too good for an enlisted," Hamilton's voice called over the radio.

My heart jumped in my throat but then died because there was no way it was Sam. But it could be Carrie. "Unless she's part of a tour or has a special dispensation I guess she'll have to wait until I'm done here." It was thirty minutes before quitting time.

"By that time, some officer will have swooped in. I'll just go out and keep her company." Hamilton cut the line.

If it was Sam... I told my first sergeant I had to use the john and I jumped into my truck and sped off toward the gate.

When I got close, my heart nearly leaped out of my mouth. There was Sam, looking like the only fresh water in the desert. It was all I could do not to run to her and be the subject of intense hazing for the rest of my time. But then I realized I gave zero fucks and jumped out of my truck and ran as fast as I could to meet her.

Those guys who'd be making jokes about me being Forrest Gump or the Blade Runner or whatever else wouldn't be tucking that beauty into bed at night.

"I've always admired that about you," she said when I reached the gate.

"My running technique? The knife hands?" I held up my hands perfectly straight and she closed one soft set of fingers around them.

"No, your amazing stamina. Not even winded." Her smile, though, took my breath away, and it was naughty enough that the gate guard started choking. I gave him a dirty look, and he saluted me. Dickhead. I'd do a surprise check of his gear later. Maybe dock him for not labeling his socks or something.

I led her away from the gatehouse and up to the truck. It was a huge violation for her to be here but I couldn't send her away.

"When are you off duty?" she asked.

"Two minutes ago."

"Seriously."

"Two minutes ago."

She gave me a look and I relented. "Okay, let me go talk to my CO. He'll want an introduction but don't spend too long shaking his hand. He's never touched anything as fine as you and he might break you with his rough handling."

"I'm looking forward to some rough handling tonight."

Jesus Mary Joseph. Instant boner. "Don't say another word."

I think the smile that broke out may have stretched clear around my face. My jaw ached for days after.

I took her to Captain Dailey's office, which was another huge breach but I couldn't leave her standing at the gate station. He could give me a dozen NJPs but it wouldn't matter because I was getting out.

"Sergeant Phillips," Captain Dailey snapped at me as I was rounding the corner of the hallway with Sam's soft hand in mine. We both stopped abruptly, the skirt of Sam's dress swirling around and tangling with my legs. The soft swish of fabric against my pants intensified my feelings of relief and satisfaction. In the future, every inch of us would be entangled. Sam snapped a salute with her wrong hand but hell, who cared. She tried. I was totally right that she'd make a great Marine wife.

Captain Dailey saluted back because that's what we did—salute people. Muscle memory couldn't be denied. We looked foolish, the three of us in some weird triangle, and Sam in a red-and-white polka-dotted dress making everything around her look boring and dull.

Dailey's eyes swung toward me, zeroed in on our joined hands and then surprised me. "I hear you have forty-eight hours of leave starting right now, Sergeant."

"What?" I said in shock, not sure I'd heard him correctly.

"Forty-eight hours. Go," he barked. I didn't wait for him to say another word. I cracked off another salute and turned and walked swiftly with Sam toward the exit. The light tapping of her heels against the tiled floor signaled that I was moving too fast for her, but since Dailey had basically told me to go home and nail Sam for the next two days, I wanted that to start now. No, yesterday.

I tucked Sam into the passenger side of my truck and drove the ten miles to my apartment complex with trembling hands. Sam was silent too. My one-bedroom apartment, while tidy, wasn't much to look at. I had a sofa, a big screen TV, a small table, two chairs and then the bed in my bedroom. The walls were beige. The sofa was brown. And Sam standing in the middle in the living room looked like a juicy piece of fruit in a shitty basket.

"What's wrong?" she asked as I stood just inside the door staring at her.

Her face was serene, and she didn't sound anxious at all even though I couldn't imagine what it took for her to come here. "I'm upset," I admitted.

She looked amused instead of disturbed. "About what?"

"So many things." I stalked toward her. Her eyes widened slightly, the humor dying away. Hot desire licked up my spine at the smoldering look she returned. "I'm mad that I didn't get to come to you. I'm upset that you got to show off your big gesture before me." I circled her, trailing a few fingers over her bared shoulder and across her exposed upper back. "I'm pissed off because I can't figure out how to lick your pussy and get my dick into you at the same time."

"You have a lot of legitimate concerns," she said, though her voice was a little thick.

"Yeah and I'm also pretty torqued that I can't decide whether I want to bend you over the sofa and push your pretty dress up or rip off your clothes and throw you down on the bed."

"A dilemma of immense proportions."

You have no idea, I thought, my uniform pants so tight that I figured the zipper pull would fly off at any moment.

"How about I take off my dress now and you can ravish me on the bed and then I'll put the dress back on and you can take me against the sofa?"

Stopping in front of her, I drew her face in my hands and soaked in her presence. "Goddamn, I love you, Samantha Anderson."

"I love you too, Grayson Phillips."

I was striding toward the bedroom with her clutched to my chest before my last name passed her lips. Her dress came off and my clothes too and then we were on each other. I tried to kiss every part of her body at once but had only one mouth. Her body writhed on the bed beneath me as I made my way to her breasts, sucking in one large erect nipple and then the other. Her gasps of pleasure as I sucked and bit and molded her supple flesh with my hands reverberated in my groin.

"We have a lot of missed sex to make up for," I informed her, resting my weight on my knees and forearms as I stroked her gently with my still-hard cock. Sliding her legs up my thighs, she hooked her ankles at the base of my spine.

"Let's not waste another minute."

It was hard not to collapse on her like a beast, but I managed to hold it together so long as she didn't touch me.

"No, baby," I said, pulling her hand away from my crotch. "You're going to make me blow too soon."

"It's been a long time for me too," she whispered. The words heated my blood almost as powerfully as her touch.

"Okay, no talking either." I lifted her up so that her mouth was even with mine and we kissed. It was like home. Every touch was made with wonder because I could hardly believe she was with me.

I reached over to grab a condom, but she stopped me. Through her lashes, she peered up and stopped my heart and made all the blood rush to my dick at the same time. "It's okay. IUD."

I think I trembled like a virgin when I entered her. It was as good as I'd remembered. Or hell, maybe better. All I knew was that my meager vocabulary had no words to describe the experience. The soft clutch of her interior flesh against my lonely sensitive dick made me gasp with pleasure. I felt her everywhere, though, not just on my cock. Her hands were roaming over my shoulders and her sharp press of her heels against my back only served to make me thrust harder and faster. Against my ear I could hear her little pants of desire. I wanted to stay like this forever, wrapped entirely around her, pumping inside of her, loving her.

I didn't last long, and I was so lost from my release that I wasn't even sure she had come until I lay gasping on top of her. Rolling to my side, I felt her shuddering, which signaled she had climaxed. Thank you, I mouthed to whatever higher deity watched over female orgasms.

"Do you mind if I explain a few things?" I asked, flipping the blankets up over our legs so she wouldn't get cold. She snuggled close, and I took her silence as a yes. "First off, I want to say that I'm sorry you ever met Ethan Drake. You don't know how sorry. When I left that afternoon, after the skydiving fuck up, I intended to have a few drinks with Bo and Noah and come back. But one beer turned into whiskeys, which turned into me being too drunk to drive back to see you."

"I know," she said. "You texted me, and it was all good."

"Ethan Drake was at the house when I got there. Drake had been dishonorably discharged right before his four-year contract was up for cocaine use. He'd been using for a while, but this time he'd gotten caught in the bathroom. That couldn't be swept under the carpet. He was…" I thought for a minute and was grateful Sam didn't jump in. I needed to collect my thoughts because what happened was my fault, not Ethan Drake's.

"He always had a way with women and was notorious for sleeping around. No one liked him much, which was why his coke use was eventually leaked to superiors. He'd done it plenty of times in the bathroom before so this time he was caught because someone was sick of his shit."

"Maybe one of the members of his platoon reported him?"

"Yeah, who knows. Did us all a favor. When I saw him, all the shit that happened with Carrie came back and I just got scared." I swallowed, but the lump in my throat wouldn't go down.

"So you asked him to come over and what?" This time I heard the pain in her voice and I felt gutted.

"God, baby, no way. I was drunk and spouting off shit to Bo. I had no idea Drake was there. I went into the house, texted you, and passed out. Next thing I knew, I was waking up in a pile of drool and Adam was standing over me telling me that Drake's at your place. I raced over there and some guy let me in. I pounded on your door but…" I left the rest unsaid.

"What happened to Ethan?"

"I went home and beat the shit out of him. Noah and Bo kicked him out." I didn't tell her that Tucker had come and struck me a few times too. "I had no idea he hit you. None."

"Did he tell you that he'd hit me? What he said to me?"

"No." I forced myself not to tense up. "But I can imagine that it wasn't good. I fucked up, Sam. I didn't send Drake to you, but I didn't prevent him from going, and it's not like I didn't have second thoughts. But I don't have those doubts now."

"He said he would tell you he succeeded."

"Ah shit, baby. I wouldn't have believed him." As I said the words I realized the truth of it. I trusted Sam and nothing Ethan Drake or anyone else could say would change my mind.

"I'm sorry, too," she said.

"What for?" This surprised me. She had nothing to be sorry for.

"Because I didn't give you a chance to explain. I wouldn't open the door and I wouldn't see you before I left."

"Baby, you got nothing to be sorry about. But…" I hesitated but figured this was the time for getting our shit out, "…what made you change your mind?"

She drew her finger over my chest, making me catch my breath and stirring parts in my lower body. I drew away slightly so I didn't start jabbing her with an inappropriate erection.

"I was just tired of sitting on my thumb, you know? I figured if you told me to take a hike, I'd just get a hotel room and go about my business."

"What business is that?" I held my breath, not sure what I wanted to hear anything other than "I love you and I want to stay in your bed forever." Too bad that wasn't a real job.

"I've applied to the Fashion Institute of Design and Merchandising here in San Diego—it's a top twenty art school, you know."

I did not know this. "Um, I was going to come to Central and go to college with you," I confessed.

"Gray Phillips. You belong in the Marines." She sat up, the sheets falling down to her waist. Was my boner inappropriate now? I couldn't tell because she was naked and her tits were heaving in front of me, and I hadn't seen her in two long, lonely months. I leaned closer and kissed her collarbone, testing the waters. When she didn't move away, I drifted lower. "Are you listening to me?"

"Well, I can hear what you're saying, but my ability to process information has shut down." My mouth was now at the top of her breast. "Have I told you how gorgeous you are?"

She hmmmed. "I don't think so. Go on." Reclining on the bed, the discussion about who was moving where with whom was brushed aside so I could properly worship her body.

"Your breasts are like...are peaches overused? I mean, because they are kind of peach in color and they taste delicious. I like a good peach." I licked the tip of one nipple and then the other, blowing on them to see her quiver in response.

"This is not one of your better dirty-talking efforts, Gray," she said, but her breathlessness gave her away.

"Okay, how about, I can't wait until you're riding my face as I eat you to a screaming orgasm?"

"I think you've used that one with me before," she joked. We both laughed.

"Only cuz it's true all of the time." I hadn't realized sex could be this much fun.

I finally let her rest after our third round, but I couldn't sleep. The last time I'd been beside her, mind buzzing, I was scared out of my mind because of my feelings for her. This time, I was still full of emotion, but it was relief, gratitude, pure pleasure. Hugging her close to me, I wondered how I could've been so stupid to allow anything to come between us, particularly me. And I vowed then and there that I'd do everything in my power to make her happy for the rest of her life.

Later Samantha awoke, probably because she was hungry. Her stomach growled, and I took that as a sign.

"Chinese okay?" I asked as I headed to the phone to order something.

"Sure. Can I use the shower?"

"Anything here you want, it's yours, baby."

She made some sound in a return—a laugh, a snort—I'm not sure. I didn't care though. I was just so fucking happy she was with me. I'd just gotten done ordering about five full dishes off the menu because I was starved and she was obviously hungry by the sound of her stomach when I heard a scream from the shower. Running toward her, I swiped the Colt, my personal piece, from the nightstand and threw open the bathroom door.

"What the hell?" I yelled.

A dripping wet hand thrust out of the shower curtain holding my shower gel. "It smells like you in here."

I turned, put my gun away, and came back. When I returned, Sam had her head out of the curtain, blinking wet drops of water out of her eyes. She looked like a kitten left out in the rain, and I wanted to lick all those drops away.

"You screamed because it smells like me? Is it that bad?" I leaned against the vanity, arms crossed and ankles crossed, torn between amusement and exasperation.

"I've always wondered if you wore a cologne but the hints of a scent were always so subtle. Sometimes I smelled it and other times I didn't. It was never overpowering. Always exactly the right amount applied. Sometimes smells get so strong at the bar, but you always had the right amount—tantalizing. I just wanted to lick you all over."

My nonchalant stance changed instantly. I stalked closer until I was just inches away. "I'm getting a clear shower curtain so I can see your sexy body while you shower."

"Why don't you just get in here?"

"Not sore? I thought I worked you hard already."

"You did, but I still want you." Her eyes were dark with sexual promise. She was love and temptation in one small, irresistible package. I shucked my clothes and climbed in with her.

Sam rubbed her hands over my chest and smiled up at me. "You know you're my adventure."

Lifting her into my arms so I could kiss her properly, I said, "And you know I'll keep you safe."

THE NEXT MORNING I TOOK her to the knitting shop.

"I'm surprised we left the apartment," Sam cooed in my ear. She leaned over the console of my truck as far as the seatbelt would allow. It was the first time I'd wished I had bench seats, but then maybe it was a good thing there was a barrier between us. I had a hard time keeping my hands off her.

"As much as I'd like to have a repeat of this morning..." I paused, remembering the vision of Sam bent over the kitchen table, her red, polka-dot dress pushed up right over her ass so I could drill her from behind. Reaching down, I adjusted my now-hard dick. At this rate, I'd have to sit in the truck for at least ten minutes before I could face Mrs. Bends and her daughter. "Anyway, I wanted to show you something."

I'd packed the rest of the knitting stuff in a bag and carried it out to the truck while Sam was showering. "What happened to the flag you were working on?"

"Oh I ended up finishing it. I just knitted a blue background and then crocheted a bunch of stars and tacked them onto the blue background. One of these days, I'm going to figure out the star pattern though and knit it. Just for fun." Her fingers were running down the side of my abdomen, tracing out the pattern of my muscles. The whisper-soft touch was distracting me. "And I gave the afghan to my local VA. It's about all I worked on these past two months. I'm behind in all my other projects."

"Ah." What the hell? That she'd finish her project before I got to her never occurred to me. She hadn't worked on it in over two years, and she'd whipped the fucker into shape in two months? I had not planned for this. Squeezing the steering wheel, I wondered where else I could take her, but we were already there.

"Oh look there's a yarn shop."

Sighing, I pulled into Knit Together.

"We don't have to stop. I can get yarn anytime." She smiled at me and stretched out her arms, making an interesting outline around her breasts. "I'm going to have a lot of time on my hands."

"What do you want to do after this?"

"Probably look for a place to live."

"There might be someone in my apartment complex who has a place. Will you let me check that out for you?"

"Sure." She smiled, and I was so overwhelmed by emotion, I couldn't really speak. Unbuckling her seatbelt, I pulled her into my lap and buried my head in her neck. She held me, soothed me, and brought me back to life again. I didn't cry...exactly, but I held her tight and hoped she realized how precious she was to me.

We may have sat like that forever if she hadn't pushed away and said, "So even though I said you didn't have to stop, do you mind if we go in? We are in the parking lot."

I chuckled and unlocked the door. Holding her to me while I climbed out, I set her down next the truck door. "Hold on." In the back seat, I pulled out the pack and then slung it over my shoulder. Placing a hand at the small of her back, I ushered her into the shop.

"Sergeant Phillips," Mrs. Bend cried out when we were inside. Sam had started to look at some yarn balls on a front table display but quickly abandoned them to look first at Mrs. Bend and then at me. I bent down so Mrs. Bend could give me an obligatory kiss in greeting. Holding out my hand to Sam, I drew her close to my side and introduced them.

"Mrs. Bend, this is my girlfriend, Sam, the one I told you about. Sam, this is Mrs. Bend. She and her daughter Dorothy have been helping me with something." I let the pack drop to the floor and then knelt down on one knee to pull out the sad mat of yarn I'd created. Mrs. Bend had her hands up by her mouth, and I could see out of the periphery of my eyes that everyone in the store had turned toward us.

Sam's head was cocked to the side as if I were some strange bug she'd found on the floor and she wasn't sure if she should crush it or sweep it outside with the trash.

Feeling embarrassed by my effort, I crushed the knitting in my hand and thought frantically of a way to get out of this. What *had* I been thinking? I started to stuff it back into the pack and stand, but Sam's hands stopped me.

"What is it?" The caring in her voice had me dropping my head. While I was pissed off at myself for spending so many years avoiding relationships because of the number Carrie had done to me, I was grateful too, because otherwise I wouldn't have met Sam, wouldn't have fallen in love with her, and wouldn't have the gift of her love in return. She'd made every effort to keep me in her life and I had to show her how willing I was to make her part of my life, forever.

Pulling out the project, I held it out to her. *That's my heart in your hands,* I thought. No one in the store said a word. It was as if we were all holding our collective breaths.

And then…then Sam started to sob. "Oh God, Sam, I'm sorry. I'm so sorry." I didn't know what I'd done, but I was damn sorry for it. Actually I'd done so many shitty things that I probably couldn't say those words enough. She allowed me to cradle her in my arms. Sound burst all around us. Mrs. Bend was trying to explain that I was a dear boy, and Dorothy was fluttering around looking for tissues.

I didn't know if I should take Sam to the back where there was a sofa or out to my truck. What I did know was that I wasn't letting go of her.

Pushing away from me slightly, Sam made the decision for me. Wiping her tears with the backs of her hand, she held the blue bit of yarn between us. "Did you make this for me?"

I nodded. "It's the stars portion of your afghan. Mrs. Bend was trying to teach me your interstitial—no, intarsia—technique. See," I pointed to a blotch of white, "that's supposed to be a star."

She started laughing and crying at the same time. "This is about the sweetest thing anyone has ever done for me." Through her tears she beamed at me. "You really do love me, don't you, Gray Phillips?"

"I really do, Samantha Anderson. More than the world has stars,

I love you."

I wasn't an officer and not much of a gentleman, but I could carry the shit out of stuff. Scooping Sam into my arms, I carried her out the Knit Together shop.

"So much better than the Lion yarn trunk show, Margo."

EPILOGUE

Samantha

"IF YOU AREN'T READY IN THE NEXT MINUTE, I'M LEAVING WITHOUT you," I yelled down the hall. My roommate Karen was still primping in the bathroom. We were both on our way to meet the boat down at the Dock. Karen's girlfriend was in the Navy. The Navy carried the Marines everywhere, or almost everywhere, so if a Navy guy comes over to the Marine base everyone thanks him for the "ride."

Pausing in front of the entryway mirror, I double-checked my appearance. Karen had used a flat iron to make big beach waves in my hair, and I'd applied eyeliner, mascara, and a little blush. I probably didn't need the blush. My cheeks were red with excitement. No lipstick, Karen counseled, because Gray would eat it all off in the first five seconds of getting off the boat. That made me more excited than it probably should have.

The six-month separation had been difficult because it came so soon, just a couple months after I'd arrived in San Diego. Gray had re-enlisted and then got sent to the Phillippines. His duties included drinking snake venom with the Philippine Army, at least according to one of his platoon members. Out of all the tall tales that his friends liked to joke about, that was actually one I believed.

Karen's girlfriend was a medic, and we'd met when I was looking for an apartment to rent. Gray said it made sense to room with someone to defray the apartment costs, particularly when I wasn't going to be spending a lot of time there. The military frowned upon single men cohabiting. It would've been easier for Karen and her girlfriend to get by together, but since Rose had come out, they'd decided not to push it.

It made for a perfect set up. Rose spent most of her time with Karen in our apartment, and I spent most of my time with Gray in his. None of us were "living" together in violation of the unwritten rules of the Corps, but I hadn't slept one entire night in my apartment. Even with Gray gone, I liked to sleep in our bed, wrapped in his scent, surrounded by his things.

It was hard on Gray to be gone. He struggled with his issues of jealousy and trust, so I did what I could to allay those concerns. When we Skyped, which we could do regularly, I gave him a general rundown of my day, including who I might have seen or run into. He never once asked, trying hard to show me how much he trusted me and how much he'd grown, but why torment him, I thought. Besides I liked sharing what I'd been doing. It made us seem closer even though we were miles apart.

Today he was coming home, though, and I wanted to make his homecoming special. I waxed, shaved, plucked, and perfumed every inch of my body. Underneath his favorite dress—the red-and-white polka-dotted one I wore when I first returned to him—I had brand new panties and a red-and-white polka-dotted lace bra. My three-inch heels would make it easier for him to kiss me, I figured. I dabbed a bit of my favorite citrus perfume on the backs of my ears and a little in the small valley of my breasts. Over the top I added a white cardigan. It was colder now, and I needed it.

Karen finally charged out of her bedroom dressed in high-waisted grey checked slacks and a fire-engine-red poet's shirt with billowy sleeves. Her hair was styled Katherine Hepburn-esque with soft waves molded close to her head. She looked like the embodiment of a 1950s glamorous actress.

Karen said that she always felt the need to look more beautiful than any other woman standing on the dock because Rose, as a lesbian in the Navy, felt like she had to do and be better than anyone else just to be perceived the same. Times were changing though. Gray didn't care and many of his contemporaries didn't either, although there were definite disagreements about women in combat infantry. Gray acknowledged, after a heated argument with Rose, that it was the men who'd need to change their attitudes but thought that it wasn't something that could be done overnight or even in Gray's lifetime. Rose and Gray agreed to disagree, but that they'd remained friends was an achievement for both.

"You look great," Karen said, giving me a once over. I smoothed back a lock of curled hair and she batted my hand down. "No mussing. That's for Gray to do."

"I'm nervous," I admitted as I drove my Rover toward the base. "I feel like we're meeting for the first time. Like it's a crazy blind date."

"I know, isn't it great?" She laughed wildly. "Your relationship can never get old. He steps off the boat and the bloodlust surges through you like you were shot with a lightning bolt."

"Can't wait." It was the truth. Karen and I had argued over who would drive, and finally I told her that if I didn't then I'd probably have Gray undressed and in a compromising position within two minutes of him being in the Rover—and only Gray would appreciate that. She'd conceded that maybe my need was just slightly more elevated than hers. Although she did ask me if I didn't self-pleasure as she figured Gray had been doing.

"As if that's even the same thing," I had scoffed.

I'd masturbated plenty while Gray was gone. We'd actually bought a couple vibrators for me to use and, while I never would admit this to anyone—not Eve, not Karen, no one—I'd used the vibrator on myself a couple of times while Gray and I Skyped. Gray just sat there, his eyes burning like crazy, headphones on so no one could hear my pants and then my pleas for him to touch me and finally my cries when I came.

We did it only twice because during second time someone must have interrupted Gray and he'd slammed his laptop shut before I'd gotten myself off. That night had been a pisser. If guys got blue balls, then I'd had a blue clit or something because I felt like I ached for days afterwards. I'd refused to do it again no matter how sweetly Gray pleaded because I didn't like that feeling of unfulfilled emptiness. But the truth was that having Gray watch me use the vibe was better than using it alone. Anytime he was with me, it was better, even if he couldn't touch me, even if he couldn't use his voice to whisper all the filthy things he'd like to do to me. Because there were only rare moments of privacy, I didn't get to hear them, although he emailed me. Oh boy did he email me. I wondered if his superiors read his messages and hoped that they didn't, or I wouldn't be able to look at any of them ever again.

"Thinking dirty thoughts about Gray," Karen teased, breaking into my mental fog. I realized we were almost at the dock.

"No, why?" I lied and then blushed.

She laughed, "Because you're squirming like a recently landed fish."

"Nice visual."

"Killed your little fantasies, right? Don't want you popping off before Gray gets off the boat."

"What about you?" Karen seemed unnaturally calm.

"I took care of myself a couple times this morning because Rose is going to need a lot of attention."

My face fell. Maybe I should've done that.

"No worries," she patted my shoulder. "Gray will be thrilled that you can't wait to jump his bones. Every couple is different and every deployment is different. Don't worry about it."

Gray

"I HAVEN'T SEEN YOU THIS excited since we went base jumping in Castle Valley two years ago," Hamilton muttered next to me.

"Base jumping has nothing on Sam." I hadn't had anyone but my parents waiting for me when I came home from a tour. This time I asked that they stay home because I just wanted to be with Sam. That she would be out there with the wives and girlfriends excited me more than I would have imagined. Yeah there had been moments when I envied the guys who were greeted by their girlfriends, wives, and kids, but in the next second I'd always wondered which of the Marines who'd stayed back home were screwing the wives and girlfriends of the deployed. And I congratulated myself on being wise and single.

Now I was one of those poor sacks whose balls were completely owned by some girl, and I couldn't be happier. "Someday, Hamilton, it'll be you."

"Nope," Hamilton muttered. "I like my balls attached to my body, thanks. I don't need to give them to some little woman back home in order to be able to function."

"You only wish you could cut off your balls and leave them on some chick's table." Fact was that Sam didn't just have my balls; she had the best part of me with her. But thoughts of my balls naturally led to a nude Sam. I had to stop thinking about the last email she'd sent back. There had been a picture of just the bottom half of her body with one of my blue physical therapy shirts draped over her thighs, pulled up up in the center to the top of her belly button. Her one hand held up the T-shirt to expose the white lace of her boy shorts and the other hand? I shuddered at the memory. The other hand was inside her boy shorts, and all I could see were the bumps of her knuckles against the cotton fabric. I got up immediately and went to the head and jerked off for about five minutes after that visual.

I can't wait for your fingers to replace mine.

I could jack off just thinking about the words that came with the photo.

"Five minutes, sweethearts, and you'll finally get off your holiday cruise. We know you have zero choice in the matter, so thank you for fucking floating with us," First Sergeant Gracias shouted as he walked by.

Leaving the boat with a hard-on was unacceptable for a Staff Sergeant. I thought of Hamilton's dirty socks, the transmission of a

1970 GTO, the shit ton of paperwork that I'd have to file when I got back to base.

And then I was walking down the ramp, eyes scanning the dock and then hooking on a red-and-white polka-dotted dress. She had her hair all done up for me, looking like a million dollars. I wanted to fling out my arms and circle around, screaming, "See her? She's mine. She's going home with me." In a rare fit of possessiveness, part of me wanted to take her right there on the dock to mark her as mine so that no one would even look at her without seeing my body covering hers. She'd probably gnaw off my balls with her teeth if I did that, though.

But right now, looking at the glow of excitement, lust and just pure happiness in her face, maybe not.

We have may said something like hello or I missed you, but all I could remember was lifting her soft body in my arms and the press of her lips against mine and then, finally, God, the lick of her tongue inside my mouth. I kissed her back with all the intensity I'd stored up for six long months. The pent-up desire bruised her lips as I held her with one arm around her waist and the other cradling her head to mine.

I loved her and I couldn't wait to get her home. The drive back to the apartment felt like it was longer than the ocean voyage but then we were in the bedroom, ripping off each other's clothes. My uniform in a heap on top of her red and white polka dotted dress.

"I'm not going to last for five minutes, but I promise to make it up to you." I grabbed her hip in one hand and my dick in the other. She was soaked and I slid in, and I finally felt like I was home. I rested my forehead against hers as we both stilled so we could just feel what it was like to be joined again—my cock sheathed by her warm pussy. Ah, so fucking perfect that I could die here a happy man.

We moved, then, again in unison as if our bodies had taken control and recalled the synchronized rhythm we'd perfected before I left. I slid both hands onto her thighs and pushed her as far open as possible because I wanted to bottom out inside of her. Her hands came to grip mine and with each bite of her fingernails she told me how much she missed me and how much she wanted this too.

"Talk to me, Gray," she begged. "Tell me how hard you've been.

How much you've missed me."

She just had to get me going. I stroked her hard, feeling our bodies slam together and reveled in the loud, wet sounds we were making. The friction caused when she clamped down on my cock as I was withdrawing made my eyes cross. I wasn't going to last much longer but if she wanted the words, I'd give them to her. "Baby, you've no idea. Every night I went to sleep, I thought about being in your tight little pussy. How it's always wet for me." Flipping one leg over my shoulder, I used my now free hand to rub her lower lips and strum her clit.

"Mmm, yes," she moaned. "Always wet for you."

"And this pussy is all mine." I spanked her clit lightly and felt her body bow in shocked and eroticized surprise. Leaning forward, I captured one upthrust nipple into my mouth and felt her convulse around me.

"Yes, and you're mine too," she declared fiercely. I was completely and utterly hers. She owned me, every part of me, and that sentiment made me feel stronger than learning how to shoot a gun or fighting insurgents or anything the Corps had taught me. She began to undulate against me, her body moving in jerky movements, caught up in the sensation of her impending orgasm. Her hands gripped my head and pulled me up for a wild and relentless kiss. Inside her mouth I tasted her want, her fevered desire, and her intense love. Her leg slipped off my shoulder and found its way around my waist until I felt the heel of her foot urging me closer to her.

"I love fucking you. I love feeling your creamy ass against my cock every morning. I love your gorgeous fucking breasts and your amazing nipples. I could suck on them and never get tired of that. I love the smell of your pussy and the taste of your come on my tongue." Her pussy's grip on my cock was like a vice.

"Me too," Sam gasped in my ear. "I love your cock in my mouth. Love it. Love your taste. I just love you, Gray Phillips."

And with that I was done for. I began thrusting into her uncontrollably. Any ability to form sentences was gone and I was left with only one thought in my head. "I love you, Sam. Love you so damn much." Slipping a hand between us, I rubbed her until I felt her release overtake her body and then I let go, pumping every ounce of my come into her body, feeling the slickness of her corresponding orgasm until I couldn't hold myself up anymore and collapsed against her body. In the aftermath, I tried to roll off but she wouldn't let go.

Her arms and legs wrapped around me and held me tight against her. "I'm never letting you go," she whispered. And her words made me shiver, not in lust but in pure fucking happiness. Our love had only grown stronger during our separation, not weaker.

After we'd had our celebration in the bedroom, I grabbed a beer, stuck something in my pocket, and picked up Sam's knitting sack. We headed down to the communal pool to enjoy the late afternoon sun. Sam had gotten accepted to FIDM and would start in the fall. In the meantime, with the help of Mrs. Bend and Dorothy, Sam had conquered intarsia stitching and few other techniques that sounded just as impossible. I happily gave up my new hobby, content to just sip a cold one and watch Sam. The rhythmic clicks of her needles were a comforting sound, and it got to the point that I couldn't even watch a game without her sitting next to me, the clacking of her needle points against each other forming the solid drumbeat of our lives.

"You make the sweater?" I asked. The white little shrug that covered her shoulders had a lot of intricate stitching that I had come to associate with her work.

"I did, like it? The bad thing about San Diego is that there aren't many times I can wear sweaters."

"I like my beanie." She'd knitted me about a dozen wool caps over the winter, and I'd needed them all because they kept getting filched. The guys in my platoon were totally fucking brazen about it too, wearing them around me and not giving a good goddamn. "And my socks. You knit some damn fine socks." Those she didn't whip out by the bushel, and I was careful to lock them up. Sam had made me several pairs of socks, all of them carefully constructed to fit my foot personally, and I swore if any one of those socks went missing, my boot would be up the ass of every man in my platoon until they were returned.

"Hamilton emailed me about your socks, you know. He wants a pair."

"Hamilton can go suck his thumb."

Sam didn't respond; she just continued to knit.

"What're you working on?" I asked.

"I got another order for a layette, so I'm making this little sweater. The booties and hat are done. I'm getting fast enough that I might break even." She laughed. "Maybe someday I'll be able to quit waiting tables to pay the rent."

I shifted in my chair, wondering if now was the time to bring up a subject that had simmered at the top of my head the entire time I was gone. It was a risky topic, and I didn't relish putting myself out there, but for once I wanted to beat Sam to the punch. She'd been the one to hit on me first. She came to see me after our rock climbing fiasco. She came out to San Diego. This one time, I wanted to be the one to make the gesture.

"You could marry me."

The sound of the needles stopped abruptly. I was hesitant to look at Sam, a little nervous about what expression she'd be wearing. Would it be astonishment? Or maybe chagrin? I tipped my head slightly so I could glance at her in my periphery. Her mouth was hanging open and her knitting had fallen unnoticed to her lap. That wasn't quite the response I was hoping for.

"Gray Phillips, did you just propose to me by the pool in front of all these people?"

It was like a trick question. I had to make sure I gave the right answer. "Yes?"

"I should stab you with one of my needles."

"That's not the answer I was hoping for." I got down on one knee, in front of the avid gazes of the sailors and Marines who lived in this apartment complex. Pulling out the ring box, I flipped it open so that the sun shown down on the pink diamond in the platinum setting. It was very different than what she'd worn before and I held my breath waiting for her answer.

The sound of her wild laugh, the one she let out when we rappelled down the cliff together that very first time, rang out in the courtyard. It was pure, unadultered joy. Goddamn, I loved her. Shoving the ring on her finger, I picked her up and twirled her around and around until we were both dizzy.

"Yes, I'll marry you." She placed a hand on either side of my face and we kissed, hungrily and lovingly and for a very long time but we didn't leave right away. Too many people came over to look at the ring, congratulate Sam and I, and generally give us the business—in jest. But it felt great. I wanted everyone to know I'd fallen irrevocably in love with this woman whose courage in life blew me away.

UNDECLARED

For four years, Grace Sullivan wrote to a Marine she never met, and fell in love. But when his deployment ended, so did the letters. Ever since that day, Grace has been coasting, academically and emotionally. The one thing she's decided? No way is Noah Jackson — or any man — ever going to break her heart again.

UNSPOKEN

Whore. Slut. Typhoid Mary. I've been called all these at Central College. One drunken night, one act of irresponsible behavior, and my reputation was ruined. Guys labeled me as easy and girls shied away. To cope, I stayed away from Central social life and away from Central men, so why is it that my new biology lab partner is so irresistible to me? A former Marine involved in illegal fighting with a quick trigger temper and an easy smile for all the women. He's sliding his way into my heart and I'm afraid that he's going to be the one to break me.

When a dangerous killer falls for a sheltered innocent, he'll cross every line just to have her...

NEW YORK TIMES BESTSELLING AUTHOR
JESSICA CLARE

USA TODAY BESTSELLING AUTHOR
JEN FREDERICK

LAST HIT

NIKOLAI

I have been a contract killer since I was a boy. For years I savored the fear caused by my name, the trembling at the sight of my tattoos. The stars on my knees, the marks on my fingers, the dagger in my neck, all bespoke of danger. If you saw my eyes, it was the last vision you'd have. I have ever been the hunter, never the prey. With her, I am the mark and I am ready to lie down and let her capture me. Opening my small scarred heart to her brings out my enemies. I will carry out one last hit, but if they hurt her, I will bring the world down around their ears.

DAISY

I've been sheltered from the outside world all my life. Homeschooled and farm-raised, I'm so naive that my best friend calls me Pollyanna. I like to believe the best in people. Nikolai is part of this new life, and he's terrifying to me. Not because his eyes are cold or my friend warns me away from him, but because he's the only man that has ever seen the real me beneath the awkwardness. With him, my heart is at risk..and also, my life.

About the Author

Jen Frederick lives with her husband, child, and one rambunctious dog. She's been reading stories all her life but never imagined writing one of her own. Jen loves to hear from readers, so drop her a line at jen@jenfrederick.com, or visit her website at www.jenfrederick.com.

Facebook: AuthorJenFrederick   **Twitter:** @JenSFred

CPSIA information can be obtained at www.ICGtesting.com
Printed in the USA
LVOW08s0336170715

446502LV00003B/263/P